DELITTO IDEALE
THE ACADEMIC EDITION

Original Italian with English Translation

Luigi Capuana

Kazabo Publishing

Foreword © 2021
English translation originally published as *Mind Games* © 2018

Garamond MT Std 12/13/18

ISBN: 978-1-948104-23-4
P012

TABLE OF CONTENTS

FOREWORD

Luigi Capuana (1839-1915) is a pivotal figure in Italian literature. Though it is more often identified with his better-known compatriot, Giovanni Verga, it was Capuana who founded the Verismo movement, the Italian answer to the Realist movement sweeping European literature in the mid-nineteenth century.

A prolific writer, Capuana published six novels and many more volumes of short stories, plays, essays and other works during his lifetime. The present work, appearing in English for the first time as *Mind Games* and originally published in 1902 as *Delitto Ideale*, is well-known in Europe but was never translated in English before.

Capuana himself was born in Sicily but lived throughout Italy, including Florence and Milan, at various times, and had a wide circle of literary friends, to whom many of the stories in the present work are dedicated. These include Federico De Roberto, Guelfo Civinini and Grazia Deledda, the first Italian woman to win the Nobel Prize for Literature.

Following this Foreword, we have included Capuana's original introduction which was dedicated to Eduardo Rod, a Swiss novelist and a friend of Capuana's. The introduction is notable for two reasons.

First, Capuana decries the hectic pace of the modern world of 1902 and suggests that, rather than being in decline, short stories ought to be the literary genre of the age. "Considering our anxious hurry to live and to enjoy ourselves, this shouldn't have happened. . . . [S]hort stories seem to reflect best the feverish demand for quickly changing impressions and sensations, and should have gained ground, instead of losing it." It seems that our modern problems and our addiction to constant stimulation and amusement are not, perhaps, as modern as we would like to think.

Perhaps more consequential from a literary standpoint, Capuana goes on to expound his theory of short stories and concludes that far too many novels are simply short stories "more or less cleverly diluted in three hundred and more pages, by way of many descriptions and alleged psychological analysis."

To Capuana, "it is easier to write a mediocre novel of five hundred pages, than an excellent short story of only ten." This thought is not original with Capuana. (In 1647, Blaise Pascal wrote, "I have made this letter longer because I did not have the leisure to make it shorter.") But it is, nonetheless, interesting to see Capuana developing this aphorism as a literary theory.

A word should be said about the openly occult themes that run through many of Capuana's stories. Realism and Verismo typically focus on life "as it is" and avoid the supernatural and the fantastical. So it may seem strange that Capuana, Verismo's founder, wrote so many stories involving supernatural occurrences. In part, this is an artifact of our modern preconceptions. In the late 19th and early 20th centuries, spiritualism was regarded almost as a type of science and many of its precepts were widely accepted and claimed adherents ranging from Arthur Conan Doyle, inventor of Sherlock Holmes, to Marie Curie, discoverer of radium and twice winner of the Nobel Prize. Capuana himself wrote two serious works on spiritualism, *Spiritismo?* (1884) and *Novelle del Mondo Occulto* (1896).

So while Capuana does not claim to be narrating actual events in his short stories, he is depicting events that, from the perspective of both Capuana and his times, could have happened. His supernatural stories are "true" in the same sense that a murder mystery is "true." No murder may have ever been committed as described in a particular novel but it is not unreasonable to imagine that a murder might have been committed that way.

More fundamentally, these supernatural situations are, for Capuana's purposes, almost secondary. Capuana, especially in *Delitto Ideale*, while not stinting on physical realism, is profoundly concerned with psychological realism. His characters are placed in unusual situations and their reactions, psychology, and inner thoughts are meticulously observed. For Capuana, his short stories are psychological laboratories where his characters are tested, sometimes to destruction. As Capuana's friend and fellow Verist, Giovanni Verga, put it, "What an unexplored and fruitful mine these short stories are, in which imagination and scientific research go hand in hand with such profound impact!"

The stories in *Delitto Ideale* revolve around the inner-life of their protagonists and evoke the gamut of emotions. Some are high comedy – a few of his characters would have gotten along perfectly well with Saki's Clovis Sangrail. Others, such as "The Boat" are touching and insightful. A few are disquieting. "The Mystery" chronicles a descent into madness worthy of Edgar Allan Poe but made all the more unsettling by its commonplace setting. But each is a captivating study of the human mind. The Verismo movement was dedicated to an almost clinical study of reality as it is rather than how we might like to imagine it. But in these stories, Capuana explores the sometimes-dangerous territory of our inner realities. The line between sanity and insanity may be thinner than we would like to think.

Chiara Giacobbe

PREFACE

PREFAZIONE

TO EDOARDO ROD

Dearest friend,

When I finished reading the simple story of the humble family and the dispute that made you write such honest and fervent prose in *Eau Courante* as to make people forget that it's only fiction – and this seems to me the most beautiful praise to which a novelist could aspire – I thought: "My friend Rod, like so many others, has long abandoned the short story!"

And because it was you, I realized that this is not a personal, almost exceptional, phenomenon, but a decisive trend in the literary works of recent years.

Is the novel killing the short story?

To an unrepentant writer of short stories like me, the facts give much to ponder. Even in the rich world of French literature, volumes of short stories are becoming increasingly rare. Long gone are the days when Guy de Maupassant conquered fame with several series of narratives – the longest of which did not surpass fifty pages – which were honored with frequent reprints.

Who is to blame for the near-abandonment of a literary genre that blossomed richly for many centuries and was greatly honored until a few years ago?

Considering our anxious hurry to live and to enjoy ourselves, this shouldn't have happened. With their short, easy narratives, smiling with irony and humor, or otherwise full of feeling and tragic horror; with their characters only briefly sketched, caught only in a glimpse; with their condensed passions, short stories seem to best reflect the feverish demand for quickly changing impressions and sensations, and should have gained ground, instead of losing it.

The opposite happened, just when the short story showed its great facility to adapt to all kinds of subjects, to be able to almost do without the usual dramas and to reach literary heights without diminishing the geniality of its form.

What a shame!

Why has the novel had the upper hand over the short story over the last few years?

I cannot identify any purely literary reasons. I see, however, that many of today's novels are actually short stories more or less cleverly diluted in three hundred and more pages by way of many descriptions and alleged psychological analysis. In a short story, the same events would require (you know this better than I) infinitely greater effort and technical prowess. The short story is the sonnet of narrative art. And you will not accuse me of exaggeration if I say that it is easier to write a mediocre novel of even five hundred pages, than an excellent short story of only ten. It is true that excellent short stories are as rare as excellent novels: but I have no hesitation in adding that a mediocre short story is worth something more than a mediocre novel, if for no other reason than its brevity as it has less time to bore the reader.

A EDOARDO ROD

Carissimo Amico,

Terminando di leggere la semplice storia dell'umile famiglia e dell'umile lite che vi ha fatto scrivere nell'*Eau courante* pagine così schiette e così evidenti da far dimenticare che si tratti di finzione d'arte—e questo mi sembra il più bel elogio a cui un romanziere possa aspirare—io pensavo:

L'amico Rod, come tanti altri, ha abbandonato la novella e da un pezzo!

E il caso vostro mi ha spinto a riflettere che non si tratta di un fenomeno personale quasi eccezionale, ma di tendenza, spiccata, del lavoro letterario di questi ultimi anni.

Il romanzo già uccide la novella?

A un novelliere impenitente come me il fatto dà molto da pensare. Anche nella ricca produzione francese i volumi di novelle cominciano a divenire di mano in mano più rari. Siamo lontani dal tempo in cui Guy de Maupassant conquistava la celebrità con parecchie serie di narrazioni, la più lunga delle quali non sorpassava le cinquanta pagine, e che ottenevano l'onore di frequenti ristampe.

A chi attribuire la colpa del quasi abbandono di un genere letterario fiorito riccamente per tanti secoli e in grande onore fino a pochi anni fà?

Nell'ansiosa fretta di vivere e di di godere che ci urge, avrebbe dovuto accadere altrimenti. Con narrazioni brevi, spigliate, sorridenti d'ironia e di umore, o piene di sentimento e di tragico raccapriccio, dove le figure tracciate alla lesta, di scorcio, dove le passioni condensate, rettificate come l'alcool, sembravano di corrisponder meglio alla febbrile richiesta di impressioni e di sensazioni rapidamente diverse, la novella avrebbe dovuto guadagnare terreno invece di perderne.

È avvenuto l'opposto, e quando più essa mostrava la sua grande facilità di adattarsi a ogni genere di soggetti, di poter quasi fare a meno dei soliti casi passionali e di spingersi verso regioni elevate, senza diminuire per questo la genialità della sua forma.

Peccato!

Per quali ragioni il romanzo ha preso in questi ultimi anni il sopravvento su la novella?

Ragioni puramente letterarie non ho saputo scoprirne. Veggo, però, che molti romanzi odierni, come contenuto, sono novelle più o meno abilmente diluite in trecento e più pagine, a furia di descrizioni e di pretesa analisi psicologica. Gli stessi fatti richiederebbero in una novella (Voi lo sapete meglio di me) sforzi d'ingegnosità tecnica infinitamente maggiori. La novella è il sonetto dell'arte narrativa. E Voi non mi accuserete di esagerazione se affermerò che è più facile lo scrivere un mediocre romanzo anche di cinquecento pagine, che non un'eccellente novella di dieci paginette soltanto. È vero che le eccellenti novelle sono rare quanto gli eccellenti romanzi: ma io non ho ritegno di aggiungere che una mediocre novella vale qualche cosa di più di un mediocre romanzo, non fosse per altro, per la brevità; non ha tempo di annoiare i lettori.

All this, said as an introduction to a volume of short stories, might seem entirely self-interested. You will not suspect me of such a thing, and I hope that none of my handful of readers will suspect it either.

But certainly, if ever, by chance, someone thinks it worthwhile to waste his time in such observations, I would like him to note the intent behind this volume, which is to show the different attitudes of which the modern short story is capable. And I would like him to notice it not in the interest of my book – by now my age and experience have cured my of such vanity – but for more important and more general reasons, i.e., those concerning the very existence of the short story.

But perhaps these naive melancholies will only engender a pitiful smile in both readers and critics. There are so many beautiful and noble things that have passed away forever. Perhaps we should let the short story, quietly and obscurely, do the same!

And forgive me, dear Rod, if, in order to have a pretext to tell you how much I admire you and cherish you, I have involved you in this pointless diatribe.

Rome, April 5th, 1902.

LUIGI CAPUANA

Tutto questo, detto in testa a un volume di novelle, potrebbe sembrare un'orazione *pro-domo sua*. Voi non lo sospetterete, e voglio augurarmi che non lo sospetterà nessuno dei miei pochi lettori.

Certamente io desiderei che qualcuno si accorgesse dell'intenzione con che è stato messo insieme questo volume per mostrare i diversi atteggiamenti di cui è capace la novella odierna, se mai, per caso, qualcuno stimasse che metta conto perdere il suo tempo in simili osservazioni. E desiderei che se ne accorgesse non per interesse del mio volume—ormai l'età e l'esperienza mi han guarito da certe fisime—ma per ragioni più importanti e più generali quelle, intendo, che riguardano l'esistenza stessa della novella.

Ma forse queste ingenue malinconie faranno sorridere di compassione lettori e critici. Sono morte tante belle e nobili cose: possiamo lasciar morire tranquillamente e oscuramente la Novella!

E scusate, caro Rod, se per avere un pretesto di dirvi che vi ammiro e che vi voglio bene, Vi ho chiamato a parte di un inutile sfogo.

Roma, 5 aprile, 1902.

LUIGI CAPUANA

THE DREAM MURDER

TO FEDERICO DE ROBERTO

"And what about justice?" Lastrucci exclaimed.

"Which one?" Morani replied. "Nobody knows anything of the justice of the world beyond. Our justice, human justice, is so rough, superficial, barbaric, that it doesn't deserve to be called *justice*. It condemns or absolves blindly, based on external facts, on testimonies that only describe material actions, which matters less in a crime. The true crime, the spiritual one, the result of thought and conscience, almost always escapes it. And so rough, human justice very often condemns when it should absolve, and it absolves, unfortunately, when it should condemn."

"There you go again with your usual paradoxes. Human justice does what it can. Would you punish even our secret thoughts?"

"Of course. A murder designed, matured through long reflection in all its smallest details and then not executed because the perpetrator's energy was exhausted in designing and preparing it, is that somehow a less blameworthy crime than a murder actually committed?"

"You are presenting an outlandish, exceptional case."

"And one more common than you'd imagine. I met a man truly worthy of the title who judged himself for such a crime. He even punished himself as if he had committed the murder he only imagined and planned."

"A man, perhaps, but a crazy man."

"A great sage, rather. His conscience would not give him peace. And since he couldn't appear in front of a judge and accuse himself – the judge would have reasoned just as you did and put him in a madhouse – to expiate his guilt, he condemned himself to the same punishment that a magistrate would have inflicted on him had he judged him according to ordinary law."

"How did he punish himself? And why did he want to commit murder?"

"Jealousy."

"I trust he at least allowed himself to plead extenuating circumstances!" Lastrucci said, smiling.

"No extenuating circumstances," Morani replied. "He was not a vulgar man. His profound culture and experience of life should have warned him against the subtle urgings of base passion. In fact, recognizing himself deluded by appearances, he judged that it should have been his duty to avoid their deceit. Instead, he made no such effort. Rather, he let himself be carried away, unresisting. This made his crime of intent wholly unforgivable in his eyes."

"I don't follow. Do you suggest we are supposed to be masters of ourselves in every circumstance?"

"My friend thought so. Our will must always control our emotions if we want to call ourselves rational creatures."

"There is quite a difference between what we *ought* to be and what we *are*. This man, who considered himself such a rational creature, reasoned very badly.

DELITTO IDEALE

A FEDERICO DE ROBERTO

—E la giustizia?—esclamò Lastrucci.

—Quale?—replicò Morani.—Di quella del mondo di là, nessuno sa niente; la nostra, l'umana, è cosa talmente rozza, superficiale, barbarica, da non meritare di essere chiamata giustizia. Condanna o assolve alla cieca, per fatti esteriori, basandosi su testimonianze che affermano soltanto l'azione materiale, quel che meno importa in un delitto. Il vero delitto, quello spirituale, risultato del pensiero e della coscienza, le sfugge quasi sempre; e così essa spessissimo condanna quando dovrebbe assolvere e assolve, purtroppo, quando dovrebbe condannare.

—Ecco i tuoi soliti paradossi! La giustizia umana fa quel che può. Vorresti dunque punire persino le intenzioni nascoste?

—Certamente. Un omicidio pensato, maturato con lunga riflessione in tutti i suoi minimi particolari e poi non eseguito perchè l'energia dell'individuo si è già esaurita nell'idearlo e prepararlo, è forse un delitto meno grave di un omicidio realmente compiuto?

—Tu presenti un caso strano, eccezionale.

—Più comune di quanto immagini. Ed io ho conosciuto un uomo, degno veramente di questo nome, che si è giudicato da sè per un delitto di tal genere, e si è punito come se avesse proprio commesso l'omicidio soltanto fantasticato e progettato.

—Era pazzo.

—Era un gran saggio, dovresti dire. La sua coscienza non gli dava pace. E siccome non poteva presentarsi a un giudice e accusarsi—il giudice avrebbe ragionato come te e lo avrebbe fatto chiudere in un manicomio—per attutire i rimorsi, si è giudicato e si è condannato da sè ad espiare la stessa pena che il magistrato gli avrebbe inflitta, se avesse potuto giudicarlo secondo la legge ordinaria.

—Come ha fatto? E perchè aveva voluto ammazzare?

—Per gelosia.

—Si sarà concesso almeno le attenuanti!—disse Lastrucci sorridendo.

—Nessuna attenuante—riprese Morani.—Oh! Non era un uomo volgare. La profonda cultura e l'esperienza della vita avrebbero dovuto metterlo in guardia contro i subdoli suggerimenti di quella bassa passione; infatti, riconoscendosi illuso dalle apparenze, pensava che sarebbe stato suo dovere sottrarsi al loro inganno. Invece, non aveva fatto nessuno sforzo; si era lasciato travolgere senza resistenza; e ciò rendeva imperdonabile agli occhi suoi quel delitto intenzionale.

—Non capisco. Siamo forse padroni di noi stessi in certe circostanze?

—Il mio amico giudicava che dobbiamo essere sempre padroni di noi stessi, se vogliamo definirci creature ragionevoli.

—Tra dovere ed essere c'è molta differenza. Quest'uomo, considerandosi creatura ragionevole, ragionava assai male.

"No. Tullio Dani acted very nobly. That's what defines his sublime exceptionality. It was like this. He had married a little late in life, when he was forty-five. His beautiful wife was twenty-eight. He was a handsome man, serious and independent. He led a happy and fulfilling life, cultivating his intellect in his favorite studies of literature and philosophy, and making long trips to Europe and America to refine his cultural appreciation. His excessive modesty prevented him from showing off his expertise by producing works of art or philosophical tracts. He never even published an article even though he could have written far better books than many held up as scholars. He had also enjoyed his life. His handsomeness had easily procured him female attention. And until he was forty-four, he had managed to keep his heart's freedom intact, perhaps because of a lack of interest produced by his passion for his studies, perhaps because he had not yet met his ideal woman. His solitary life – he was orphaned very young and had no close relatives – had never weighed on him. He fulfilled his obligation to his fellow man with charity and never waited to be asked. Instead, he spent time among those suffering and always had an open hand for those in the most lonely and resigned misery.

"At the age of forty-four, it came to him that bachelorhood was becoming a burden more than a joy. He felt that he had satisfied the needs of the intellect well enough, but had overlooked those of the heart.

"When he told me of his imminent marriage, he asked me, 'Do you think there's too much disparity between my age and that of my future wife?'

"'Not really,' I had said.

"This idea, which made him hesitate for several months, returned to his mind six months later, when he felt the first pangs of jealousy and seemed to age ten years overnight. I urged him to consult a doctor, as I believed he was seriously ill and perhaps even in danger.

"'I'm perfectly fine,' he would reply.

"'Your wife is worried,' I told him once.

"'For so little?' he responded in a tone of irony and sadness.

"I didn't dare insist further, suspecting there might be intimate reasons for his decline that he could not explain to me. The young bride seemed to adore him. Blond, small, educated, and able to appreciate his intelligence and his immense goodness, I thought her enraptured by the virility of this tall, strong man, by the brightness of spirit that shone in his dark eyes, and by the intelligence betrayed by his wide forehead. I knew she had loved him before she was loved, and that this circumstance had greatly contributed to his finally deciding to marry her.

"A year later, typhoid suddenly took that young life. Tullio's grief for that loss was so extraordinary that I, recalling many details I had noticed and several of his peculiar answers, was tempted to suspect him of exaggerating it on purpose to erase the impressions his earlier actions had left in my mind.

—No. Tullio Dani ha fatto una nobilissima azione. La sua sublime eccezionalità consiste appunto in essa. Ascolta. Aveva preso moglie un po' tardi, a quarantacinque anni; e la sua signora, bellissima, ne aveva appena vent'otto. Bell'uomo anche lui, serio, indipendente, aveva potuto soddisfare ogni suo desiderio, coltivando lo studio prediletto della letteratura e della filosofia, facendo lunghi viaggi in Europa e in America per aumentare la sua cultura, che l'eccessiva modestia gli ha impedito di mostrare agli altri con opere d'arte o di riflessione. Non ha mai pubblicato neppure un articolo, e avrebbe potuto scrivere libri assai meglio di tanti altri. Aveva anche goduto la vita. La sua bellezza gli avea procacciato facilmente molte donne. E fino ai quarantaquattro anni era riuscito a conservare intatta la sua libertà di cuore, forse per un sentimento di egoismo prodotto dalla passione dello studio, forse perchè fino allora non gli era successo d'incontrare la sua donna ideale. La solitudine della sua vita—era rimasto orfano giovanissimo e non aveva stretti parenti—non gli era parsa mai grave. Pagava unicamente con la carità il suo debito di uomo sociale; e non attendeva che la gente si rivolgesse a lui. Andava incontro a coloro che soffrivano, e tra questi sapeva indovinare coloro che soffrivano di più in miseria solitaria e rassegnata.

Dopo i quarantaquattro anni, egli cominciò ad accorgersi che il celibato stava per divenirgli pesante. Sentiva di aver sodisfatto a bastanza le esigenze dell'intelletto, e di aver trascurato troppo quelle del sentimento.

Annunziandomi il suo prossimo matrimonio, mi aveva domandato:

—Ti sembra che ci sia molta sproporzione tra la mia età e quella della futura mia moglie?

—No davvero—risposi.

Questa idea che lo aveva tenuto esitante parecchi mesi, dovette ripresentarsi alla sua mente sei mesi dopo, quando sentì i primi sintomi della gelosia che parve invecchiarlo di dieci anni in pochissimo tempo. Credendolo colpito da una malattia che gli insidiasse la vita, lo sollecitavo caldamente di consultare un medico e di curarsi.

—Sto benissimo—rispondeva.

—Tua moglie è preoccupata—gli dissi una volta.

—Per così poco?—soggiunse con accento d'ironia e di tristezza.

Non osai insistere oltre, sospettando intime ragioni inesplicabili per me. La giovane sposa mi sembrava in continua adorazione davanti a lui. Bionda, piccola, gracile, sufficientemente colta da potere apprezzarne l'elevatissima intelligenza e la immensa bontà d'animo, io la credevo vinta dal doppio fascino della virilità di quell'uomo alto e forte, e della luminosità dello spirito che gli splendeva negli occhi nerissimi e nell'ampia fronte. Sapevo che lo aveva amato lei prima di essere amata, e che questa circostanza avea molto contribuito ad affrettare la decisione di lui.

Un anno dopo, la febbre tifoidea troncava quasi improvvisamente quella giovane vita. Il dolore di Tullio per tale perdita fu così straordinario, che io, ricordando molti particolari da me notati e parecchie sue strane risposte, fui indotto a sospettarlo esagerato ad arte per cancellare le impressioni che essi mi avevano lasciato nell'animo.

"I was his childhood friend. Since his passion for travel had diminished, we saw each other almost every day. And so, I was an intimate observer of the terrible drama that had quickly taken over his life. However, knowing his taciturn nature when it came to his personal feelings, I was surprised to find myself the sole keeper of the secret that had upset his happy existence.

"One morning, he appeared at my house with a big stack of documents in his hands.

"'I need your help. I know it's a great deal to ask, but I'd like you to act as the administrator of my property for several years.'

"'Are you leaving for a long journey?' I asked.

"'No.'

"After a short pause, he added, 'I am not entrusting you with a secret. What I'm about to say, you are free to repeat if it seems appropriate. In fact, as the early Christians did, I'd prefer to make a public confession. I fear, however, my actions would be wrongly interpreted and appear ridiculous. But I know that you will understand and empathize with me.'

"I stared at him anxiously and, with a brief nod, I invited him to continue.

"'I have been a miserable coward!' he said forcefully. 'I have committed the infamy of saddening and slandering her with vile suspicions, the best, the most holy creature I knew in this world. Death was right to deprive me of such great treasure: I was no longer worthy to possess her. And I have done something even worse. I am a murderer. . . though only in my mind. But this detail means nothing. I enjoyed the wicked satisfaction that the crime would give me had I only had the strength to commit it, and I feel a very deep remorse, as if I had really committed it. I can't be touched by human justice. But I feel no less of a murderer for this. I have, inexorably, judged myself, and I condemned myself to the punishment that I would have received if my hand had put into effect what my thought had long pleasure in planning with the finest malice.'

"'Oh, Tullio!' I exclaimed.

"'Are you surprised at discovering how low someone who has spent his life pursuing the highest ideals of art and thought can fall? The misery of the human spirit is so great that you should rather be surprised that I have not fallen even lower! Know, however, that if I did not actually kill, it was not because my will prevented it.'

"He stopped for a moment, shook his head, squeezed his eyes a little, and then resumed. 'Even I can't explain how I began to suspect. I should have reacted quickly against those first impressions, produced by clues that were recognizably false. My narcissistic love, my slightly wounded pride, pushed me, instead, to doubt that recognition, to fixate on those meaningless clues, and to search for new ones, with an intense and painful pleasure. Perhaps they were only the fruit of my imagination, or perhaps a cruel fate maliciously taunted me with a hundred facts, which I let carry a vast significance very different from the meaningless nothings they actually were. My wife, innocent and unsuspecting, could not avoid certain circumstances that fatally conspired to give life to the hell shadows that darkened my heart.

Ero suo amico d'infanzia. Da quando gli era passata la smania dei viaggi, ci vedevamo quasi tutti i giorni; e soltanto così avevo potuto intravvedere il terribile dramma che si era rapidamente svolto nella vita intima di lui. Conoscendo però la sua indole taciturna per quel che riguardava certi fatti personali, non mi attendevo più di poter essere un giorno o l'altro l'unico confidente di quel segreto che avea sconvolto all'ultimo la sua felice esistenza.

Una mattina lo vidi apparire in casa mia con un grosso plico di carte in mano.

—Ho bisogno del tuo aiuto. Vengo a chiederti il grave sacrificio di essere per parecchi anni l'amministratore dei miei beni.

—Intraprendi un lungo viaggio?—domandai.

—No.

E, dopo breve pausa, soggiunse:

—Non ti faccio una confidenza; quel che ora ti dirò potrai ridirlo, se ti sembra opportuno. Vorrei anzi, come i primi cristiani, confessarmi in pubblico, ma temo di veder male interpretata la mia azione, di apparire ridicolo. Tu saprai capirmi e compatirmi.

Lo guardai ansioso, e con un breve gesto di assenso lo invitai a proseguire.

—Sono stato un miserabile vigliacco!—egli disse energicamente.—Ho commesso l'infamia di rattistare, calunniandola con indegni sospetti, la più buona, la più santa creatura che io abbia conosciuta in questo mondo. La morte è stata giusta privandomi di così gran tesoro; non ero più degno di possederlo. Ho fatto anche peggio; sono stato assassino… con l'intenzione soltanto; ma questa circostanza non significa niente. Ho goduto la malvagia sodisfazione che quel delitto mi avrebbe dato nel caso che avessi avuto la forza di compirlo, e ne sento vivissimo rimorso, quasi lo avessi davvero compiuto. La giustizia umana non può colpirmi; io però non mi reputo meno assassino per questo. Mi sono giudicato da me, inesorabilmente, e mi son condannato alla pena che avrei meritata se la mano avesse posto in atto quel che il pensiero si è a lungo compiaciuto di architettare con la più raffinata malizia.

—Oh, Tullio!—esclamai.

—Ti meravigli di scoprire caduto tanto in basso colui che ha desiderato in tutta la sua vita i più eccelsi ideali d'arte e di pensiero? La miseria dello spirito umano è così grande, che dovresti piuttosto meravigliarti di non vedermi caduto ancora più in basso! Sappi però che, se non sono stato effettivamente assassino, la mia volontà non c'entra per nulla.

Si fermò un istante, scosse la testa, strizzando un po' gli occhi, poi riprese:

—Non riesco a spiegarmi neppure io come ho cominciato a sospettare. Avrei dovuto reagire sùbito contro le prime impressioni prodotte da indizi riconosciuti falsi. L'amor proprio, l'orgoglio lievemente ferito mi spinsero invece a dubitare di quel riconoscimento, a rimuginare quegli indizi, a ricercarne con intenso e doloroso piacere altri nuovi. Forse li creò la mia fantasia, o forse un crudele destino mi ingannò con perfidia con cento piccoli fatti facili ad apparire molto diversi da quello che erano in realtà…. Mia moglie, innocente, e senza nessun sospetto, non poteva evitare certe circostanze che congiuravano fatalmente a dare corpo alle ombre e mettermi l'inferno nel cuore.

I should have asked her for explanations, warned her, admonished her. But I didn't, hoping to catch her in some act that would make her infidelity plain and undeniable. And the more my spying and my ambushes yielded nothing, the more I convinced myself that her diabolical malice would rob me of the atrocious vengeance I had already planned. I won't go into all the details. The memory is unbearable to me, now that I understand my own deception. What matters now is that you know of the terrible revenge that I planned day and night against her supposed accomplice.'

"'As for her, against my will, I was gradually won over by tenderness. I forgave her for the sake of the love she had felt for me before I recognized it in myself. I forgave her for her beauty, for her youth, for her naivety, which had made her sad fall possible. Instead, all my hate focused on her seducer, or at least the man I believed was her seducer, who had no excuse of any sort, who must have done evil knowingly, and who had enjoyed the exquisite pleasure of damaging my honor and my happiness, in fact, as I imagined, mainly with this objective in mind. I wanted to kill him and leave no trace so that no one would ever know who had done it. My long search for the best means helped me ease my suffering. I had even chosen the weapon: a razor. For a month I played the part of his friend. There is no point in telling you his name. It's bad enough that I believed him capable of such infamy. I will not offend him further by telling others that I could believe such a thing of him. Jealousy's worst torment is that you never have certainty. You feed on doubts and suspicions that you would like to see eliminated, and at the same time, you fear to eliminate them. Because one day they may help you find certainty, no matter how dreaded. So, while waiting for the terrible moment when all my doubts were resolved, I planned my project. I doted on even its smallest details, and soon I felt the same wild pleasure, in planning the crime, that its actual implementation would have given me. In the streets, in my study, in bed beside her, pretending to be asleep, I would assault my hated victim. I would plunge the sharp blade into his neck and cut the carotid so quickly that he would barely have time to realize he was dying. I would feel the warm spray of his blood on my hand. I would hear the wheeze of his cut throat. I could see the convulsions as his body fell to the floor with a hollow thud.

"'For two long months I tasted, ten, twenty times a day, this fierce, murderous joy. Ten, twenty times a day, I witnessed this chilling imaginary spectacle. It became so real to me that I would snap out of my gory reveries with the same thrill of horror and brutal satisfaction that I would have had had I just committed the deed. It is no exaggeration to say that I have committed not one, but a hundred crimes, because each of those obsessive reenactments was an ever improved and more effective variant of the one before.

"'In the end, I was so satisfied with those brutal imaginings, that the need to actually enact my vengeance diminished. My fevered thoughts had exhausted my physical energies. I was so internally pleased with this mental murder that I needed no other material satisfaction. How could the actual doing of the thing give me any more sincere and acute pleasure than I already had?

Avrei dovuto chiederle spiegazioni, avvertirla, ammonirla; non volli, sperando di sorprenderla in qualche atto che non le permettesse sotterfugio alcuno per continuare ad ingannarmi. E più le mie ricerche, i miei agguati non ottenevano nessun convincente risultato, più io mi ostinavo a immaginare che la sua diabolica malizia riuscisse a farmi sfuggir di mano l'atroce vendetta che avevo già nell'animo. Non posso diffondermi in minuti particolari; il ricordo mi è insopportabile ora che sono convinto del mio inganno. Importa soltanto che tu conosca la vendetta meditata giorno e notte contro il creduto suo complice.

In quanto a lei, inaspettatamente mi ero sentito a poco a poco sopraffare dalla tenerezza; la perdonavo per l'amore che aveva avuto per me quando ancora ignoravo di essere amato da lei; la perdonavo per la sua bellezza, per la sua giovinezza, per l'inesperienza della vita, che aveva dovuto agevolarne la triste caduta. Tutto il mio odio si concentrava sul creduto seduttore che non poteva avere scusa di sorta alcuna, che doveva aver operato il male sapendo di far male, e con lo squisito piacere di farlo a danno del mio onore, della mia felicità, anzi principalmente per questo. Volevo toglierlo dal mondo senza che si potesse mai scoprire chi lo avesse colpito. E la lunga ricerca del mezzo arrivava talvolta fino a calmare il mio dolore. Avevo scelto l'arma: il rasoio. Da un mese mi mostravo suo amico. È inutile dirti il suo nome; è già molto l'averlo creduto capace di un'infamia; non voglio offenderlo ancora col far sapere ad altri che ho potuto crederlo tale. Il peggior tormento prodotto dalla gelosia è quel non sentirsi mai sicuri, quel vivere di dubbi e di sospetti che si vorrebbero veder distrutti, e che si teme di veder distrutti perchè un giorno essi potrebbero servire a farci raggiungere la temuta ma desiderata certezza. Perciò io attendendo il terribile momento in cui non avrei potuto dubitare più, maturavo il mio progetto, lo studiavo nei minimi particolari, e arrivavo al punto di sentire nella concezione del delitto la stessa selvaggia voluttà che mi avrebbe dato la sua attuazione quando l'istante della certezza sarebbe arrivato. Per le vie, nel mio studio, a letto accanto a lei fingendo di dormire profondamente, io assalivo l'odiato, gli sprofondavo nel collo l'affilata lama del rasoio che doveva recidergli la carotide con tale rapidità da non fargli quasi accorgere di morire; e sentivo sulla mano convulsa il caldo schizzo del sangue, e udivo il rantolo della gola squarciata, e vedevo l'annaspare di quel corpo che stramazzava con sordo rumore sul selciato. Ho assaporato, per due lunghi mesi, dieci, venti volte al giorno, questa feroce gioia assassina; ho assistito dieci, venti volte al giorno, al tetro immaginario spettacolo di quella morte; e tale crescente evidenza esso aveva raggiunto all'ultimo, che io mi risvegliavo dall'impressione con lo stesso brivido di orrore e di brutale sodisfazione che mi sarebbe dato la realtà. Potrei dire di avere commesso non uno ma cento delitti, perchè ognuna di quelle ossessionanti rappresentazioni era una variante sempre più perfezionata, sempre più efficace della precedente; e così, alla fine, fui talmente pago di quelle fantasticate sensazioni, da sentir venir meno il bisogno di attuare la mia vendetta; lo sforzo del pensiero avea esaurito ogni mia fisica energia. Mi ero così internamente compiaciuto di ammazzare pensando, da non provar più nessun bisogno di altra soddisfazione materiale.... La realtà avrebbe, forse, potuto darmi soddisfazione più sincera e più acuta?

"'It was for this reason, and this reason alone, that I didn't become a murderer in the strictly legal sense of this word. By pure chance, I eventually realized that a series of unlikely circumstances had contributed to my delusion and had deceived me.

"'Oh! It's so horrible! What had been the point, then, of my deep philosophical studies, of my detached observations, my intense meditations? I knelt by my wife's deathbed and asked her forgiveness. But in the final throes of her illness, she could not understand me. In her delirium, she kept repeating: 'Tullio, what have I done? Why don't you love me anymore?' And so, she died with this loving condemnation on her lips.'"

"'And so?' I said, as I saw him falling into a grave sadness. 'All this is natural, it's human.'

"'Human? There is nothing human about crime if it remains unpunished!' he exclaimed, proudly raising his head. 'Whoever desires somebody else's woman, commits adultery. Whoever thinks of killing, commits murder. And I am a murderer.'"

"'Tullio! Tullio!' I reproached him."

"'I haven't lost my mind!' he replied. 'For the peace of my spirit, for the ideal of justice I have chosen my path: to judge and condemn myself with the same impartiality as I would judge any person accused of the same crime. The day after tomorrow, I will leave for the place in which I have chosen to expiate my crime. My imprisonment will not differ in any way from that decreed by law. It will be hard, inexorable. In a few days, I'll become my own jailer.'"

"Your friend Tullio Dani was crazy!" repeated Lastrucci, who up until then had been listening intently. "And has he completed his sentence?"

"Not yet!" Morani replied.

Per questo, per questo soltanto, io non sono stato omicida nel volgare senso di questa parola! Appunto allora il caso mi faceva scoprire quale serie di incredibili circostanze aveva contribuito a illudermi, a trarmi in inganno. Oh!... È orribile! A che cosa mi era servito dunque l'aver tanto studiato, osservato, meditato? Ho chiesto perdono a mia moglie inginocchiato davanti alla sponda del suo letto di morte. L'intelligenza offuscata dal male le ha impedito di comprendere. Nei vaneggiamenti del delirio, ella ripeteva continuamente:—Tullio, che cosa hai contro di me?... Che ti ho fatto? Perchè non mi ami più?—Ed è morta con questo affettuoso rimpianto su le labbra.

—Ebbene?—dissi io, vedendolo caduto in grave depressione.—Tutto ciò è naturale, è umano.

—Non può essere umano il delitto se rimane impunito!—egli esclamò, rilevando alteramente la testa.—Chi desidera la donna altrui, commette adulterio. Chi pensa di ammazzare, commette omicidio. Ed io mi sento omicida.

—Tullio! Tullio!—lo rimproverai.

—Non ho perso il senno!—egli riprese.—Per la pace del mio spirito, per la giustizia ideale ho voluto far questo: giudicarmi e condannarmi con la stessa imparzialità e serenità con che avrei giudicato qualunque persona accusata del mio stesso delitto. Dopodomani partirò per il luogo da me scelto per espiarvi la pena. La mia prigionia non differirà in niente da quella legale. Sarà dura, inesorabile, ed io diverrò tra pochi giorni il carceriere di me stesso....

—Era pazzo il tuo Tullio Dani!—ripetè Lastrucci stato fin allora ad ascoltare intentissimo.—Ed ha finito di espiare?

—Non ancora!—rispose Morani.

THE MYSTERY

TO GIUSEPPE DRAGONETTO

"I would like to explain myself better, dear Doctor, but I can't. The more I think about my case, the more I try to see through the fog enveloping my mind, the more I feel my reason shaken. Am I already at the edge of madness? Another step and my reason will be lost forever in the darkness of unconsciousness! It's terrible, Doctor! No, say nothing, just listen to me; be patient. Since my illness is all here, in my head, and has no physical symptoms, you can learn nothing without listening to what I have to say. And to speak, or rather to make the effort to think and to speak with some order, I should not be interrupted. My brain doesn't work properly: It has some strange, intermittent lapses. The problem consists of this: I no longer distinguish between dream and reality, between facts I imagined in moments of strange excitement and facts that have actually happened. . . Just so! You smile in disbelief. You think I am mistaken? If only you were right!

"About some of these events I have no doubts.

"Let's note the date: nine months ago. Let's note the place: Florence. I had arrived the night before. Two days before then, I was in Naples, and I'd decided to stay there until mid-June. In the spring, Naples is a paradise. I had gone there to enjoy this paradise, and for no other reason.

"I had spent half a day at the aquarium among the wonders of the underwater life. Suddenly, as if someone had whispered in my ear, I thought, 'Go to Florence! Go to Florence!' I was standing in front of a beautiful bed of sea anemones and corals moving, palpitating with their filamentous ridges. And between the corals and the sea anemones, magnificent octopuses, of which I cannot remember the name now, stretched their tentacles, swelled, opened like living fans, narrowed and almost disappeared, blending with the rosy vegetation. Other small mollusks, sea horses, if I am not mistaken, hydras and jellyfish, climbed and descended through the clear water behind the large crystal glass; hermit crabs, with their homes made of large shells, wandered here and there, now fast, now slow, on the gravelly ground. And, again, that suggestion, that unexpected inspiration: 'Go to Florence!'

"Prior to that, I had not even considered going there. But, wait, I remember now: As I watched intently that marvelous water show, two ladies had stopped for a moment near me. They were from Florence; one could tell by their accents. One of them had a melodious voice that moved me to look at her. And I was disappointed. Her voice had made me think of a young and fresh beauty. But no! She was neither young, nor beautiful. It may be that the suggestion: 'Go to Florence!' was produced by the fascination of that sound. I said fascination, and I mean it, because I could not escape from its power.

L'INESPLICABILE

A GIUSEPPE DRAGONETTO

—Vorrei spiegarmi meglio, caro dottore, ma non sono capace. Più ripenso al mio caso, più tento di veder bene tra la nebbia che mi avvolge la mente, e più sento sconvolgermi l'intelligenza. Sono già al confine della pazzia? Un altro passo e la mia ragione si smarrirà per sempre nella tenebra dell'incoscienza? È terribile, dottore! No, non mi dite niente, state ad ascoltarmi; abbiate pazienza. Siccome il mio male è tutto qui, nella testa, e non ha sintomi fisici, voi non indovinereste nulla se io non parlassi. E per parlare, anzi per far lo sforzo di pensare e di parlare con qualche ordine, ho bisogno di non essere interrotto. Il mio cervello non funziona regolarmente; ha strane intermittenze. L'imbroglio consiste in questo: io non distinguo più tra sogno e realtà, tra fatti fantasticati in momenti di strana esaltazione e fatti realmente avvenuti…. Così, proprio così! Voi sorridete incredulo. Mi sbaglio? Tanto meglio.

Su alcuni avvenimenti non ho nessun dubbio.

Notiamo la data: nove mesi fa. Notiamo il luogo: Firenze. Ero arrivato la sera prima. Due giorni prima, mi trovavo a Napoli, deciso a starvi fino alla metà di giugno. Nella stagione di primavera Napoli è un paradiso. Vi ero andato per godermi questo paradiso, e per nient'altro.

Avevo passato mezza giornata nell'Aquario tra le meraviglie della vita sottomarina…. Improvvisamente, quasi mi fosse stato suggerito all'orecchio da qualcuno, io pensai:—Va' a Firenze! Va' a Firenze!—Mi stava davanti agli occhi una bella aiuola di attinie e di coralli che si agitavano, che palpitavano con le loro creste filamentose: e tra i coralli e le attinie, magnifici polipi, di cui ora non ricordo il nome, allungavano i tentacoli, si gonfiavano, si aprivano simili a viventi ventagli, si restringevano e quasi sparivano confondendosi con la vegetazione rosata. Altri piccoli molluschi, cavallini di mare, se non sbaglio, idre, meduse, salivano e scendevano nella limpidissima acqua dietro il grosso cristallo; paguri, che si eran formati una casa con grosse conchiglie, erravano qua e là, ora lenti ora rapidi, sul suolo ghiaioso, movendo le gambe rimaste fuori dal guscio. E, di nuovo, quel suggerimento, quella inattesa ispirazione: Va' a Firenze!

In quei giorni, io non vi avevo pensato neppur di sfuggita. Ma, ecco, ora ricordo bene. Mentre guardavo intentamente quel maraviglioso spettacolo acquatico, due signore si erano fermate un istante vicino a me. Fiorentine, si capiva dall'accento. Quale di esse aveva quella voce così melodiosa, da spingermi a guardarla? Ed ero rimasto deluso. La voce mi aveva fatto supporre una bellezza giovane e fresca. Invece! Colei non era giovane, nè bella. Può darsi che il suggerimento:—Va' a Firenze!—sia stato prodotto dal fascino di quel suono. Fascino, ho detto benissimo; giacchè non potei sottrarmi alla sua azione.

"When I left the aquarium, the marvelous marina beside it was suffused by the tender light of the setting sun. The avenues of the Villa of the Aquarium were almost deserted, filled with mysterious shadows and coolness, and in the distance, Vesuvius with a thin plume of smoke, golden from the last rays of the sun.

I looked distractedly at the divine vista that I had been coming to admire every day, never tiring of it, discovering it always renewed by the constantly-varying play of light. And again, I thought, 'Go to Florence!'

"Does this suggestive insistence seem strange to you? Oh, it wouldn't have seemed strange to me either, if not for what happened later! I left the next day, without wondering at my decision, almost as if the trip to Florence had already been a part of my itinerary. Only once I had arrived did I ask myself, 'And why did I come here?' And I left the hotel and took the first road that came before me. Five minutes later, I was in Piazza dell'Indipendenza.

"Oh, this wasn't a dream! I remember very well; I am sure that is was real.

"The blond lady passed by me, saturating the air with her perfume, under her parasol striped in yellow and white, bordered with lace. Her dress was of light fabric, also with yellow and white stripes, but narrower, elegantly enveloping her slim body. I hadn't noticed her face, so quickly she had passed me. I could see, however, under her parasol, golden reflections from her thick hair, gathered on the nape of her neck, from which a few strands floated free, like a living thing.

"I was tempted to follow her, to catch up with her, if only to satisfy my curiosity as to whether her face was as elegant as her silhouette.

"At that point, she had turned into Via Enrico Poggi – a secluded, quiet street, with houses that looked like little villas – and was ringing the bell at a door. She had turned at the sound of my steps, a bit annoyed, it seemed to me, that someone had followed her. So I could ascertain that she was indeed beautiful. An instant's vision! As the door opened, I could see an entry hall with marble busts, large vases with plants and, at the end, a colored stained-glass window. Then the door closed.

"I retraced my steps slowly, troubled by that brief vision, almost as if a part of me had followed her into that house. I suddenly felt the vivid sensation of seeing again, in my mind's eye, that entry hall, and of walking in those rooms, beyond the colored stained-glass window, following that stranger.

"Did I really enter that place, not on that same day, but a few weeks later? It must have been so: Otherwise, how could I see now, as if I were there, that sitting-room upholstered with blue damask, with her portrait on the wall; that Murano lamp with large rosy leaves curling around its arm and climbing along the stem capriciously; the small table, filled with knick-knacks; and the small armchairs covered with a paler shade of blue damask?

Quando uscii dall'Acquario, l'incantevole tratto di marina là accanto era suffuso della tenera luce del tramonto; i viali della Villa quasi deserti, e pieni di misteriose ombre e di frescura; e laggiù, il Vesuvio con un sottile pennacchio di fumo, tutto dorato dagli ultimi raggi del sole, e quasi sorgente dalle onde per ottica illusione.... Guardai distrattamente il divino scenario che venivo ad ammirare ogni giorno insaziabilmente, scoprendolo rinnovato sempre dalla varietà della luce, secondo le ore della giornata.... E tornai a pensare: Va' a Firenze!

Non vi sembra strana questa insistenza suggestiva? Oh, non sembrerebbe strana neppure a me, se poi non fosse accaduto quel che accadde! Partii il giorno dopo, senza maravigliarmi della mia risoluzione, quasi la gita a Firenze fosse stata segnata nell'itinerario del mio viaggio. Soltanto arrivato colà, mi domandai stupito:—Che cosa son venuto a farvi? Ormai!—e uscii dall'albergo e infilai la prima via che mi capitò davanti. Cinque minuti dopo, mi trovavo in *Piazza dell'Indipendenza.*

Oh, questo non è sogno! Ricordo benissimo, ho coscienza della realtà....

La bionda signora mi era passata accanto inondando l'aria del suo profumo, sotto l'ombrellino con strisce gialle e bianche ornato di pizzo. La veste di leggerissima stoffa, con strisce gialle e bianche anch'essa ma più strette, ne modellava elegantemente la persona sottile. Non avevo potuto osservarla in viso, così rapidamente mi aveva oltrepassato. Vedevo, sotto i riflessi dell'ombrellino, l'oro dei suoi copiosi capelli rialzati su la nuca, dai quali sfuggivano alcune ciocchettine che tremavano a ogni passo, come cosa viva.

Fui tentato di seguirla, di raggiungerla, per la sola curiosità di conoscere se l'aspetto corrispondeva alla elegantissima linea della persona.

In quel punto, ella svoltava per via *Enrico Poggi*—via appartata, silenziosa, con case che paiono villini—e suonava a un portoncino. Si era voltata al rumore dei miei passi, un po' contrariata, mi parve, che qualcuno l'avesse seguita. Così potei accertarmi che ella era bellissima. Visione di un istante! All'aprirsi del portoncino avevo intravveduto un andito con busti in marmo, grandi vasi con piante e, in fondo, una vetrata con vetri colorati. Il portoncino si era richiuso.

Tornai indietro lentamente, turbato dalla rapida visione, quasi qualche parte di me fosse penetrata là, dietro a colei, ed io ne sentissi la mancanza. Giacchè sùbito provai la viva sensazione di rivedere con l'immaginazione quell'andito e d'inoltrarmi dietro alla sconosciuta per le stanze, oltre la vetrata colorata.

Quel giorno no, ma qualche settimana dopo, sono io davvero entrato colà? Dev'essere stato così, perchè altrimenti come avrei ora quasi davanti agli occhi quel salottino tappezzato di damasco azzurro, col gran ritratto di lei, in piedi, appeso alla parete di faccia; quella lampada di Murano con grandi foglie rosee che si accartocciavano attorno ai bracci e si arrampicavano al fusto capricciosamente; e il tavolinetto ingombro di ninnoli; e le poltroncine di un azzurro più pallido del damasco delle pareti?

"How could I remember, even in the smallest details, the conversation we had four or five days later? In my mind, I can still hear it. Yet, in certain moments I doubt of my memory. Could it be that I dreamed that conversation, or that I imagined it with such intensity as to believe it actually happened? How can I remember that lady dressed differently, in a flowing, cream-colored dressing gown, all vaporous with rare laces, with the thin fingers of her white hands full of rings, with that big pearl hanging from a star of diamonds pinned to the left side of her chest, almost below her shoulder? How can I have in my ears the exotic sound of her voice, which gave new charm to the Italian language? And finally, if all this wasn't real, how could I recall from that conversation facts that I did not previously know but must have happened?

"'I recognized you immediately,' she said.

"'Why didn't you tell me?'

"'Because, in that house, I didn't want to speak in front of the person who introduced us.'

"'Are you sorry?'

"'No. It is useless to be sorry for what can't be avoided. I accept things easily, philosophically, I would say, if saying so wasn't too much to say for a woman.'

"'Would you have avoided me, if you could?'

"'Of course. Men like you are a disaster in a woman's life.'

"'Why?'

"'Because they soon claim to love her, deluding themselves, perhaps, of being able to inspire a feeling that would flatter their own vanity. You have on the tip of your tongue a declaration that you are not uttering just for appearances' sake, because we only recently met.'

"'You are partly correct. Not appearances, but fear of not being believed prevents me from speaking.'

"'So you are waiting for a more appropriate occasion, correct?'

"'It's impossible now.'

"'You're apparently ignoring that I have a husband.'

"'No; they call you Lady, not Miss.'

"'I see; my husband doesn't seem like an obstacle to you.'

"'It's never one, when love wants.'

"'For some women, that is true.'

"'And for you?'

"'I. . . I believe that the individual has no higher duty in life than what happiness requires; and that of this happiness the individual alone is the final judge.'

"She spoke slowly, and not because speaking Italian was difficult for her. It seemed that every word she pronounced had a hidden meaning and that she wanted to give me time to understand it well before I answered. I was in a hurry to show her that I had interpreted her sentence as being in my favor. She interrupted me: 'You are foolish, like all men.'

Come mai potrei ricordarmi precisamente la nostra conversazione, di quattro o cinque giorni dopo? Mi sembra di riudirla. Eppure in certi momenti dubito della mia memoria. Può mai essere che io abbia sognato quel colloquio o che lo abbia fantasticato a occhi aperti e con tale intensità da crederlo, poi, realmente avvenuto? In che modo dunque io rivedo la signora vestita diversamente, con ampia vestaglia color crema, tutta spumante di pizzi rari, con le sottili dita delle bianchissime mani cariche di anelli, con quella grossa perla pendente da una stella di diamanti attaccata su la parte sinistra del petto, quasi sotto la spalla? In che modo ho negli orecchi il suono esotico della sua voce che dava alle parole della nostra lingua un fascino nuovo? E, finalmente, se non fosse stato vero, in che modo nel dialogo trovo accennati fatti che non ricordo e che pure debbono essere avvenuti?

—Vi ho sùbito riconosciuto—ella diceva.

—Perchè lo avete taciuto?

—Perchè non mi interessava di farvelo sapere, in quella casa, davanti alla persona che vi presentava a me.

—E vi è dispiaciuto?

—No. È inutile dispiacersi di quel che non si può evitare. Io mi rassegno facilmente; filosoficamente direi, se non fosse un po' troppo per una donna.

—Avreste voluto evitarmi potendo?

—Certamente. Gli uomini come voi sono una sciagura nella vita di una donna.

—Perchè?

—Perchè presto affermano di amarla, illusi forse, o vanitosi d'ispirare un sentimento che lusingherebbe il loro amor proprio. Voi avete sulla punta della lingua una dichiarazione che soltanto le convenienze di un primo colloquio v'impediscono di farmi.

—Indovinate, in parte. Non le convenienze però, ma il timore di non esser creduto mi impedisce di parlare.

—Attendete per ciò, è vero? occasione più opportuna.

—Ormai è impossibile.

—Voi forse ignorate che ho marito.

—No; vi chiamano signora, non signorina.

—Capisco; il marito non vi sembra un ostacolo.

—Non è mai tale, quando l'amore vuole.

—Per certe donne, sì.

—E per voi?

—Io... io credo che l'individuo non ha altra norma di vita all'infuori di quella che la sua felicità richiede; e che di questa felicità è giudice inappellabile egli solo.

Parlava lentamente e non perchè l'esprimersi in italiano le richiedesse uno sforzo. Sembrava che ogni parola da lei pronunziata avesse un riposto significato e che ella volesse darmi tempo d'intenderlo bene, prima di rispondere. Ebbi fretta di mostrarle che avevo interpretato in favor mio la sentenza. M'interruppe:

—Siete fatuo, come tutti gli uomini.

"Is it clear? Is it accurate? The introduction, in the house she mentioned, I don't remember it at all. But that conversation is fixed here, word for word, with the sound of her voice, with the accent, with the attitude of the whole person, the proud gestures of her right hand, where a strange ring in the form of a snake twisted around the middle finger forming five or six rings, with the flattened head bending on the side of her nail. So many details that cannot be imaginary. Yet I'm not sure this visit really happened. From time to time, a doubt crosses my mind; that I might have seen that ring, by chance, on another hand, and that I might have heard those words from another mouth, on another occasion, or I might have read them in a novel.

"Why? Because I cannot explain the memory, very clear, very precise, of a solitary walk on the *Viale dei Colli*, where I saw her again a few days later, again as a stranger whose charm attracted me, but without feeling a strong desire to approach her, indeed feeling an instinctive resistance against that charm. She was not alone that day. And I, having followed her for a bit, guessing from some gestures that the three ladies were talking about me, had stopped, annoyed at my seeming to them, it appeared, impudent. If I had been introduced to her, if I had really had that conversation with her in her house, why I hadn't I at least greeted her?

"And no, I'm not confusing the dates. Between the first and the second meeting there was an interval of two or three days. But every time I think about the past, both the conversation and the second meeting have the same sense of reality. Are they both true? Are they both false?

"Nothing kept me in Florence. I had come on a subtle and almost inexplicable whim, and I didn't tour any churches, didn't visit any galleries or museums, didn't stop in front of the monuments. I merely wandered, absent-minded, in the streets. But from time to time, I realized that among the people passing by, I sought one, the one I hadn't seen for a week.

"I was obsessed with her. I wandered in Piazza dell'Indipendenza, I often crossed Via Enrico Poggi, eager to run into her. And I recall often asking myself: 'Why don't you go back to her house?'

"So I *was* in her house; I could not remember this if I hadn't really been there.

"I know what you are going to say: Memory is weak and unreliable! Or perhaps such confusion seems to you explainable by some illness of my nerves. But I was not ill. My nerves have always kept in perfect balance before and after. That is, until a few months ago, until the day when I began to suspect that my mind was confusing things only thought and imagined with facts that had actually happened. And at first, the hesitations, the uncertainties in my judgment were brief; they didn't overly concern me. But, gradually, they worsened. Now I can't make any distinction between reality and imagination. And the idea, the suspicion that I could really have committed. . . It's horrible, Doctor! Let me continue.

"I remember another conversation with her, on a terrace, or in the studio of a painter in Via San Paolo. A bit of uncertainty here, too, but only about the place. It's natural. The image of her erases every other detail. Could I see anything else beyond her?

È chiaro? È preciso? La presentazione, in quella casa da lei accennata, io non la ricordo affatto; ma la conversazione è fissata qui, parola per parola, col suono della voce, con l'accento, con l'atteggiamento di tutta la persona, coi fieri gesti della mano destra, dove uno stranissimo anello in forma di serpente si attorcigliava, flessibile, al dito medio formando cinque o sei anelli, con la testa schiacciata che si piegava di lato alla radice dell'unghia. Tanti particolari non può averli inventati la mia fantasia. Eppure io non sono certo che questa visita sia proprio avvenuta. Di quando in quando, un dubbio mi attraversava la mente: che quell'anello io lo abbia veduto, per caso, in un'altra mano, e che quelle parole io le abbia udite da un'altra bocca, in altra occasione; o le abbia lette in qualche romanzo.

Perchè? Perchè non so spiegarmi il ricordo, nettissimo, precisissimo, di una passeggiata solitaria per il *Viale dei Colli* dove io la rividi alcuni giorni dopo, sempre come una sconosciuta il cui fascino mi attirava, ma senza che ancora sentissi un forte desiderio di avvicinarla, anzi provando un istintivo movimento di resistenza contro quel fascino. Non era sola quel giorno; ed io, seguìtala un po', indovinando da alcune mosse che le tre signore parlavano di me, mi ero fermato, indispettito di riuscire, a quel che sembrava, importuno; e avevo interrotto la salita. Se fossi stato presentato a lei, se avessi avuto davvero quella conversazione con lei in casa sua, perchè non l'avevo almeno salutata?

Non confondo le date. Tra il primo e il secondo incontro ci fu un intervallo di due o tre giorni…. Ma ogni volta che mi metto a ripensare il passato, la conversazione e l'incontro hanno lo stesso valore di realtà. Sono tutti e due veri? Tutti e due falsi?

Niente mi tratteneva a Firenze. Vi ero venuto per subitaneo e quasi inesplicabile capriccio: e non entravo in nessuna chiesa, non visitavo gallerie o musei, non mi fermavo davanti ai monumenti. Erravo per le vie con aria sbadata. Se non che, di tratto in tratto, mi accorgevo che tra le persone dei passanti ne ricercavo una, colei, che più non avevo riveduta da una settimana.

Ne ero impazzito. Mi aggiravo per *Piazza dell'Indipendenza,* attraversavo spesso la via *Enrico Poggi* smanioso di imbattermi in lei. E mi sembra che mi domandassi spesso:

—Perchè non ritorni a casa sua?

Dunque c'ero stato; non potrei rammentarmi di questo, se non ci fossi stato davvero.

Capisco quel che volete dirmi: La nostra memoria è labile! o tale confusione vi sembra spiegabilissima con qualche complicazione nervosa sopravvenuta. Ma io non sono stato malato. I miei nervi hanno conservato sempre un equilibrio perfetto, prima e dopo. Cioè fino a pochi mesi fa, fino al giorno in cui mi sono accorto che avveniva nella mia mente una confusione tra fatti soltanto pensati, immaginati, e fatti realmente accaduti. E, sul principio, l'esitazione, l'incertezza di giudizio erano rapide, mi lasciavano tranquillo. Poi, a poco a poco. Ora non riesco più a fare distinzione alcuna. E l'idea, il sospetto che io abbia davvero potuto commettere…. È orribile, dottore! Lasciatemi continuare.

Ho il ricordo di un'altra conversazione con lei, su una terrazza, o nello studio di un pittore in via S. Paolo. Un po' di incertezza anche qui, ma intorno al luogo. È naturale; l'immagine di lei cancella ogni altro particolare. Potevo vedere qualche cosa all'infuori di lei?

And it is a memory of a pointless conversation, such as that between people who meet for the first time. Or did she only pretend she hadn't met me before, and I humored her so as not to make her look like a liar?

"'Do you prefer painting or music?'

"'I like them both,' I answered. 'Some paintings, like this one', (or perhaps I said, 'like the one we have before our eyes.' No matter. We were speaking of a painting that was a harmonious combination of colors, maybe of a Florentine procession of the Fourteenth Century? Yes, yes, I think it was that.) 'Some paintings are like music for our eyes. The two arts, sometimes, become one. Doesn't Beethoven's pastoral give you the impression of a painted landscape?'

"'With a bit of effort, yes.' She smiled.

"This time she wore a blue dress, with a white and gold silk bib, and a collar of the same fabric. And beneath the hat, made of black tulle with yellow embroidery, the curled hair on her forehead shone even more golden, and her eyes seemed bluer, clearer, smiling like spring skies.

"So how could I tell her the next day – yes, the next day, because at first we discussed the picture we had seen together – how could I say, 'You are made of ice. You have in your heart the snows of your native Russia. Why do you make me suffer? Why won't you speak a word of hope?'

"'Because such words are never spoken; they can only be guessed.'

"I was startled, and I took her ringed hand. She didn't offer it to me, but she didn't withdraw it, either. This indifference prevented me from kissing it. I looked at the little snake dotted with rubies.

"'Is it a symbol?' I asked.

"'Maybe. But it is certainly an admonishment: Be careful!'

"What charm in her voice, her look!

"'Let me worship you!' I exclaimed.

"'I cannot stop you.'

"'What will I be for you?'

"'Who knows?'

"'Have we met in vain?'

"'Maybe.'

"'Not for me!'

"'People say so many things without knowing they lie!'

"I trembled, intimidated by her glacial gaze, with a sense of rebellion and rage deep in my chest. So the lions and tigers must tremble under the charm of the tamer who strikes them with the whip and makes them curl up in a corner of their iron cage.

"'Listen!' I exclaimed. 'You attracted me from afar, through some mysterious force. I had no intention of coming here. A sudden impulse commanded me: *Go to Florence!* And I came and saw you on the very day of my arrival, as if I had made a special trip just for you. I remain here only for you. Break this spell. Free me, witch!'

Ed è ricordo di conversazione futile, quale tra persone che si trovano insieme la prima volta. O ella finse di non avermi conosciuto prima, ed io fui costretto a secondarla per non infliggerle una smentita?

—Preferite la pittura o la musica?

—Tutt'e due—risposi—Certi quadri, come questo che abbiamo visto ora ora (o forse dissi: come questo che abbiamo sotto gli occhi? Non importa. Si parlava di un quadro che era un'armoniosa festa di colori, di una Processione fiorentina del quattrocento? Sì, sì, mi pare appunto di questo.) Certi quadri sono anche una musica per gli occhi. Le due arti si confondono insieme talvolta. La pastorale del Beethoven non fa l'impressione di un paesaggio dipinto?

—Con un po' di buona volontà, sì. E sorrise.

Questa volta portava un abito di colore azzurro, con sprone sul petto di seta chiara, lameggiata di oro, e collare della stessa stoffa; e sotto il cappellino di tulle nero con ricami gialli, i capelli arruffati su la fronte spiccavano con toni dorati più ardenti, e gli occhi sembravano più azzurri, più limpidi, sorridenti come cieli di primavera.

Com'è dunque che io potei dirle il giorno dopo—il giorno dopo, perchè da prima riparlammo del quadro veduto insieme—com'è che potei dirle:

—Voi siete di ghiaccio. Avete nel cuore le nevi della vostra Russia. Perchè mi fate soffrire? Perchè non mi dite una parola di speranza?

—Perchè certe parole non si dicono mai; s'indovinano.

Ebbi un sussulto, e le presi la mano inanellata. Non me la concedette, ma non la ritirò. Questa indifferenza m'impedì di baciargliela. Guardai il serpentello col dorso punteggiato di rubini.

È un simbolo?—domandai.

—Forse. Un'ammonizione, certamente: Abbi prudenza!

Che fascino nella voce e nello sguardo!

—Lasciatevi adorare!—esclamai.

—Non posso vietarlo.

—Che sarò per voi?

—Chi lo sa!

—Ci siamo incontrati invano?

—Può darsi.

—Per me, no!

—Si dicono tante cose senza aver coscienza di dire una falsità!

Tremavo, intimidito dal suo sguardo glaciale, con un senso di ribellione e di furore in fondo al petto. Così devono tremare i leoni e le tigri sotto il fascino della domatrice che li percuote con lo scudiscio e li fa rannicchiare in un angolo della gabbia di ferro.

—Sentite!—esclamai—Mi avete attratto da lontano, per via di una forza misteriosa. Non pensavo affatto di venire qui. Un impulso improvviso mi suggerì: Va' a Firenze! E sono venuto e vi ho veduta lo stesso giorno del mio arrivo, quasi fossi accorso apposta per voi. Sono rimasto qui unicamente per voi. Rompete l'incanto; liberatemi! Siete una maga?

"I loved her and hated her. I was completely in her power, both happy and terrified.

"But did I really have this conversation with her? Sometimes, it seems to me that I spent long hours in my hotel room imagining these meetings, these conversations, indulging myself by creating adventures straight out of a romantic novel after the door on Via Enrico Poggi had closed behind her that first time and she was gone, gone and I never saw her again.

"It is all unbelievable, is it not? Yet it is so. But what about everything else? Have I really spent nine months in a dream world suffering constant hallucinations? Ahh! My forehead! My temples! Such tightening, such stabbing pain! Am I insane, Doctor? Tell me! No! Don't! Tell me at the end when you can begin to heal me. Otherwise, I will kill myself. I can't go on like this.

"I should not doubt myself. It's absurd. Certainly, it is possible to imagine events when moved by the intense desire of an instant, while thinking: 'Oh, imagine if this were to happen!' – and it might be possible, for a moment, to convince yourself that the thing you so intensely desire had actually become reality. Believing it for months, however, and taking action as a result of the imagined event, enjoying it, suffering because of it, having your whole life upset because of it. . . No, it's even more absurd!

"I can't be sure if I saw her again at the *Parco delle Cascine*, in a carriage, with a handsome man who spoke to her warmly, gesticulating, laughing. What was he telling her? She was listening to him, reclining almost lying down, her face turned up towards him, seemingly astonished at what she was hearing, her eyes intent and her head nodding slightly.

"They stopped for a minute in front of the monument to that Indian prince and I got a good look at her. She started at the pallor of my face and my acid gaze. And yet, she again pretended not to recognize me. And again, I humored her deceitfulness. Why?

"The carriage went on and I saw her disappear up the boulevard. I had death in my heart. Who was this man? A husband? A lover? I said aloud, suddenly resolute: 'She must tell me.'

"If I hadn't felt I had the right to ask her, if I had not been sure I was owed a response, would I ever have conceived the thought: *She must tell me?*

"So why do I often doubt that I went to Via Enrico Poggi that very same day? I did go, that is certain; but did I really ring the doorbell? Did she receive me? Or did my imagination create the dialogue that I remember word for word, so clearly that even now I seem to hear my voice and hers with the most minute details of accent and intonation? Can one really imagine such a thing?

"She started as I entered the room. I was having great difficulty in restraining myself, but seeing her startled, I forced on myself a calm I did not feel.

"'I trust you will allow me an indiscretion,' I said.

"'You want to know who he was?'

"'Yes, who was he?'

"'A fellow citizen, from Saint Petersburg.'

"'Nothing else?'

"'If so, that secret belongs to me.'

"'Can't you see how jealous I am?'

L'amavo e la odiavo. Mi sentivo in piena balìa di costei, e n'ero felice e avevo paura.

Ma è vero che io ho avuto quest'altra conversazione con lei? In certi momenti mi sembra che io sia soltanto rimasto lunghe ore nella camera del mio albergo a fantasticare questi incontri, queste conversazioni, compiacendomi di creare le avventure di un romanzo possibile, dopo che il portoncino di via *Enrico Poggi* si era chiuso dietro a lei, ed ella era sparita e non avevo potuto rivederla.

Non è incredibile? Eppure è così. Ma il resto? Sono dunque vissuto nove mesi in continuo sogno, in continua allucinazione? Se sapeste quel che provo qui alla fronte, e alla tempia! Una stretta, fiere trafitture! Non sono già pazzo, dottore? Ditemelo No: me lo direte all'ultimo, e tenterete di guarirmi O mi ammazzerò Non può durare a questo modo!

Non dovrei dubitare; è assurdo. Si possono fantasticare alcuni fatti, intensamente, secondo il desiderio dell'istante, pensando:—Oh, se avvenisse così e così!—e credere per un momento che il desiderio vivissimo si fosse mutato in realtà. Crederlo a lungo però, agire in conseguenza dell'avvenimento fantasticato e goderne e soffrirne e sentirne così sconvolta la vita, quasi tra esso e la realtà non ci fosse stato intervallo nè contraddizione... è anche più assurdo!

Non posso sospettare che io non l'abbia riveduta alle *Cascine*, in carrozza, con un bell'uomo che le parlava calorosamente, gesticolando, ridendo. Che cosa le raccontava? Ella stava ad ascoltarlo quasi sdraiata, con la faccia rivolta verso di lui, stupita di quel che udiva; si scorgeva dagli occhi intenti e dai lievi accenni del capo.

Si fermarono un minuto davanti al monumento del principe indiano; e fu così che io potei osservarla bene e notare che il pallore del mio volto e il fosco lampeggiare dei miei sguardi avevano attirato la sua attenzione. Perchè anche questa volta ella finse di non riconoscermi? Perchè anche questa volta io secondai la sua finzione?

La vidi sparire allo svolto del viale; avevo la morte nel cuore. Chi era colui? Il marito o un amante? Dissi sùbito, risoluto: Dovrà confessarmelo.

Se io non mi fossi riconosciuto in diritto di domandarglielo, se io non avessi avuto la certezza che avrei potuto domandarglielo, avrei mai pensato: Dovrà confessarmelo?

Intanto perchè spesso mi nasce il dubbio se io sia andato quello stesso giorno in via *Enrico Poggi*? Ci sono andato, questo è certo; ma ho proprio suonato il campanello del portoncino? Sono stato ricevuto da lei? O la mia immaginazione ha creato il dialogo, che pure rammento parola per parola, tanto da riudire oggi la mia voce e quella di lei con le più minute particolarità di accento e di gesti? Si può giungere a questo estremo d'illusione?

Appena mi vide entrare ella fece una mossa di sorpresa. Non ero più capace di contenermi; quella sua mossa però m'impose di forzarmi ad essere calmo.

—Mi permetterete un'indiscrezione—dissi.

—Chi era colui? Ho indovinato.

—Non siete maga per nulla. Sì, chi era colui?

—Un mio concittadino, di Pietroburgo.

—Nient'altro?

—In ogni caso, è un segreto che mi riguarda.

—Non vedete dunque che io fremo di gelosia?

"'You're mistaken. Only the possession of a woman may somehow justify jealousy. Only barbarians are jealous. The human creature can't belong to anyone. It is free. Being jealous means being absolute master of a heart, a soul. It's beastly; a harsh word, to be sure.'

"'And what word do you have for someone who takes violent possession of a heart, of a soul, only to mistreat and torture?'

"'I respect the rights of others as I respect my own. Have I done anything to seduce you? Two months ago, I didn't even know you existed.'

"'You know what your beauty has done to me.'

"'Only from you. But I have no obligation to believe you, because I have no way of discovering if you are telling the truth or lying to achieve your own ends.'

"'What must I do to be believed?'

"'Nothing. Certainty is impossible.'

"'Are you really so skeptical?'

"'So reasonable, you should say.'

"'You put my soul in hell!'

"'Perhaps you should see a priest.'

"I saw her through new eyes. Her beautiful face flickered with an expression of cruelty, a malignant ferocity, a sadistic, ruthless enjoyment of my torment. Her blue, clear eyes seemed to be clouded by a sudden swirl of darkness. On the sides of her rosy lips, two small, hard lines appeared, giving her face the appearance of a mask.

"I stared at her, unsettled. The transformation lasted but an instant. And then she smiled, offering me her hand and adding, 'You are a child!'

"I barely had the strength of will to answer, but I managed to exclaim, "'I want to be believed!'

"'I want the moon!' she replied, imitating my tone.

"'What should I do?'

"'Go on loving me! It is very flattering for a woman.'

"'Oh, Kitty!'

"I had never before called her by her given name, and it seemed to me that I was revealing to her my immense love in a way I had never been able to do until that day.

"She smiled again. But as soon as I tried to kiss her hand, she stood up, stern and forbidding. I can still see her, in front of me, with her hands out, rejecting me in a gesture of dismissal.

"Should I doubt all this? No, no! For what reason would I have invented such a conversation? Not once, but a hundred times I've gone through it in my mind, without changing even a syllable, and not once, but a hundred times, faced with the reality of the facts, I have felt a sense of perplexity, of uncertainty, an ineffable pain that clutches my forehead like a vice and drives nails into my temples.

"Do you believe in magic? I do. I believe that man can acquire, through initiation, an almost unlimited power over nature and other people. A power, either beneficial or evil, but more often evil, unfortunately. Have you read the novel by Huysman, *Là-Bas?*

—Avete torto. Soltanto il possesso di una donna può giustificare in qualche modo la gelosia. Bisogna essere barbari per essere gelosi. La creatura umana non può appartenere a nessuno: è libera. Esser gelosi significa esser padroni assoluti di un cuore, di un'anima. È bestiale, scusate la cruda parola.

—E impossessarsi violentemente di un cuore, di un'anima, maltrattarli, torturarli come lo chiamate?

—Io rispetto il diritto degli altri quanto il mio. Ho fatto forse qualche cosa per sedurvi? Due mesi fa ignoravo fin la vostra esistenza.

—Voi sapete già quel che ha operato la vostra bellezza.

—Me lo avete detto voi; non ho obbligo di credervi, perchè non ho la possibilità di accertarmi se dite la verità o se mentite per raggiungere uno scopo qualsiasi.

—Che cosa debbo fare per essere creduto?

—Niente. Non c'è modo di arrivare alla certezza.

—Siete così scettica?

—Così ragionevole intendete dire.

—Mi avete messo l'inferno nell'anima!

—Ci sono degli esorcismi, affermano i preti, per debellare l'inferno.

La vedevo in nuovo aspetto. Sul bellissimo viso tremolava un'espressione di crudeltà, di maligna ferocia, di spietata raffinatezza nel godere del tormento altrui. I ceruli occhi limpidissimi sembravano intorbidati da improvviso rimescolamento fangoso. Ai lati delle rosee labbra apparivano due pieghettine lievi ma rigide che davano alla fisonomia il carattere ripugnante di una maschera.

Rimasi a guardarla, interdetto. La trasfigurazione durò un baleno. Sorrise, mi stese una mano e soggiunse:

—Siete un bambino!

Non avevo forza di risponderle.

—Voglio essere creduto!—esclamai.

—Voglio la luna!—rispose, contraffacendo il mio accento.

—Che cosa debbo fare?

—Continuate ad amarmi! È assai lusinghiero per una donna.

—Oh, Kitty!

Era la prima volta che la chiamavo per nome, e mi parve di rivelarle così l'immenso amor mio, come non avevo saputo mai fare fino a quel giorno.

Sorrise nuovamente; ma tosto che feci atto di voler baciarle le mani, si rizzò in piedi, severa. Mi par di vederla qui, davanti a me, con le mani vietanti, col gesto di congedo.

Dovrei dubitare? No, no! Per qual ragione avrei inventato questo significativo dialogo? Non una ma cento volte l'ho ripensato, senza mutarvi neppure una sillaba; e non una ma cento volte alla convinzione della realtà del fatto son seguiti sempre quel senso di perplessità, di incertezza, quella sensazione ineffabilmente dolorosa che mi stringe la fronte con un cerchio di ferro, che mi conficca due chiodi qui alle tempia.

Credete voi alla magia? Io sì. Credo che l'uomo possa acquistare, per via d'iniziazione, un quasi illimitato potere sulla natura e sui suoi simili; benefico e malefico; malefico più spesso, sventuratamente. Avete letto il recente romanzo dell'Huysman, *Au de là?*

It's not a novel like the others; it is ancient and contemporary history at the same time. Oh! My faith in magic doesn't come just from that book. French newspapers, months ago, wrote extensively of the atrocious revenge one of these magicians took against an unhappy man who had incurred his wrath, a priest, according to the stories. For a moment, put aside your scientific prejudices, and think about my case. I was in Naples, calm, carefree. And I hear a voice suggesting, or I should say, ordering: 'Go to Florence!' Blaming a fascination with a melodious voice heard by chance in the aquarium is inadequate. This explanation occurred to me just now and I wanted to share it with you, because I must tell you all so that you can properly diagnose my illness. But the real explanation is this. I have been aware of it since the day that I told Kitty, 'Break this spell. Free me, witch!' The mystery, however, remains. Why did she choose me as her victim? Me, a person unknown to her, far away, that had done her no wrong? I did later. I was ruthless, if it is true that. . . But you will judge. Let's proceed in order, if I can.

"In just over three months my passion had reached a state of madness. The resistance with which she opposed me, the few concessions that she granted me, followed instantly by even stronger resistance, kept me in a state of excitement that anyone who hasn't loved that way cannot understand. And jealousy. Now there was also jealousy to fan the flames that burnt in my heart! She had said, 'If so, that secret belongs to me.' So I had guessed correctly! What other kind of secret could exist between her and the young man from the carriage in the *Parco delle Cascine*? I obsessed about it for a week: I would seek him, ask him impertinently, 'Are you her lover?' I would insult him, challenge him. And I told Kitty of my plans. She laughed at me.

"'Ah, don't laugh, please!' I had begged.

"She became suddenly serious. 'I don't put my freedom in anybody's hands! What right do you have to extort a confession from me?'

"'I love you!'

"'To me, that's not a reason.'

"'You said, *Keep on loving me!*'

"'Since it seems to please you.'

"'What am I to you, then?'

"'One who says he loves me.'

"'Nothing else?'

"'This, too, is a secret that belongs to me. A day may come, a moment, when it pleases me to reveal it to you.'

"'How cruel you are!'

"'Sincere, rather.'

"During this brief exchange, she stared at me with those clear, blue eyes, which nonetheless deeply disturbed me as if they reinforced the power of her spell. That day, she really looked like a witch, a sorceress, dressed in her dark, transparent dressing gown over a yellow silk lining, with black lace covering her hands and highlighting her rings and bracelets, so strangely shaped, like branches of mystical plants with emerald leaves.

Non è un romanzo come gli altri; è storia antica e contemporanea nello stesso tempo. Oh! La mia fede nella magìa non proviene soltanto da quel libro. I giornali francesi, mesi fa, hanno parlato a lungo dell'atroce vendetta di uno di questi maghi contro un infelice che era incorso nell'ira di colui, prete, a quel che dicevano. Fate tacere per un momento i vostri pregiudizi scientifici, riflettete intorno al mio caso. Io ero a Napoli, tranquillo, spensierato. E mi sento consigliare, mi sento anzi ordinare, non è eccessiva la parola: Va' a Firenze!—Quella spiegazione che mi davo poco fa, la malìa della melodiosa voce udita per caso nell'Acquario, è insufficiente. Mi si è presentata discorrendo, ed ho voluto manifestarvela, perchè debbo dirvi tutto quel che può aiutarvi nella diagnosi del mio male. Ma la vera spiegazione è là; ne ho avuto coscienza sin dal giorno in cui dissi a Kitty:—Rompete l'incanto! Liberatemi!—Il mistero però non si schiarisce. Perchè ella ha scelto me per sua vittima? Me ignoto a lei, lontano, che non posso averle fatto niente di male? Glien'ho fatto dopo. Sono stato inesorabile, se è vero che.... Giudicherete. Procediamo intanto ordinatamente, finchè mi riesce.

In poco più di tre mesi, la mia passione era giunta al parosismo. La resistenza che colei mi opponeva, le scarse concessioni che si degnava di farmi, seguite sùbito da altre e più vive resistenze, mi tenevano in uno stato di eccitazione di cui non può farsi nessuna idea chi non ha amato a quel modo. E la gelosia era sopravvenuta a metter legna al fuoco che mi divampava nel cuore, terribile! Ella aveva detto:—In ogni caso, è un segreto che mi appartiene.—Dunque avevo indovinato! Qual altro genere di segreti poteva mai esistere tra lei e quel giovane veduto in carrozza con lei alle *Cascine*? Avevo farneticato una settimana: Cercarlo, domandargli impertinentemente:—Siete suo amante?—Insultarlo, sfidarlo. E avevo insistito presso Kitty. Mi aveva risposto ridendo.

—Ah, non ridete, per carità!—le avevo detto supplicandola a mani giunte.

Si era fatta seria tutt'a un tratto:

—Io non metto la mia libertà alla mercè di nessuno! Con qual diritto pretendete di strapparmi una confessione, ammesso che ne abbia una da farvi?

—Vi amo!

—Non è una ragione per me.

—Mi avete detto: Continuate ad amarmi!

—Visto che vi fa piacere!

—Che cosa sono dunque per voi?

—Uno che dice di amarmi.

—Nient'altro?

—Anche questo è un segreto che mi appartiene. Può arrivare un giorno, un momento che stimerò opportuno di rivelarvelo.

—Come siete crudele!

—Sincera piuttosto.

E mentre ella pronunziava queste brevi risposte, mi fissava con gli occhi cerulei, limpidissimi, che però mi turbavano profondamente quasi rafforzassero l'opera della sua malìa. Quel giorno sembrava proprio una maga, con quella scura vestaglia trasparente su fodera di seta gialla e con pizzi neri che le coprivano le mani e facevano risaltare gli anelli delle dita e i braccialetti ai polsi, di foggia stranissima, quasi rami attorti, di simboliche piante—immaginavo—con foglioline di smeraldi.

"Her words gave me hope. But a false hope? So I asked her: 'Have you seen him again?'

"'He was here half an hour ago.'

"'Would you promise me. . .'

"'Not to see him again? And if I loved him?'

"Even if she had she actually told me that she loved him, I could not have been more crushed. I went pale, as pale as death. In that moment, I really did think that I might die.

"Did she have pity on me? Did she lie to comfort me?

"'I don't love him, no! Are you happy?'

"I jumped up with such energy that she couldn't prevent me from taking her hand and covering it with kisses. My God! How cold it was! It seemed drained of blood, pale white with no trace of veins under the delicate, shiny skin.

"This iciness is fixed in my mind. It's not merely a persistent hallucination. Yet I have come to doubt this, too. Why? Here is why: I remember meeting her one day in the gardens of Palazzo Pitti and she was accompanied by the same two friends as before. She passed in front of me without looking at me, and lifted up a hand to point out something, I don't know what. And, on seeing that bloodless white hand, I thought: *It must be as cold as ice*! If I had really kissed it, I would have thought: *It is as cold as ice*! I would have remembered the impression that hand had made.

"Ah, if you could only feel this splitting headache! If you could feel these nails inside my temples! I wish I could stop thinking! Without thinking I would have some relief! But we approach the end. I will endure this torture. You will find a cure that will make my thoughts sleep. Is there a cure? Ah! Very well!

"I was feeding on hate, jealousy, unbridled love. I wanted to run away, but I couldn't. I stayed for long hours in my hotel room; I wandered in Piazza dell'Indipendenza, passing hour after hour in front of that fatal door on Via Enrico Poggi, without daring to ring the bell, as if that door had never been opened to let me in, and in the anxiety that perhaps it would never open for me again!

"Isn't it strange that I would torture myself this way, if all I had to do was stretch out my hand, ring the bell, cross the entry hall with the busts, the sempervivum and cactus vases, the colorful medieval glass at the end, and be introduced into the blue living room?

"I passed by that house, over and over, obsessed by suspicion. Perhaps, in this very moment, he is there! Even now, he may be holding her in his arms! Perhaps she abandons herself to him, madly! Or maybe she makes him suffer, like me, savoring the evil enjoyment of her power over him.

"I rang the bell violently. The bell vibrated for a long while, and I repented of having announced myself so. The servant girl was slow to answer and this made me imagine she had ordered her maid to pretend she was not at home. Instead, she welcomed me cheerfully.

"'Oh! Why the dark look?'

"'The only means to make me radiant with happiness, as you know, is in your hands.'

Non erano state incoraggianti, subdolamente incoraggianti le sue parole? Allora io le domandai:

—Lo avete riveduto?

—È stato qui mezz'ora fa.

—Volete farmi la grazia di promettermi....

—Che non lo rivedrò più? E se lo amassi?

Mi avesse detto effettivamente lo amo, non avrei potuto sentirmi trafiggere con maggiore strazio. Impallidii, mi parve di morire!

Ebbe pietà di me in quel punto? Mentì per confortarmi?

—Non l'amo, no! Siete contento?

Scattai con tale impeto ch'ella non fece in tempo per impedirmi di prenderle una mano e di coprirgliela di baci. Dio mio! Com'era fredda quella mano! Infatti pareva esangue, tanto era bianca, senza traccia di vene sotto la pelle fina e lucente.

Ho vivissimo il ricordo di questa sensazione di cosa ghiacciata. Non è un'aberrazione della mia fantasia. Eppure sono arrivato a dubitare anche di essa. Perchè? Ecco: rammento di averla incontrata un giorno nei giardini di *Pitti* con le sue due amiche dell'altra volta. Mi passò davanti senza guardarmi, e levava appunto in alto una mano per indicare non so che cosa; ed io, vedendo quella mano così bianca che pareva esangue, pensai così: Dev'essere fredda come il ghiaccio!. Se l'avessi realmente baciata, avrei pensato: È fredda come il ghiaccio! Avrei ricordato la impressione ricevuta.

Ah, se poteste sentire che male mi produce questo cerchio qui! Se poteste sentire come mi si conficcano più addentro i chiodi delle tempie! Vorrei non poter pensare! Soltanto non pensando avrei un po' di requie! Ma ci avviciniamo alla fine. Sopporterò questa tortura; voi troverete un rimedio per addormentarmi il pensiero. C'è un rimedio? Ah! Benissimo!

Vivevo di odio, di gelosia, di amore sfrenato. Avrei voluto fuggire lontano, ma non potevo. Restavo per lunghissime ore nella camera del mio albergo; mi aggiravo per *Piazza dell'Indipendenza* passavo e ripassavo davanti al fatale portoncino di via *Enrico Poggi* senza osare di stendere la mano al campanello, quasi quel portoncino non fosse mai stato aperto per lasciarmi entrare, e con l'angoscia che forse non si sarebbe aperto mai, mai per me!

Non è strano che mi torturassi per questo, se ormai bastava che stendessi la mano al campanello per venire introdotto nel salottino azzurro, varcando l'andito coi busti, coi vasi di spetriste e di cactus, e in fondo, la vetrata medievale colorata?

Passavo e ripassavo, sconvolto dal sospetto:

—In questo momento forse egli è là! Forse la stringe tra le braccia! Forse ella si abbandona a lui, follemente! O, forse lo fa soffrire al pari di me, assaporando il maligno godimento della sua potenza di nuocere!

Suonai violentemente. Il campanello ondulò a lungo per l'andito, mentre io mi pentivo di essermi annunziato a quel modo; e il ritardo del servitore che doveva venir ad aprire mi faceva imaginare che ella avesse ordinato di fingere che nessuno era in casa. Invece ella mi accolse con aria lieta.

—Oh! E venite qui così fosco?

—L'unico mezzo di farmi accorrere raggiante di felicità, voi lo sapete, è in mano vostra.

"'I may not use it. A terrible fate persecutes me.'

"'You, you, are the terrible fate!'

"'It's true! And I don't know if I should be sad, or moved by it any longer. Against the inevitable, one does not fight.'

"Her face now had a different expression, and this made me think that the happy countenance with which she had welcomed me had been dishonest.

"'Were you alone?'

"'Alone with my thoughts, as the characters of certain plays say.'

"She made an effort to look cheerful again. And this, too, made me suspicious. I looked around, to see if I could find in the living room some sign of disorder, in the chairs, in the armchairs, that she hadn't had the time to hide. Nothing!

"'What are you looking for with those jealous eyes? Your supposed rival?' And after a short pause, she added, 'He killed himself yesterday. For me, he wrote in his note. What a fool! You would not do such a thing.'

"'Perhaps,' I said grimly.

"And I left her. She had seemed to me covered in the blood of the poor man who had killed himself for her. And she had no note of compassion in her voice. Not the glimmer of a tear in her clear blue eyes. She was unmoved! What terrible creature was this? Did the spell she cast feed on human blood?

"'Perhaps,' I had said.

"But I felt she was relentlessly pushing me toward the abyss, toward death. Who knows how much blood was already on her hands? And I didn't want to die! To love her, to possess her, to feel her tremble under the force of my will, to tame her, to destroy her, *that* is what I wanted!

"To destroy her! For several days I was obsessed by this idea. To avenge the others and myself, to prevent her from exerting her evil influence on yet another innocent! At the same time, I felt I was committing a great sacrilege merely by contemplating harming her perfect beauty. Who was I to demand her love? Wasn't it enough that she had allowed me to continue to love her and to repeat my feelings as often as I liked? 'A day may come, a moment!' Didn't this mean 'You may hope'?

"I searched for news of the suicide in the newspapers. There was no mention of it. Had she lied to me? I realized that she hadn't said whether he had killed himself in Florence or in some other Italian city. Perhaps he had gone back to Saint Petersburg, hoping to escape her lethal power. But in vain! An inexorable Atropos, she had cut the thread of his life from afar. And I wouldn't be able to escape from her either, if I delayed, if I hesitated to decide. And I did decide, one night, after a long struggle between the anguish of insomnia and that of a passion that may have been love, or hate, or both together. And with that, I fell into such a deep sleep that the hotel staff became concerned. When they finally decided to check on me, it was two in the afternoon.

"I felt perfectly calm, and I was not surprised by this. My first thought, as soon as the waiter awakened me, had been, *Destroy her!*

"Apparently my subconscious had continued the debate while I slept and had matured and reinforced my decision.

—Non posso adoperarlo. Una fatalità mi perseguita.

—Siete voi, voi, la terribile fatalità!

—È vero! E non so più attristarmene, nè commovermene. Contro l'ineluttabile non si combatte.

La sua fisonomia aveva mutato espressione; la qual cosa mi faceva pensare che l'aria lieta con cui ella mi aveva accolto non fosse stata sincera.

—Eravate sola?

—Sola coi miei pensieri, come dicono i personaggi di certi drammi.

Voleva riapparir gaia. E anche questo mi mise in sospetto. Guardavo attorno, se mai scoprissi nel salotto un indizio di disordine, nelle seggiole, nelle poltrone, non potuto riparare per la fretta. Niente!

—Che cercate con quegli occhi gelosi? Il vostro preteso rivale?—E, dopo una breve pausa, soggiunse:—Si è ucciso ieri; per me, ha lasciato scritto. Che pazzia! Voi non ne commettereste una simile.

—Forse!—risposi cupamente.

E la lasciai. Mi era parsa coperta dal sangue del misero che si era ucciso per lei. E non aveva nell'accento nessun fremito di compassione! Non una lagrima negli occhi azzurri limpidi, impassibili! Che terribile creatura era ella dunque? Aveva bisogno di sangue umano per le sue orrende incantagioni?

—Forse!—mi era fuggito.

Ma sentivo che mi spingeva furiosamente verso l'abisso, verso la morte. Chi sa di quanti altri disastri era colpevole! Ed io non volevo morire! Amarla, possederla volevo, sentirla tremare sotto la forza della mia volontà, domarla, annullarla, volevo!

Annullarla! Per parecchi giorni fui sotto l'ossessione di questa idea! Vendicare gli altri e me, impedirle di esercitare sopra nuove innocenti creature la sua malefica influenza! Nello stesso tempo, mi sembrava di compire un gran sacrilegio attentando soltanto col pensiero alla sua perfetta bellezza. Chi ero io da pretendere di essere riamato da lei? Non era anche troppo ch'ella mi avesse permesso di continuare ad amarla e di ripeterglielo quante volte mi fosse piaciuto?—Può arrivare un giorno, un momento!— Non significava: Sperate?

Cercai nei giornali la notizia di quel suicidio; nessuno ne faceva cenno. Aveva ella mentito? Riflettei che non mi aveva detto che colui si fosse ammazzato a Firenze o in qualche altra città italiana. Era tornato, probabilmente a Pietroburgo, lusingandosi di sfuggire al letale potere di lei. Ma inutilmente! Ella aveva reciso il filo di quella vita come una inesorabile parca, da lontano! Neppure io avrei potuto evitarla, se tardavo ancora, se non mi decidevo. E mi decisi, una notte, dopo lungo dibattermi tra le smanie dell'insonnia e della passione che più non distinguevo se fosse amore o odio, o l'uno e l'altro insieme. E mi immersi sùbito in un sonno così profondo da impensierire le persone dell'albergo. Quando risolsero di accertarsi se stavo male, erano le due pomeridiane.

Mi sentivo calmo, e non me ne maravigliavo. Il mio primo pensiero, appena scosso dalla voce del cameriere, era stato:

—Annullarla!

Certamente il mio spirito aveva continuato durante il sonno l'intenso lavorìo della giornata precedente, e aveva maturato e rafforzato la mia decisione.

"I don't know what use you will make of what I am about to tell you. If it triggers certain professional or ethical obligations on your part, I understand. Do what you have to do. I took that into account. Whatever happens, it will never cause me the anguish that I suffer by remaining silent.

"Please believe me when I say I can see that terrible scene in my mind's eye as if it had happened just a few hours ago. Nevertheless. . . Oh! I find this all so terrifying, Doctor!

"Did she have a foreboding? An inkling of what was to come? She didn't sit next to me in her usual place, but behind the table, with the excuse of lighting a cigarette. I refused the one she offered me, very thin, too fragrant for my taste.

"'Have you nothing to say? What are you looking at? This brooch?'

"'It looks like a small dagger.'

"'It is an ornament from the Caucasus. Many women wear them there.'

"'Made of silver?'

"'Of steel, well tempered.'"

She inhaled slowly through her lit cigarette, her eyes narrowing in pleasure, then added, 'I have news that will please you.'

"'Finally!'

"'It isn't what you imagine. I'm leaving.'

"I stood up, opening my eyes wide.

"'It's not true!' I stammered.

"'Why should I lie to you?'

"'And me? What about me?'

"Every possibility had gone through my mind except that she would leave, escaping my revenge! I believed that she was announcing it almost to laugh at me, to taunt me, because now I would never be able to shake off the sinister power of her spell, that mysterious spell which would work even more terribly from afar. Indeed, if instead of 'I'm leaving,' she had told me at that moment 'Tomorrow the sun will no longer shine and all will be buried in eternal darkness,' even believing her, I would have been much less frightened.

"'What about me?' I repeated.

"'What can I tell you? You'll do as you like. You'll forget me, first of all.'

"'Please, make me forget you first! Release me from your spell!'

"'It is so easy to forget.'

"'Not when one loves the way I love you! Even now, you don't believe me? And yet, you see my agony!'

"I was barely able to speak. I panted and wheezed. My eyes were dimming, a faintness took me. I had to lean on the table not to fall.

"'You know, I saw one of your great actors doing something like that. You Italians have no rivals in expressing your moods.'

"It was like telling me: *You are a comedian*!

Io non so qual uso voi farete della rivelazione che sto per farvi. Se la vostra professione di dottore v'impone dei doveri, adempiteli senza esitare. Ho preveduto questo caso. Qualunque cosa sia per accadere, non potrà mai raggiungere quel che dovrei continuare a soffrire tacendo.

Notate: ho la visione netta, evidentissima della terribile scena, come se fosse accaduta poche ore fa. Ciò nonostante…. Oh! È spaventevole, dottore!

Aveva ella qualche tristo presentimento? Non si sedette accanto a me al solito posto, ma dietro al tavolino con la scusa di accendere una sigaretta. Io rifiutai quella che mi era stata offerta, sottilissima, troppo profumata per il mio gusto.

—Non dite nulla? Che guardate? Questo spillone?

—Sembra un pugnaletto.

—È un ornamento femminile di certe regioni del Caucaso.

—D'argento?

—Di acciaio, e ben temprato.

Tirò due o tre boccate di fumo, socchiudendo gli occhi deliziata, poi soggiunse:

—Vi do una notizia che vi farà gran piacere.

—Finalmente!

—Non quella che voi imaginate. Parto.

Balzai in piedi, sbarrando gli occhi.

—Non è vero!—balbettai.

—Perché dovrei mentirvi!

—E io?

Ogni possibilità mi era passata per la mente all'infuori di questa ch'ella partisse, che si sottraesse così alla mia vendetta!Credetti che me lo annunziasse quasi ad irrisione, per sfida, mentre io non avrei potuto mai levarmi di addosso il funesto dominio del suo filtro, del suo misterioso potere, che forse avrebbe operato più terribilmente da lontano. Infatti, se ella mi avesse detto in quel momento, invece di: Parto!—Domani non spunterà più il sole, tutto rimarrà sepolto in tenebra eterna!—anche credendole, ne sarei stato assai meno atterrito.

—E io? Io?—ripetei.

—Che volete che ne sappia? Farete quel che vi piacerà. Mi dimenticherete, innanzi tutto.

—Fatemi prima dimenticare! Datemi qualche vostra magica bevanda di oblìo!

—Si dimentica così facilmente!

—Non quando si ama come io vi amo! Neppure in questo momento mi credete? E mi vedete agonizzare!

Parlavo a stento, ansavo; sentivo nel petto un rantolo di morte; gli occhi mi si erano annebbiati, un languore mi invadeva. Dovetti appoggiarmi al tavolinetto per non cadere.

—Ho visto uno dei vostri grandi attori fare qualche cosa di simile. Siete inarrivabili voialtri italiani nella espressione di certi stati d'animo.

Era come dirmi: commediante!

"I tore the brooch from her gown and brandished it menacingly.

"'Bravo!' she exclaimed, 'Strike me!'

"And she rose and offered me her breast covered with lace.

"I had the strength to smile, to answer her, hiding my true feelings: 'You know I couldn't do that! Ah, Kitty!'

"'You do not love me, then, enough to kill? Your love is pathetic!'

"She provoked me; she taunted me. Was she really so sure I could not strike her? She removed the cigarette from her mouth, slowly exhaling the smoke from her lips and rosy nostrils with a voluptuous pleasure. Then she opened her arms, repeating, 'Strike!'

"'Yes, it's true,' I said, 'if I loved you without reservation. . .'

"I approached her, gently pushing aside the lace with one hand while positioning the brooch over her heart with the other.

"'. . . I would do. . . this!'

"The brooch effortlessly sank into her chest all the way to the hilt.

"She didn't cry out. She made no noise at all. Her eyes rolled up and she slumped over me. A slight tremor convulsed her and she lay still, unmoving.

"I have no recollection of succeeding events except that I spent the night at the church of San Domenico, on the road to Fiesole, sitting on a low wall, while the moon flooded the countryside with a bright, peaceful light. I remember the crickets chirping in the surrounding meadows and a dog barking, at intervals, far away.

"Sometime around noon, I returned to Florence and went to bed with a fever.

"Over the next few days, I followed the newspapers voraciously. But, to my astonishment, there was nothing of the murder of a beautiful Russian lady living on Via Enrico Poggi.

"Three days later, still not quite myself, I left my bed and asked a coachman to take me to Via Enrico Poggi without giving a precise address. The street was silent, as usual. All the doors were closed, the windows shuttered. There was nothing to indicate that something horrible had happened on that street, in that familiar house.

"I knew that murderers often feel an irresistible compulsion to return to the place where they had committed their crime, and I thought: *It is true! It's true!* Because a strong impulse dominated me, an imperative command: 'Get out of the carriage! Ask someone! You must know!'

"And I tell you, my greatest terror was not that I would receive confirmation of my crime, but the opposite.

"I repeatedly rang the bell at the door. No one came to open it.

"A woman coming out of the next house stopped, looked at me hesitantly, and then said, 'I'm afraid there is no one there.'

"'A lady was living here. . .'

"'She left a while ago. The house is not rented now.'

"'A while ago?' I asked, surprised.

"'Oh yes! At least three weeks.'

"I felt my heart skipping. And it is from that moment that the pain grips my forehead and I can feel nails driven into my temples.

Afferrai lo spillone, lo brandii minacciosamente.

—Bravo!—esclamò—Ferite!

E si rizzò e mi offerse il seno coperto di trine.

Ebbi la forza di sorridere, di rispondere con profonda dissimulazione:

—Sapete bene che non posso!Ah, Kitty!

—Non mi amate fino al delitto? Misero amore, il vostro!

Mi provocava, mi aizzava. Era proprio sicura che non avrei potuto colpirla? Con una mano si tolse la sigaretta di bocca, esalò lentamente con voluttuosissimo godimento il fumo dalle labbra ristrette e dalle rosee narici, e aperse le braccia, ripetendo:

—Ferite!

—Sì, è vero—dissi—Se vi amassi in modo estremo....

Mi accostai, scartai con una mano la trina, appuntai lo spillone in direzione del cuore....

—... farei... così!

Lo spillone era penetrato senza nessuna resistenza fino alla capocchia....

Non gridò. Travolse gli occhi e mi si rovesciò addosso, con un lieve sussulto per tutto il corpo.

Che cosa io abbia fatto dopo non so. Ricordo soltanto che passai la nottata presso San Domenico su la strada di Fiesole, seduto su un muricciolo, e che la luna inondava la campagna col suo pieno lume sereno, e che i grilli zirlavano tra le erbe dei prati attorno e che un cane abbaiava, a intervalli, lontano.

Ricordo che, a giorno alto, tornai a Firenze e che dovetti mettermi a letto con la febbre.

Volli leggere i giornali. E vidi con stupore che nessuno di essi parlava dell'assassinio della bella signora russa in via *Enrico Poggi*.

Tre giorni dopo, non interamente guarito, mi levai da letto, e mi feci condurre colà da un cocchiere, senza dare indicazione precisa. La via era silenziosa, come al solito; tutti i portoncini chiusi; tutte le persiane delle finestre o chiuse o socchiuse. Nessun indizio che in quella via, in quella nota casa fosse avvenuta qualche cosa di straordinario.

Sapevo che gli assassini sentono una irresistibile attrazione verso i luoghi dov'essi hanno commesso un delitto, e pensavo: È vero! È vero! giacchè un vivo impulso mi dominava, un imperativo suggerimento mi diceva:

—Scendi dalla carrozza! Domanda a qualcuno! Saprai!

E il terrore che mi invadeva non era quello di ottenere la certezza del mio delitto, ma l'opposto.

Suonai replicatamente al portoncino. Nessuno venne ad aprirmi.

Una donna che usciva dalla casa accanto si fermò a guardarmi esitante, poi mi disse:

—Sa? Non c'è nessuno.

—Abitava qui una signora....

—È partita, da un pezzo. L'appartamento è sfitto.

—Da un pezzo?—domandai stupito.

—Eh! Da tre settimane, almeno. Mi sentii dare un tuffo al sangue. E da quell'istante ho questo cerchio, qui, attorno alla fronte, e questi chiodi confitti nelle tempie.

"How was it possible? Had I not killed her only days before? And yet, she had left three weeks ago! What, then? What have I been doing these last two months? Was everything I told you simply a figment of my imagination even though every detail, every recollection rings true? I saw her, I talked to her, I heard her voice. There is no doubt that she lived there, in that house on Via Enrico Poggi. It is certain that I've been in that little blue drawing room many times.

"I visited the house on the pretext of renting it. There was no longer any furniture, only the bare walls. And yet her perfume lingered, and the scent of her cigarettes. If I had not been there before, how could I have recognized it?

"The trouble is here, in my head. Doctor, I beg you, free me from the vice that grips my forehead! Tear these nails from my temples! I don't want to lose my mind. It's all too horrible! If she isn't dead, if she somehow survived the cold steel plunged into her breast. . . then it is true. She is a witch, and it is she who torments me. Don't shake your head. It is she! What evil did I do her? I loved her! Yes. Immensely!"

Com'era possibile! Non l'avevo uccisa giorni addietro? Partita da tre settimane! O dunque? In che modo io sono vissuto questi ultimi due mesi? In che modo tutto quel che vi ho narrato si è andato formando nella mia mente con la suprema evidenza della realtà? Io la ho vista, le ho parlato, ho udito la sua voce. È certo che ella abitava colà, in quel villino di via *Enrico Poggi*. È certo che io sono stato più volte in quel salottino azzurro.

Visitai la casa, con il pretesto di prenderla in affitto. Non c'erano più i mobili, niente; solo le dure pareti. E c'era tuttavia il suo profumo, il profumo acutissimo di quelle sue sigarette. Se non fossi stato là altre volte, avrei potuto riconoscerlo?

Il guasto è qui, nel mio cervello. Dottore, liberatemi da questo cerchio alla fronte! Strappatemi questi chiodi dalle tempie! Non voglio impazzire! È orribile! Se non è morta, se ha potuto sopravvivere al colpo dello spillone conficcatole nel seno… è lei, la maga, che continua a tormentarmi! Non crollate la testa. È lei! Che male le ho fatto? L'amavo! Oh! Immensamente!

THE BOAT

TO JOLANDA

Although she had been in Catania for eight days now, my wife was still fascinated by the sight of the sea which was new to her. As I played tour guide and led her around showing her churches, monuments, and shops, she kept pulling my arm, almost like a child demanding satisfaction, and whispering in my ear, "Let's go to the marina!"

"We were there an hour ago!"

"So what? Oh, the sea! I can't get enough of it! Shall we go?"

I felt her excitement, walking arm in arm with her, from her anticipation of the next sight of the sea. And the moment she caught a glimpse of it, through the arches of the viaduct and the trees of the Villa Pacini, she would burst out in exultation that made me smile and seemed, at least to me, a classic product of feminine excitability.

Just to be contrary, I would say something like, "There it is! It's still the same: water, water, water!"

"It's not true. It changes from one hour to the next. An hour ago it was blue; now, look, it's the color of ash."

"It's the effect of the light."

"*Bravo*! You astound me! Thank you for the explanation. But you can't see it very well from here. Let's go onto the quay."

"I know! Let's take a boat and tour the harbor!"

"No, I'm afraid."

"Afraid of what?"

"Of the water. If a storm came. . ."

"Storms don't break out suddenly."

"What if the boat capsized?"

"Impossible! A boat seems as if it is cradled by the waves when the sea is as quiet as it is now."

"I'm afraid."

"Think again! When we leave, you will regret not having enjoyed the great pleasure of a boat trip."

"I'm sure I will." Then she added, "If we went with one of those big ships, with a steamer, I would feel safe. But look at these boats, they look like walnut shells! How many are there in a row? Don't they look like big fish on the surface of the sea? They shake and jump like living things. . . I'd be happy to go on a ship, on a steamer, but these!"

"You're wrong. In a storm, small boats are more seaworthy than big ships. When steamers are about to sink, the passengers and crew save themselves – as you know perfectly well – using small boats like these. Come on! You really should overcome these silly fears."

IN BARCA

A JOLANDA

Sebbene fosse a Catania da otto giorni, mia moglie era ancora affascintata dallo spettacolo del mare, nuovo per lei. Ogni momento, mentre la conducevo attorno per farle osservare chiese, monumenti, negozi, mi si attaccava al braccio e, con accento da bambina che vuol essere accontentata, mi sussurrava all'orecchio:

—Andiamo alla Marina?

—Ci siamo stati un'ora fa!

—Che importa? Oh, il mare! Mi sembra di non aver potuto ancora ammirarlo a bastanza. Andiamo?

La sentivo trasalire, sotto braccio, dal godimento anticipato che la prossima vista del mare le avrebbe prodotto. E appena ne scorgeva un pezzetto attraverso gli archi del viadotto e i rami degli alberi di Villa Pacini, prorompeva in esclamazioni che mi facevano sorridere e già mi sembravano esagerazioni femminili. Per contraddirla, allora le dicevo:

—Ecco! È sempre lo stesso: acqua, acqua, acqua!

—Non è vero. Cambia aspetto da un'ora all'altra. Un'ora fa era azzurro; ora, guarda, è cenericcio.

—Effetto della luce.

—Bravo! Grazie della spiegazione! Ma di qui non si vede bene; andiamo laggiù, sulla panchina del Molo.

—Perchè non usciamo in barca fuori del porto?

—Ho paura.

—Di che cosa?

—Dell'acqua. Se arrivasse una tempesta….

—Le tempeste non scoppiano all'improvviso.

—Se la barca si capovolgesse….

—In che modo? Le barche sembrano cullate dalle onde quando il mare è tranquillo come in questo momento.

—Ho paura.

—Stai attenta! Quando saremo andati via, rimpiangerai di non aver gustato il gran piacere di una gita in barca.

—Lo credo!—E soggiungeva:—Se andassimo con uno di quei grossi bastimenti, con un piroscafo, mi sentirei sicura; ma con queste barche che sembrano tanti gusci di noce! Quante ce ne sono, in fila, là! Non sembrano grossi pesci a fior d'acqua? Si agitano, saltellano come cosa viva…. Oh, su una nave, su un piroscafo, sì!

—Hai torto. Nelle tempeste, le barche tengono il mare assai meglio di quei grandi legni. Quando questi stanno per affondare, passeggeri ed equipaggio si salvano, lo sai bene, su fragili imbarcazioni. Dai! Dovresti vincere così sciocca paura.

"Perhaps another time. Now be quiet. Let me admire the view."

Standing there, her beautiful black eyes drinking in the immense expanse of the Ionian Sea, sparkling in the sunshine, she was overwhelmed by her emotions. And I, watching her, envied her the joy this novel experience provided her. It was a joy that I could not fully comprehend, as I became accustomed to the sea in my student days though, like my wife, I was born in the Troina Mountains, in the hinterland of Sicily.

***

During our honeymoon, that spectacle had made a deeper impression on Paolina than anything else. She couldn't stop talking about it.

"What had you imagined?" I would ask her, teasing her a bit.

"Something huge, immense. . . and still I could not imagine this. Now, the more I look at it, the more I contemplate it, and the more I see details that had escaped me before. You say, 'The sea is blue like the reflection of the sky.' But it isn't true. The sea is a hundred different colors, blue, turquoise, purple, light green, dark green, yellow, gray, white. . . It is a hundred colors. If I had not seen it, I wouldn't have believed it. And now that I feel like I am a little more acquainted with it. . ." she finally said one morning.

"Ah! You've decided!"

"Yes, I asked the maid for some information: We could go on a boat to Ògnina, and return in a few hours, after having lunch there."

"And if a storm should come?"

"Don't laugh at me!"

"And if the boat should capsize?"

"We would drown, hugging each other tight. . . Goodbye cruel world!"

"How did you become so brave all of a sudden?"

"I was afraid for your sake. But as you say that there is no danger. . ."

I looked at her with amazement and with great joy. Relief, I should say.

I believe that the honeymoon is often the first and the most irreparable disappointment in married life. The passage from the imagined ideal to stark reality is so abrupt and so unexpected that it leaves a deep mark on the soul, something that shapes the future unhappiness of the two creatures that, perhaps a bit foolishly, have been joined forever.

I myself, in those eight days of hotel life, had picked up from Paolina's behavior, if not exactly a bad impression, a confused sense of. . . I wouldn't know how to define it. It seemed to me that she lacked tenderness, trust, and that her spirit was more superficial, more childish than she had ever let me see in a year of engagement and almost daily intimacy. At times, I would be surprised to discover a dull and inexplicable grudge against her in the depths of my heart. And I would be offended by it, as if it were an injustice against the beautiful eighteen-year-old creature that I would have wished were different than what sex and age had made her.

—Un'altra volta. Ora sta' zitto; lasciami ammirare.

Dal muraglione della panchina del Molo, spalancava i begli occhi neri sulla immensa distesa del Mar Jonio scintillante di sole, e non aveva parole nén gesti per esprimere le sue diverse sensazioni. Ed io, osservandola, le invidiavo la gioia della novità di quelle sensazioni che quasi non riuscivo a comprendere, abituato ormai, sin da quando ero studente, alla vista del mare, sebbene fossi nato, come mia moglie, in cima alle montagne di Troina nell'interno della Sicilia.

***

La più profonda impressione del nostro viaggio di nozze era stata per Paolina quello spettacolo; non finiva di parlarne.

—Che cosa ti eri immaginata?—le domandavo, canzonandola un po'.

—Qualcosa di grande, d'immenso… e non sono arrivata alla realtà. Ora più lo guardo, più lo contemplo, e più vi scorgo particolari che da prima mi erano sfuggiti. Tu dici:—Il mare è azzurro come il cielo che vi si riflette.—Non è vero. Il mare è di cento colori, qua azzurro, là turchino, più in là violetto, più in là verde chiaro, verde cupo, giallastro, grigio, bianco…. di cento colori. Se non lo avessi visto, non lo avrei creduto. Ed ora che ho preso un po' di confidenza con lui…—soggiunse finalmente una mattina.

—Ah! Ti sei decisa!

—Sì, mi sono informata dalla cameriera dell'albergo: potremmo andare in barca fino a Ògnina e tornare, in poche ore, dopo aver fatto colazione là.

—E se arrivasse una tempesta?

—Non ridere di me!

—E se la barca si capovolgesse?

—Annegheremmo, abbracciati stretti… e addio!

—Sei diventata coraggiosa tutt'a un tratto?

—Avevo paura per te. Giacchè ora dici che non c'è pericolo….

La guardai maravigliato e con una vivissima gioia; sollievo, dovrei dire.

Io credo che il viaggio di nozze sia, spesso, la prima e la più irrimediabile delusione della vita matrimoniale. Il passaggio dall'ideale fantasticato alla realtà è così brusco e così inatteso, che lascia un'orma profonda nell'animo, qualche cosa che forma poi l'infelicità delle due creature che si sono unite, forse un po' sbadatamente, per sempre.

Appunto in quegli otto giorni di vita di albergo, io avevo ricevuto dal contegno di Paolina, se non una cattiva impressione, un senso confuso di… non saprei come dire. Insomma, mi era sembrato ch'ella mancasse di tenerezza, di abbandono, e che il suo spirito fosse più superficiale, più fanciullesco ch'ella non avesse mai lasciato trasparire in un anno di fidanzamento e di quasi quotidiana intimità. In certi momenti, sorprendevo in fondo al mio cuore un sordo e allora inesplicabile rancore contro di lei; e me ne indignavo come di un'ingiustizia verso la bella creatura di diciotto anni che io desideravo diversa da quello che il sesso e l'età la rendevano.

Was I not much more childish and more superficial than she was, feeling a sort of jealousy toward the sea that excited her so much with its immensity? Was I not ridiculous? Yes, ridiculous, especially in those last few days, when I would accompany her to the beach with a bored attitude, and would have fun teasing her, taunting her, without hiding the fact that her insatiable love for the sea was beginning to seem to me unworthy of her.

"I was afraid for your sake!"

Those words had been a sudden revelation. Not just because of the tone she'd given her words, but for the affectionate gaze that she had given me when she said them.

I took her arm, and shortly thereafter, we were at the marina looking for a boat and a boatman that would take us to Ògnina, as Paolina had planned.

***

By chance, that morning we found neither boats nor boatmen. Maybe because it was Sunday, maybe because the good weather had given many others the same idea, maybe because most sailors had gone out fishing.

"It's impossible! Today of all days!" Paolina exclaimed.

At last, an old man, after a brief consultation with two other old men who smoked quietly in a corner and hadn't even bothered to acknowledge our request, came to offer us his boat.

"Will you be able to row on your own?" I asked.

"Get in!" His abrupt gesture and the tone of his voice made it clear that my doubts had wounded his pride.

The sea couldn't have been calmer. The boat glided on its surface with a slight rustle. The shore flowed beside us just a short distance away, sloping upward and covered with pieces of black lava rocks, it hid the countryside beyond. Caves opened here and there. Flocks of wild wood pigeons flew intermittently out of them, while the cormorants were following us, the tips of their wings silently touching the water.

Paolina was ecstatic, and I had to stop her from trying to touch the iridescent, opaline jellyfish at the water's surface, crystalline mushrooms carried by the current. I was amazed that she felt none of the symptoms of seasickness.

"Are you happy with this trip?"

"It's delightful!"

"Here is Ògnina," said the boatman.

***

We were only halfway through our lunch, when the old man, who had gone to visit an acquaintance, came to announce, "We should leave right away. The wind is rising, and the sea is getting rough."

In fact, the sea looked as if it were shuddering. It rippled and lifted with frequent foaming crests.

"Let's go soon," the old man insisted.

"Will we be in danger?" Paolina asked.

"No, ma'am. But it's better to hurry. With the sea, you never know. . ."

46

Non ero io assai più infantile e più superficiale di lei, sentendo una specie di gelosia del mare che la entusiasmava tanto con la sua immensità? Non ero ridicolo?—sì, ridicolo—specialmente in quegli ultimi giorni, quando la accompagnavo alla spiaggia con aria annoiata, e mi divertivo a punzecchiarla, a canzonarla, a non nasconderle che la sua insaziabilità cominciava a sembrarmi indegna di lei?

—Avevo paura, per te!

Queste parole intanto erano state un'improvvisa rivelazione, soprattutto per l'accento con cui ella le aveva dette e per l'affettuosissimo sguardo con cui le aveva accompagnate.

Le presi il braccio, e poco dopo eravamo alla Marina in cerca di una barca e di un barcaiuolo che ci portasse a Ògnina, come Paolina aveva progettato.

* * *

Per caso, quella mattina non trovavamo barche nè barcaiuoli disponibili, forse perchè era domenica, forse perchè il bel tempo aveva suggerito a parecchi altri la stessa idea, forse perchè la maggior parte dei marinai erano usciti per la pesca.

—Pare impossibile! Proprio oggi!—esclamò Paolina.

All'ultimo un vecchietto, dopo di essersi consultato con due altri vecchi che fumavano tranquillamente in un angolo e non si erano neppur degnati di rispondere alla nostra richiesta, venne ad offrirci la sua barca.

—Basterete a remare voi solo?—gli dissi.

—Salite!

E il gesto e la voce del vecchio rivelarono l'orgoglio offeso da quel dubbio da me espresso.

Il mare non poteva essere più tranquillo. La barca scivolava sulla superficie con un leggero fruscio. E la riva scorreva di fianco a noi a poca distanza, salendo con nere rocce di lava che già nascondevano la campagna. Grotte si aprivano qua e là; stormi di palombi selvatici sbucavano da esse, di tratto in tratto, mentre gli alcioni ci accompagnavano sfiorando l'acqua con ali spiegate che non producevano nessun rumore.

Paolina era in èstasi, ed io dovevo impedirle di chinarsi ogni volta ch'ella tentava di afferrare qualcuna delle meduse erranti a fior d'acqua, opaline, iridate, simili a funghi cristallini portati via dalla corrente.

Mi maravigliavo ch'ella non sentisse nessun sintomo di mal di mare.

—Sei contenta di questa gita?

—Che delizia!

—Ecco Ògnina—disse il barcaiolo.

* * *

Eravamo appena a metà del nostro pranzo, quando il vecchio, che era andato a trovare un suo conoscente, si presentava annunziandoci:

—Bisogna partire sùbito. Si è alzato un po' di vento, il mare si guasta.

Infatti pareva che avesse dei brividi; si increspava, si sollevava con frequenti crestine spumanti.

—Facciamo presto—insisteva il vecchio.

—Ci sarà pericolo?—domandò Paolina.

—No, signora; ma è meglio far presto. Col mare non si sa mai….

The waves began tossing the boat the moment we left the dock. Paolina gazed into my eyes as if to scrutinize me, and then looked at the boatman, who was pulling hard on the oars and fighting the rising crests of the waves. I was beginning to worry about her. This time surely she would suffer from seasickness.

The boat jumped, descended, and climbed again. Sprays of foam came over the gunwale.

Now the sea was becoming even rougher. The boatman was barely making any way. He was panting and sweating. He looked at the horizon and shook his head. Some of the rocks I had noticed on the way out were no longer visible, submerged under the waves that followed one after the other, overlapping and foaming.

"Ah, Holy Virgin! . . . ah, Holy Agatha!" the boatman mumbled.

This was not encouraging. But I tried to smile at Paolina, and to cheer her by radiating a confidence I did not feel.

"Bloody. . .! Damn. . .!" the boatman swore under his breath, as the sea became even rougher.

"Are you afraid?" I asked Paolina.

"No."

"Hold on to the bench."

"Don't worry, it isn't necessary."

"Blessed Saint Agatha! Holy Mother of Grace!" the old man kept mumbling. He was having difficulty resisting the force of the waves and could no longer go straight.

"Watch out!" I shouted.

Hearing my cry, he pulled hard on the oars, and with two or three powerful curses, the rock we were about to hit was mercifully avoided. With great good luck, I had noticed it barely in time as the waves, crashing on the other side, had left it visible for a split second. This was very dangerous.

"What happened?" Paolina asked.

"Nothing. Keep more to the left," I added, addressing the boatman.

"That would be even worse," he replied. "Ah, no! Ah! Ah!" he grunted rhythmically, reinforcing his efforts.

In the midst of all this, I was amazed to see Paolina smiling calmly. At first in a whisper and then more loudly, as if the shudders and crashes of the little boat gave her pleasure, she began to sing. I can't remember exactly what it was she was singing, but firmly fixed in my mind, I still have the impression of that clear, firm voice raised in song, a sweet melody by Bellini, or perhaps by Verdi, set against the crashing waves. I had to force myself not to show her that I feared for our lives, between the shuddering sea and the old, half-exhausted boatman, who offered prayers to the Holy Virgin and the Blessed Agatha interspersed with the most blasphemous of curses. We were still five hundred yards out from the end of the dock, and Paolina, having finished her melody, had started to sing another, even more cheerful and upbeat, seemingly unaware of the rising violence of the sea.

The end of the dock was crowded with people staring anxiously at our boat as it fought the waves.

"Veer away from the shore!" I heard someone cry out. "Pull harder! Have courage!"

Partimmo un po' sballottati. Paolina mi guardava negli occhi quasi per scrutarmi, e poi guardava il barcaiuolo, che faceva forza coi remi per resistere agli urti crescenti delle ondate. Io cominciavo a impensierirmi per lei. Questa volta certamente il mal di mare l'avrebbe fatta soffrire.

La barca balzava, si avvallava, si rialzava. Sprazzi di spuma arrivavano agli orli di essa.

Tutt'a un colpo il mare diventò più agitato. Il barcaiuolo stentava a farci procedere; ansimava, sudava, guardava attorno, lontano, e scoteva la testa. Certi scogli a fior d'acqua, che io avevo notati nell'andare, non si scorgevano più, sommersi sotto le ondate che si succedevano fitte, accavallandosi, spumeggiando.

—Ah, Madonna Santa!… Ah, sant'Agata benedetta!—brontolava il barcaiuolo.

Non era incoraggiante; ma io mi sforzavo di sorridere a Paolina, e di farle animo con gli sguardi.

—Sangue di…! Corpo di…!—bestemmiava sotto voce il barcaiolo, come più il mare si faceva cattivo.

—Hai paura?—domandai a Paolina.

—No.

—Tieni forte al panchetto.

—Sta' tranquillo, non occorre.

—Sant'Agata benedetta!… Madonna delle Grazie!—tornava e brontolava il vecchio, che sosteneva male le spinte delle onde e non riusciva più a procedere diritto.

—Attento!—urlai.

Al mio grido egli fece uno sforzo, accompagnato da due o tre energiche bestemmie, e così lo scoglio che stavamo per investire fu, fortunatamente, evitato. Io lo avevo scorto mentre le ondate, rovesciandosi dall'altra parte, lo avevan lasciato per un istante scoperto. Era uno di quelli a fior d'acqua, pericolosissimo.

—Che cosa è successo?—domandò Paolina.

—Niente. Restate più a sinistra—soggiunsi, rivolto al barcaiuolo.

—Sarebbe peggio—rispose.—Aah! Aah! Aah!

E aiutava con la voce lo sforzo di tutta la persona.

Allora fui stupito di veder Paolina calma, sorridente, e di udirla, prima, canticchiare a mezza voce, poi cantare a voce spiegata, quasi gli sbalzi della barca fossero cosa gradevole. Ora non ricordo più che cosa ella cantasse, ma ho ancora nell'animo l'impressione di quella voce limpida, ferma, che gettava in mezzo al rumore delle onde agitate una dolce melodia del Bellini, o forse piuttosto del Verdi. Io dovevo farmi violenza per non farle capire che cominciavo a temere qualche pericolo con quel barcaiolo vecchio, mezzo sfinito, che alternava con maggior frequenza invocazioni alla Madonna e a sant'Agata e brutali bestemmie. Eravamo lontani mezzo chilometro dalla punta del Molo; e Paolina, terminata una melodia, aveva impreso a cantarne un'altra più allegra, più squillante, senza mostrar di curarsi della crescente violenza del mare.

La punta del Molo era affollata di gente che pareva seguisse ansiosa con gli occhi la nostra barca lottante contro le onde.

—Vira, vira più al largo!—udii gridare.—Forza! Coraggio!

When we finally were close enough, a sailor threw us a rope that the old man grabbed. He jumped out, first on the dock, and kneeling down, he touched the ground with his forehead, thanking the Holy Virgin and St. Agatha for saving him.

The moment Paolina stood on the dock, she went pale and fainted into my arms.

***

"How could you do this to me? You!"

I was incredulous.

As it happened, she had a much better understanding than I of the danger we had been in. But to help me keep my courage, she had refused to show herself terrified and had, instead, remained calmly at her post, singing courageously.

"I was terrified by the idea of drowning! How did I have the strength? I don't even know myself. . . I loved you so much in those moments!"

"And afterwards? Now?" I asked, hugging her and covering her with kisses.

Her only answer was a gesture, a quick, unforgettable gesture.

E quando fummo vicini, un marinaio ci gettò una fune che il vecchio afferrò. Saltato per primo sulla banchina si buttava in ginocchio, scoppiando in lagrime, e toccava con la fronte il terreno, ringraziando la Madonna e sant'Agata dell'averlo salvato!

Paolina, appena posto piede a terra, impallidiva improvvisamente e mi si sveniva tra le braccia.

* * *

—Come hai potuto far questo? Tu!

Mi pareva incredibile.

Ella aveva compreso assai meglio di me il pericolo in cui ci eravamo trovati; e intanto, per non farmi perdere coraggio col mostrarsi atterrita, si era messa a cantare, stando ferma al suo posto.

—Mi sentivo morire dalla paura di annegare! Come abbia avuto quella forza non lo so neppur io…. Ti volevo tanto bene in quel momento!

—E dopo, ora?—dissi abbracciandola e coprendola di baci.

Fece soltanto un gesto, un rapido indimenticabile gesto.

HIDDEN FORCES

TO GUELFO CIVININI

Fine. Aldo Sàmara and his fiancée had given up on their wedding trip.

Èlvia had been delighted to see her proposal accepted. The idea of staying in hotels and mingling the first sweet impressions of their married life with the intrusive looks of waiters and travelers was distasteful to her.

Aldo Sàmara, who, due to an unlikely chain of events, had never satisfied his dream of visiting Venice, had hoped to associate the memory of this fantastic city with that of the day he achieved his supreme happiness. He had, therefore, shown some slight hesitation in agreeing to a proposal that seemed only to confirm that fate conspired to prevent him from finally visiting the City of Canals every time he was on the point of closing his suitcase.

"Do you mind?" Èlvia had asked.

"Oh, no, not if it pleases you!"

"Venice will always be there, nobody is going to steal it from us," she had added, smiling. "We can go later."

"It won't be the same thing."

"Maybe it will be better. We will be less distracted from admiring its beauty."

"You are right. . . You are always right! However. . ."

"'However!' Let's hear it!"

"It may be a prejudice, or a personal impression, but a honeymoon spent at home doesn't seem to me a honeymoon at all. We won't be able to hide in the house, close the door to our relatives, to our friends, to your girlfriends – to your girlfriends in particular. How, then, will the first month of our marriage be different from all the rest when we are again caught in the swirl of social life, and especially the frenzy of business? It will be so even though we intend to lead a modest life, as our condition requires."

"And why should it be different?" replied Èlvia.

"You are right. . . Yes, you are always right! However. . ."

"*Another* however?"

"One day, on one of our walks in the countryside last fall, you pointed out a villa, the one with the towers that looked like a medieval building on top of a hillside and half-hidden among the trees, and you whispered to me, 'Over there!' Do you recall? Ah! The flash in your eyes, and your smile! I have thought of that many times, and one day – I believe I told you – I indulged myself by visiting it."

"You've never told me anything about this."

FORZE OCCULTE

A GUELFO CIVININI

D'accordo, Aldo Sàmara e la sua fidanzata avevano rinunziato al loro viaggio di nozze.

Èlvia era stata lietissima di veder accettata la sua proposta. Le repugnava quell'andare a disperdere per gli alberghi, sotto gli sguardi importuni dei camerieri e dei viaggiatori, le prime dolci impressioni della loro vita di sposi.

Aldo Sàmara, che per una strana serie di circostanze non aveva fin allora potuto effettuare il suo sogno di visitare Venezia, si era proposto di associare il ricordo della fantastica città con quello del giorno in cui avrebbe raggiunto il più elevato scopo della sua esistenza; e per ciò aveva mostrato un po' di esitazione nell'acconsentire a una proposta che gli sembrava confermare quella specie di fatalità che gli impediva ogni volta di partire per Venezia quando quasi sul punto di chiudere le valige o di avviarsi per la stazione.

—Ti dispiace?—aveva detto Èlvia.

—Oh, no, se fa piacere a te!

—Venezia è sempre là, non ce la porta via nessuno—aveva aggiunto Èlvia sorridendo.—Potremo andarci dopo.

—Non sarà la stessa cosa.

—Sarà forse meglio. Saremo meno assorti, meno distratti nell'ammirarne le bellezze.

—Hai ragione.… Hai sempre ragione! Però….

—Sentiamo!

—Può darsi che sia un pregiudizio, o un'impressione mia personale, ma la luna di miele passata in città non mi sembra più luna di miele. Non potremo segregarci in casa, chiudere la porta ai parenti, agli amici, alle tue amiche soprattutto. Quel primo mese del nostro matrimonio in che cosa differirà poi dagli altri, quando la vertigine della vita sociale, degli affari specialmente, riprenderà te e me, per quanto abbiamo l'intenzione di condurre una vita modesta, come la nostra condizione richiede?

—E perchè mai dovrebbe differire?—replicò Èlvia.

—Hai ragione.… Hai sempre ragione! Però….

—Un altro però?

—Ricordi? Un giorno, in una delle nostre passeggiate in gran comitiva per la campagna, lo scorso autunno, tu mi facesti osservare quella villa mezza nascosta tra gli alberi, in cima a una collinetta, e mi dicesti sottovoce:—Colà!—Il lampo degli occhi e il sorriso finirono di esprimere l'intimo significato di quella parola. Vi ho ripensato parecchie volte, e un giorno—mi pare di avertelo raccontato—ho commesso la fanciullaggine di andare a visitare la villa turrita che, vista dallo stradone sembrava un edifizio medioevale.

—Non me n'hai detto mai nulla.

"Did I not? Perhaps I felt that I acted foolishly. It is a small villa and about a hundred years old. Some *mezzadri* – sharecroppers – live on the ground floor. The owners never go there, not even to visit. 'Why?' I asked. 'Who knows?' one of the sharecroppers answered. 'And would they be willing to rent it?' 'Certainly. We have the keys, to air the rooms. Do you want to see them?' There are five on the first floor and two on the upper floor, in the area that one would call the tower. Airy rooms, clean, with decent furniture, a little dated, from about thirty years ago. And such silence, such peace! There's a wonderful view to the east, of the Latium hills. To the west, Rome with the dome of St. Peter towering in the blue sky. . . In a week, that small villa could be ready to receive us," concluded Aldo, winking.

"Yes, yes," said Èlvia. "It's a beautiful idea."

***

Aldo Sàmara had decided to leave most of the rooms unchanged and preserve their period atmosphere. Except for the bedroom, they all remained exactly as he had found them on his first visit. Nothing was moved on the advice of the sharecroppers who told them that the owners preferred that the furniture remain undisturbed as much as possible.

It certainly wasn't because the furnishings were in any way valuable. They consisted of tables and chairs, chests of drawers, sofas, armchairs, some lithographs and engravings in ebony frames, some mediocre copies of religious scenes originally painted by Guercino and Carlo Dolce, and two mirrors that had been rendered almost unusable by years of exposure to humidity.

Yet, Èlvia and Aldo had immediately made themselves at home in this atmosphere of a faded past – of *tiredness,* as she called it – although they were keenly aware of the contrast with the cheerful homes from which they had just come, filled with all the gay freshness of modern furnishings.

The first two days had passed as if in a dream. The bride and groom spent their days enjoying leisurely walks and admiring the local scenery. But on the third day, in the afternoon, a fine, persistent drizzle had confined them to the house. They had amused themselves a bit by reading one of the many new novels bought for the occasion. The sudden shadow of evening had surprised them as they gazed out the drawing room window, absorbed in the ever-intensifying rain that veiled and blurred the surrounding countryside and the hills of Lazio far away.

Aldo was holding Èlvia by the waist, her head resting on his shoulder. But suddenly, she started.

"What?"

"Nothing. . . I don't know!"

Meanwhile, her eyes opened wide, she turned to peer into the room already invaded by darkness.

"Well?" Aldo said.

"I felt a shiver, as if someone had laid a freezing hand on my shoulder."

"You must have been imagining something."

—Probabilmente perchè mi pareva di aver commesso una fanciullaggine. È una villetta dei primi anni di questo secolo. I mezzadri abitano al pianterreno. I padroni non vanno mai a villeggiarvi e neppure a visitarla di tanto in tanto.—Perchè?—domandai—Chi lo sa?—rispose la mezzadra.—E sarebbero disposti ad affittarla?—Certamente. Abbiamo le chiavi noi, per dar aria alle stanze. Vuol vederle?—Sono cinque al primo piano e due al piano superiore, in quella che vorrebbe essere una torretta; stanze ariose, pulite, con discreta mobilia un po' invecchiata, di trent'anni addietro o poco più. E un silenzio, una pace! Vista maravigliosa dal lato di levante, con tutti i colli laziali torno torno; da ponente, Roma con la cupola di San Pietro troneggiante nell'azzurro…. In una settimana, quella villetta potrebbe esser pronta a riceverci—concluse Aldo insinuante.

—Sì, sì—rispose Èlvia.—È una bella idea.

* * *

Aldo Sàmara aveva voluto lasciare a quelle stanze l'impronta caratteristica del tempo in cui erano state mobiliate; ed eccettuata la camera degli sposi, esse erano rimaste quali egli le aveva trovate nella sua prima visita, senza spostar nulla, anche perchè i mezzadri avevano raccomandato, in nome dei padroni, di conservare, per quanto più era possibile, la disposizione degli oggetti che vi si trovavano.

Non erano affatto preziosi i tavolini, i canterali, i divani, le seggiole, le poltrone, le litografie e le incisioni in cornici di ebano, i quattro o cinque quadri a olio, di soggetto sacro, mediocrissime copie di originali del Guercino e di Carlo Dolce, i due specchi ridotti quasi inservibili dall'umidità.

Eppure Èlvia ed Aldo si erano adattati sùbito a quell'aria di vecchiezza—di stanchezza, diceva Èlvia—quantunque si sentissero stranamente trasportati in un ambiente completamente diverso da quello delle loro case sorridenti di tutta la gaia freschezza dell'ammobiliamento moderno.

Le prime due giornate eran passate come in sogno. I due giovani sposi avevano avuto appena tempo di dare un'occhiata al paesaggio e di fare qualche breve passeggiata all'aperto. Ma, il terzo giorno, nelle ore pomeridiane, una pioggerella fina, insistente, li aveva confinati in casa. Si erano un po' svagati leggendo alcuni capitoli di uno dei tanti romanzi nuovi comprati per quell'occasione, e le ombre della sera li avevano sorpresi dietro i vetri della finestra del salotto, silenziosi, intenti a guardare la pioggia che veniva giù più fitta, velando e quasi sfumando la campagna attorno e i colli laziali lontani.

Aldo avea cinto col braccio la vita di Èlvia, ed ella si era abbandonata carezzevolmente col capo su la spalla di lui. Tutt'a un tratto, ella trasalì.

—Che cosa è stato?

—Niente…. Non so!

Intanto spalancava gli occhi spauriti, voltandosi a guardare nella stanza già invasa dall'oscurità.

—Insomma?—fece Aldo.

—Un brivido per tutta la persona, come se qualcuno mi avesse posato una mano diaccia su la spalla.

—Chi sa che cosa fantasticavi!

"I wasn't imagining anything, I was just looking outside."

"Let's have some light."

They lit both the lamps and brightness filled the living room but she was still not completely reassured. They resumed their interrupted novel, Aldo reading aloud, and occasionally lifting his eyes to glance at Èlvia's face. Èlvia listened, with her elbows resting on the table top and her chin on the back of her hands, but with a distracted air. Two or three times, he caught her glancing anxiously from side to side. So he chided her gently, "You're not a little girl! Come, come! . . . Or do you feel ill?"

"I am very embarrassed," Èlvia answered, "to explain to you what I feel. . . Nonetheless, I must tell you. I've felt something similar the first night we arrived, when you went down to talk with the sharecroppers and left me alone for a few moments."

"And what did you feel?"

"A shiver, as if I had been touched by someone repulsive. . . invisible."

"Oh. . .!"

"It is silly. . . I don't know what to say. . . You, too?" exclaimed Èlvia, as her husband's expression became increasingly serious and he adopted the puzzled air of someone studying something highly unusual.

Aldo hesitated.

"You, too!" she insisted, grabbing his hand, terrified.

"I was merely trying to determine," said Aldo, attempting to hide his embarrassment, "what could have produced in you such a strange reaction. Is it the old console? The mirror? Those darkened paintings, stained by ancient dust and humidity? The high ceilings? Perhaps the new wall paper?" A young lady's nerves are impressionable, her imagination too easily excited. . .

But, even as he spoke, Aldo could not hide that he, too, felt an indefinable sense of disgust, as if he had been brushed by someone utterly foul and invisible. He shut the book, stood up and, forcing himself to smile, said, "It's not raining anymore!"

He opened the window. The sky was clear. The clouds still gathered over the mountains on the horizon far away. The silver of moonlight flooded the countryside and the unmistakable smell of the recent rain filled the air.

He closed the window, took Èlvia's arm, and led her into the dining room. The table was already set for dinner.

"How strange this villa is in the evening!" Nannina, the maid, said, as she placed the food on the table.

"Why do you say so?" Èlvia asked.

"I can't really say. . ." Nannina said.

You too? Aldo thought.

***

—Non pensavo niente, guardavo fuori.

—Facciamo accendere i lumi.

Tutta la gran luce che due lumi diffusero poco dopo nel salotto non valse però a rassicurarla pienamente. Avevano ripreso la continuazione della lettura interrotta. Aldo leggeva ad alta voce, alzando, di tratto in tratto, gli occhi in viso a Èlvia, che coi gomiti appoggiati sul piano del tavolino e col mento sul dorso delle mani congiunte, stava ad ascoltare. Evidentemente era un po' distratta. Due o tre volte, Aldo aveva notato che ella, pur restando immobile, girava le pupille attorno, con aria di diffidente paura; e credette opportuno di sgridarla con dolce severità.

—Non sei una bambina! Eh, via!… O ti senti male?

—Sarei proprio imbarazzata—rispose Èlvia—se dovessi spiegarti quel che provo…. Ora voglio dirtelo—soggiunse:—Ho provato qualcosa di simile sin dalla prima sera che arrivammo qui, quando tu, sceso a parlare col mezzadro, mi lasciasti sola per qualche istante.

—Che cosa provasti?

—Un senso di freddo, come al contatto di persona sgradevole… invisibile.

—Oh!…

—Sarà una ridicolaggine… che vuoi che ti dica?… Anche tu?—esclamò Èlvia, vedendo diventare serio serio il marito e prendere l'atteggiamento di chi sta in osservazione di qualcosa d'insolito.

Aldo tardò a rispondere.

—Anche tu?—ella replicò afferrandolo, atterrita, per una mano.

—Volevo spiegarmi—disse Aldo con qualche imbarazzo—che cosa può mai averti prodotto tale strana suggestione in questo salotto. La vecchia consolle? Lo specchio? Quei quadri anneriti e dai quali non si è potuto togliere la polvere resa aderente dal tempo e dall'umido? Il soffitto troppo alto? La tappezzeria nuova delle pareti? I nervi di una giovine signora sono impressionabilissimi, la immaginazione troppo facile ad essere eccitata….

Ma, così parlando, Aldo nascondeva a stento che aveva in quell'istante anche lui un'indefinibile sensazione di malessere, precisamente come pel contatto di persona disaggradevole, invisibile. Chiuse il libro, si alzò da sedere, e sforzandosi di sorridere, disse a Èlvia:

—Non piove più!

E aprì la finestra. Il cielo era sereno. Le nuvole si addensavano sui monti in fondo all'orizzonte, e la luna inondava con la sua luce argentea la campagna, che esalava l'odore speciale dei terreni bagnati da pioggia recente.

Richiusa l'imposta, egli prese Èlvia sottobraccio, e la condusse nella sala da pranzo. La tavola era già apparecchiata per la cena.

—Com'è curiosa questa villa, di sera!—esclamò Nannina, la donna di servizio, portando in tavola.

—Perchè dite così?—domandò Èlvia.

—Mah!…—fece Nannina.

—Anche lei?—pensò Aldo.

* * *

He thought about a book he had read years before by an English author or authors – he seemed to remember they were two – that tried to prove scientifically that God exists and that the soul is immortal. They argued that even our most insignificant thoughts, as well as our words and actions, are recorded, fixed in the cosmic matter of the universe as on a photographic plate.

It was from this idea, which had remained fixed in his mind, that he began to formulate a probable explanation for this now-undeniable phenomenon while he lay curled up in his bed and pretending to sleep. It must be that the walls of that house were saturated with recorded thoughts and acts from times past, and with such force as to produce these terrifying sensations.

He recalled what the sharecropper had said about the state of abandonment in which the owner had left the villa for years and years, never returning to stay or even to keep an eye on it. Now it seemed to him, though it had not struck him at the time, that the sharecropper had hesitated before answering. Aldo decided to probe further that morning, before Èlvia rose from bed.

During his long, sleepless night, he seemed to sense a sort of vibration in the walls and ceiling, beyond the doors, and even in the adjoining rooms. A gentle, dull vibration, imperceptible to the ear but somehow none the less real. Every nerve in his body felt the frisson of this vibration as though he were in direct contact with the source.

Over the last year, he had become increasingly interested in certain phenomena that only a handful of scientists had dared to research. He began to suspect that he was now facing one of these phenomena. He simply refused to accept he had been influenced by the nervous fantasies of his new wife and her maid.

"Did you sleep well?" Èlvia asked him as he slipped out of bed that morning.

"Like a log. And you?"

"I didn't sleep a wink. I was very close to waking you up."

"Why?"

"Don't scold me! I was afraid."

"Again?" he exclaimed, pretending to be slightly annoyed at this feminine weakness. "While you are dressing," he added, "I'll go smoke a cigar outside. I'll send Nannina in to you."

He could get nothing out of the sharecroppers. When they took the job, the villa had already been locked up and uninhabited for years.

"Since the owners don't care, why don't you live in the upper rooms?"

"The rooms on the ground floor are more convenient for us."

"Before me and my wife, has anyone else rented the villa?"

"Yes, four years ago, two foreigners, an old man with his daughter, a beautiful creature. They left after a week."

"Why?"

Egli si era rammentato di un libro inglese letto anni addietro, col quale si pretendeva di dare una prova scientifica dell'immortalità dell'anima e dell'esistenza di Dio. L'autore, o gli autori—erano due, se ricordava bene—credevano di aver dimostrato che fin i più impercettibili movimenti del nostro pensiero, nonché gli atti e le parole, vengono registrati e fissati nell'universa materia cosmica come su una lastra fotografica, anzi meglio che su una lastra fotografica. E partendo da questa nozione che gli era rimasta in mente, rannicchiato nel suo cantuccio di letto e fingendo di dormire, aveva iniziato a fantasticare, durante la nottata, una probabile spiegazione di quel fenomeno ormai innegabile perchè avvertito contemporaneamente da tre persone. Le pareti di quella casa dovevano essere certamente sature di misteriosi fluidi, di pensieri e di atti registrati, e con tale forza da produrre terrificanti sensazioni rivelatrici.

Gli erano tornate in mente le parole del mezzadro riguardo all'abbandono in cui i padroni lasciavano quella villa da anni ed anni, senza mai venire a darvi un'occhiata. Ora gli sembrava di non aver notato allora certe esitazioni nelle risposte del mezzadro e della sua moglie, e si proponeva di interrogarli quella mattina, prima che Èlvia si alzasse da letto.

E durante la lunga nottata insonne non gli era anche parso di sentire una specie di formicolìo dappertutto, nelle pareti, nel soffitto, dietro gli usci, nelle stanze accanto; un formicolìo sordo sordo, che l'orecchio non percepiva ma che intanto non gli sembrava meno reale, quantunque percepito dai nervi di tutto il suo organismo quasi per immediato contatto?

Egli s'interessava molto, da un anno in qua, di certi fenomeni di cui soltanto da poco tempo alcuni scienziati osavano occuparsi, e cominciava a sospettare di trovarsi di fronte a uno di tali fenomeni; perchè non poteva credere di essersi lasciato suggestionare dal nervosismo di Èlvia e della donna di servizio.

—Hai dormito bene?—gli domandò Èlvia vedendolo saltar giù dal letto.

—Ho fatto tutt'un sonno. E tu?

—Io non ho chiuso occhio. C'è mancato poco che non ti svegliassi.

—Perchè?

—Non sgridarmi; avevo paura.

—Ancora?—egli esclamò, fingendo di mostrarsi un po' in collera per questa debolezza femminile.—Intanto che tu ti vesti—poi soggiunse—scendo a fumar un sigaro all'aria aperta. Ti mando Nannina.

Non aveva potuto cavare nulla di bocca ai mezzadri. Quando essi avevano preso quella mezzadria, la villa era chiusa e abbandonata da un pezzo.

—Giacchè i padroni non se ne curano, perchè non abitate nelle stanze superiori?

—Queste al piano terreno sono più comode per noi.

—E dite, prima di me e della mia signora, nessun altro ha preso in affitto la villa?

—Sì, quattro anni fa, due forestieri, un vecchio con la figlia, bellissima creatura, che volle andar via dopo una settimana.

—Perchè?

"It's hard to say. They may have told us, but who could understand them? They left one morning, almost at a run, grumbling to each other and making wild gestures. But the old man had to be crazy. He spent his days, from morning to night, picking weeds and bringing them home in bunches. His daughter would paint."

That day passed quietly. They had almost forgotten the unpleasant impressions of the night before since the rooms, flooded by sunlight, seemed quite cheerful. But once the sun had set, they began to change. And lighting any number of lamps was no help at all. Something indefinable, inexplicable was vibrating from the walls, from the objects in the room. Even the air they breathed thrummed with energy.

Not wishing to appear a frightened little girl, Èlvia dared not confess to Aldo the feeling of oppression that invaded her. And Aldo could never have confessed to her the repugnance every room of the villa now held for him once the sun had set. Èlvia clung to him, wanting to be held in his arms to find a refuge there. Aldo was happy to oblige, caressing her, kissing her, and whispering sweet words to her from time to time. But as the evening progressed, they became more and more silent, even though they still had so many things to say to each other in these hours of companionship, amidst the great peace of the vast countryside!

Aldo could no longer doubt the reality of these sensations. Like him, Èlvia was a steady, healthy person. It was true that he had interested himself in abnormal phenomena, but only by reading what prestigious scientists wrote about them, both pro and con. He had certainly never tried to observe them directly, although people who wanted to initiate him into the mysteries of mesmerism and spiritism had often invited him to do so. Èlvia had sometimes teased him about his studies and shown herself to be something of a skeptic. He couldn't decide whether what both of them – and Nannina – were sensing in the villa came from excessive nervousness or from preconceptions capable of altering the ordinary functions of their senses.

***

They had spent the whole day wandering through the countryside. After having breakfast at a dairy farm, they walked along little roads and paths going up the hills, picking wild flowers, stopping to rest in the peasant houses encountered here and there, taking snapshots with their Kodaks, each of them choosing different views to see who could produce the most artistic landscape. They had returned to the villa a bit weary but very contented about the beautiful hike, and fighting cheerfully about the results of their photos. What a pity they would have to wait for their return to Rome to develop them!

That evening, they had sat down at the table with great appetite, though dinner was not yet ready.

"Are you sleepy?" Aldo asked, noting his wife's drooping eyelids. "Èlvia! What's wrong?" he cried, as her eyes rolled up until only the whites were visible.

She gave no answer. Stiffly sitting in her chair, her brows furrowed, she seemed to stare intently through her closed eyelids at something only she could see.

—Lo dissero forse; ma chi li capiva? Scapparono quasi, brontolando, facendo certi gesti! Già quel vecchio doveva essere mezzo matto. Andava attorno da mattina a sera, raccogliendo erbacce, riportandone a casa mazzi, fasci interi. La figlia dipingeva.

La giornata passò tranquilla. Èlvia e lui avevano quasi dimenticato le tristi impressioni della sera prima, perchè le stanze illuminate dal sole, assumevano durante il giorno aspetto gaio. Ma la sera, dopo il tramonto, sembrava si trasformassero; e non serviva accendere molti lumi. Qualcosa d'indefinibile, d'inesplicabile vibrava dalle pareti, dagli oggetti; si sarebbe detto anche dall'aria che vi circolava.

Èlvia, per vergogna di apparire paurosa come una bambina, non osava confessare ad Aldo l'opprimente sensazione che la invadeva; ed Aldo si guardava bene dal confessarle la repugnanza che gli ispirava, di sera, tutta la casa, in qualunque stanza essi si intrattenessero fino all'ora di cenare e di andare a letto. Èlvia si stringeva a lui, voleva esser presa tra le braccia, quasi per trovarvi un rifugio; ed egli era contento di tenerla così, di accarezzarla, di baciarla, di mormorarle dolci parole a intervalli. Giacchè, a mano a mano che la sera più s'inoltrava, essi si sentivano costretti a restare silenziosi; e avevano ancora—pensavano—tante dolci cose da dirsi in quelle ore di raccoglimento, in mezzo alla gran pace della vasta campagna!

Aldo non poteva più dubitare che si trattasse di sensazioni reali. Èlvia era una persona solida, in salute, come lui. Egli, è vero, si era occupato di fenomeni anormali, ma solamente leggendo quel che ne scrivevano, pro e contro, scienziati d'alto valore. Non aveva mai provato provato a osservarli direttamente, quantunque spesso invitato da persone che volevano iniziarlo ai misteri del magnetismo e dello spiritismo. Èlvia lo aveva qualche volta punzecchiato per questi suoi studi, mostrandosi piuttosto incredula. Egli non poteva perciò capire se che quel che essi e Nannina sentivano nella villa provenisse da eccessiva nervosità o da preconcetti capaci di alterare le ordinarie funzioni dei loro sensi.

* * *

Avevano trascorso l'intera giornata vagando per la campagna. Fatto colazione in una vaccheria, si erano inoltrati per sentieri e sentieroli verso le colline, cogliendo bellissimi fiori selvatici, fermandosi, per riposarsi, nelle case dei contadini incontrate qua e là, prendendo istantanee coi loro Kodack, fotografando ognuno un punto di vista diverso per vedere chi di loro due avrebbe saputo scegliere il paesaggio più artistico; ed erano tornati tardi alla villa, un po' stanchi ma contentissimi della bella escursione, e litigando allegramente sui risultati delle fotografie dei rispettivi Kodack. Peccato che bisognasse attendere il ritorno a Roma per svilupparle!

Intanto si erano seduti a tavola con grand'appetito, quantunque la cena non fosse ancora pronta.

—Hai sonno?—domandò Aldo, scorgendo che sua moglie stentava a tener aperte le pàlpebre.

—Èlvia!... Èlvia!...—egli gridò vedendole travolgere gli occhi fino al bianco.

Ella non rispondeva. Rigida, eretta sul busto, con gli occhi chiusi e le sopracciglia corrugate, sembrava guardasse attentamente e vedesse a occhi chiusi.

Aldo immediately realized that it was a case of spontaneous catalepsy and he was terrified. He had no idea of its cause or what consequences might follow. He kept calling out to her and shaking her by the arm, horrified by her contorted expression: "Èlvia! Èlvia!"

Making an animal sound, Èlvia stood up and stumbled backwards over her chair, her hands raised in defense or rejection and turning her head from side to side as if to avoid seeing something. With a cry, she fell into Aldo's arms and opened her eyes.

"What happened?" she asked, astonished.

"You fell asleep," Aldo stammered, so as not to frighten her. "I was about to lay you down on the sofa."

Èlvia remembered nothing. *What had she seen?* Aldo didn't press her. But he was now certain that some terrible tragedy must have occurred in the villa. He, too, could sense a mysterious power that made the very walls vibrate with an ancient terror, a terror that grew stronger by the day. Would he succumb next?

To his astonishment, Èlvia was perfectly calm that evening, showing no signs of fear either during dinner or after. She was, in fact, more cheerful than usual. Except that, suddenly, as she rose from the table, she asked, "Tell me: where did I read or where have I seen performed. . ."

"What?"

"It's strange!" she exclaimed after a brief pause. "I remember a specific scene, from, oh, I no longer remember which drama, or novel. . . But why is it coming back to my mind so alive, so fresh, as if I had recently read it or seen it performed?"

"What scene?"

"Eh. It's. . . it's the scene where that husband orders his wife, whom he believes guilty: 'Punish yourself!' And she doesn't want to die by poison or dagger. And she wants to cry, to call for help. And she bangs on the locked doors, and on the windows, which are nailed shut. . . until finally, she can no longer speak and she dies of terror, watched by her inexorable husband, who has brought her to this distant villa. Where did I read this? Or where did I see it performed? It's strange! Strange!"

"Let it go!" Aldo interrupted her. "Let's talk about something else. Aren't you bored here by now?"

"No. And you?"

That unexpected phenomenon of serenity made Aldo Sàmara even more suspicious. Though it seemed irrational, he feared that his Èlvia was at the mercy of the mysterious forces dominating the upper rooms of the abandoned villa. And so, he decided to remove her from the reach of their disturbing power.

Having returned to Rome, he was long obsessed by the absurd thought that an evil influence had overcome both of them. After a few months of tormented doubts, however, he managed to convince himself that he had been mistaken.

Aldo capì sùbito che si trattava d'un caso di catalessi spontanea e ne fu atterrito, non potendosi render conto del motivo per cui accadeva, nè delle conseguenze che avrebbero potuto seguirne. E continuava a chiamare, scotendola pel braccio:—Èlvia! Èlvia!—

Poi le labbra di lei si mossero; suoni inarticolati le uscirono di bocca. In piedi, con le mani in avanti, ella indietreggiava, voltando il capo da una parte come per evitar di vedere. Diede un grido, cadde tra le braccia di Aldo che furon pronte a riceverla. E aprì gli occhi.

—Che succede?—domandò, stupita.

—Ti sei lasciata sorprendere dal sonno—balbettò Aldo per non spaventarla.— Volevo metterti a giacere sul canapè.

Èlvia non si rammentava di niente. Che cosa aveva visto? Aldo non glielo domandò. Ma egli era ormai certo che in quella villa era dovuto accadere qualche terribile tragedia rimasta ignorata. Le pareti vibravano terrore. Si sentiva sopraffare anche lui dalla misteriosa forza ogni giorno più. Sarebbe caduto in catalessi pure lui?

Con sua grande meraviglia, quella sera Èlvia fu tranquillissima. Non mostrò di sentire nessuna impressione di paura durante la cena nè dopo. Fu anzi più allegra del solito; se non che, tutt'a un tratto, nell'alzarsi da tavola domandò:

—Dimmi: dove ho letto o dove ho veduto rappresentare….

—Che cosa?

—È strano!—ella esclamò dopo breve pausa.—Mi torna in mente una scena di non so più qual dramma, di non so più qual capitolo di romanzo…. Come mai mi ritorna in mente così viva, così fresca, quasi l'avessi letta recentemente o veduta rappresentare?

—Quale scena?

—Mah! È strano! Mi sfugge…. Di quel marito che ordina alla moglie creduta colpevole:—Punisciti da te stessa!—E lei non vuol morire di veleno nè di pugnale; e vorrebbe gridare, chiamare aiuto; e urta agli usci chiusi a chiave, e picchia alle imposte delle finestre inchiodate… e perde la parola e muore di terrore davanti all'inesorabile marito, che l'ha condotta in una villa lontana! Dove ho letto questo? O dove l'ho veduto rappresentare? È strano! È strano!

—Lascia andare!—la interruppe Aldo.—Dimmi piuttosto un'altra cosa: Non ti sei già annoiata di star qui?

—No. E tu?

Quell'inatteso fenomeno di serenità mise in maggior sospetto Aldo Sàmara. Gli parve di vedere la sua Èlvia in balìa delle misteriose forze spadroneggianti nelle stanze superiori della villa abbandonata, e volle sottrarla e sottrar se stesso al loro occulto potere.

Tornàti a Roma, egli soffrì per qualche tempo l'irragionevole ossessione di una malefica influenza che avrebbe nociuto a tutti e due; ma, dopo alcuni mesi di chiusa ansietà, ebbe a convincersi perfettamente che si era ingannato.

But, at long intervals, Èlvia would suddenly remark, just as she had on that night: "Tell me: Where did I read. . . Or where did I see it performed?. . . It's strange! Strange!"

From that time on, Aldo Sàmara repeatedly studied the book written by the two British scientists. He had become a believer.

Soltanto, accadde—due o tre volte, a lunghi intervalli,—che Èlvia ripetesse, come quella sera:

—Dimmi: Dove ho letto…. O dove ho visto rappresentare?… È strano! È strano!

Da allora in poi, Aldo Sàmara ha riletto più volte il libro di quei due scienziati inglesi, e metterebbe la mano sul fuoco per attestare che essi hanno ragione.

THE CONSULTATION

TO AMILCARE LAURIA

Seeing the doctor come in, the beautiful lady rose from the chair in which she had been comfortably lying in wait.

An old friend of the family, he smilingly nodded to her not to move, and hurried to grasp the hands she was offering to him.

The living room, kept in darkness by heavy window curtains, was crowded with chairs, armchairs, little tables covered with precious knickknacks, and Japanese vases filled with yellow roses which spread a very fragrant perfume. Two old tapestries were suspended against a backdrop of a fine brocade fabric wall covering. All this, in that evening hour, lent the room an unusual air of mystery, enhanced by the severity of the beautiful lady's appearance. The doctor had immediately noticed the lack of the usual kind smile with which she usually welcomed him even when she was ill in bed, and at the same time, a quick glance made him realize that the consultation for which he had been invited had to be a pretext. He wondered what this could possibly be about. Women often turn to a doctor rather than to their confessor in certain delicate circumstances.

"Please forgive me if I delayed my coming for a few hours. Our profession," said the doctor, "never leaves us full freedom."

"No need to apologize," she said, shaking his hands again.

"You are not sick, it seems to me."

"Physically, maybe not; but I'm so disturbed in my spirit that I'm afraid of getting sick."

"What is this about?"

"My happiness."

"In that case, you are your own best counselor."

"I have a terrible scruple."

"I'd be delighted if I could help in making it disappear. Are you addressing your doctor or your friend?"

"Both."

"Then your friend is more important than your doctor."

"I am consulting my friend because he is a doctor."

"Oh! My responsibility grows, because the friend's heart may harm the physician's science. It's a serious matter, it seems."

"Extremely! I'm on the verge of making a big decision and I can't decide. There is that terrible scruple that stops me; it makes me hesitate. I wouldn't want to commit a crime."

"Oh," the doctor said, astonished. "You couldn't hurt a fly."

"Voluntarily, no; but by thoughtfulness, by mistake. . ."

"Speak, and count on my devotion, my affection, if not my science."

UN CONSULTO

AD AMILCARE LAURIA

Vedendo entrare il dottore, la bella signora si era alzata dalla poltrona dove stava abbandonatamente sdraiata da un pezzo, in attesa.

Vecchio amico di casa, egli le accennò sorridendo di non muoversi e affrettò il passo verso di lei che gli stendeva le mani.

Il salotto, tenuto in penombra dalle pesanti tende di stoffa delle finestre, ingombro di seggiole, di poltrone, di tavolinetti sovraccarichi di preziosi gingilli e di vasi giapponesi colmi di rose gialle che spandevano per l'aria acutissimo profumo, con due antichi arazzi alle pareti sullo sfondo della tappezzeria di broccato, prendeva in quell'ora vespertina, un'insolita aria di mistero, accresciuta dalla severità dell'aspetto della bella signora. Il dottore avea subito notato la mancanza dell'abituale gentile sorriso con cui ella lo accoglieva anche quando stava a letto malata, e nello stesso tempo una rapida occhiata gli aveva fatto comprendere che il consulto per cui era stato invitato a venire da lei doveva essere, più che altro, un pretesto. Di che cosa poteva voler consultarlo? Se lo domandava, pensando che spesso le donne amano di rivolgersi piuttosto al medico che non al confessore in certe delicate circostanze.

—Mi perdoni se ho ritardato di qualche ora la mia venuta. La nostra professione— disse il dottore—non ci lascia mai piena libertà.

—Non ha bisogno di scusarsi—ella rispose, stringendogli nuovamente le mani.

—Non sta male, mi pare.

—Fisicamente, forse no; ma sono così turbata di spirito che ho paura di ammalarmi.

—Di che si tratta?

—Della mia felicità.

—In questo caso, la miglior consigliera è lei stessa.

—Ho un terribile scrupolo.

—Sarei lietissimo, se potessi riuscire a dileguarlo. Si rivolge al medico o all'amico?

—A tutti e due.

—L'amico vale più del medico in questo caso.

—Consulto l'amico perchè è medico.

—Ahi! La responsabilità cresce, perchè il cuore dell'amico può nuocere alla scienza del medico. È cosa grave, a quel che pare.

—Gravissima! Sono sul punto di prendere una gran decisione e non so decidermi. Quel terribile scrupolo mi trattiene, mi fa esitare. Non vorrei commettere un delitto.

—Oh!—fece il dottore, stupito.—Lei non è capace di far male a una mosca.

—Volontariamente, no; ma per leggerezza, per sbadataggine....

—Parli, e conti su la mia devozione, sul mio affetto, se non sulla mia scienza.

"I count on that above all. I want a word of certainty, of absolute certainty."

"Who can be sure of giving that?"

"I read a book that shocked me. Ignorance really is a good thing! I had never understood that before now."

"Even ignorance has its drawbacks. An educated lady like you knows that every matter in this world can be looked at from different points of view; so from one it can seem white, and black from the other, or gray or red or yellow."

"My case is less complicated: either white or black. My heart makes me see white; the mind, after that unhappy reading, black. Which should I heed?"

"A woman must always heed her heart."

"Probably you wouldn't say so, if you knew. . ."

"Indeed. Let's not get lost in preambles."

"Are you in a hurry?"

"Only to save you, if possible, from your moral suffering that I can see is very painful, since I don't see the sweet smile on your lips that usually makes you even more beautiful. Don't take this as a compliment, merely an observation I made as I came in."

"A dying soul can't smile, Doctor."

"Let's not exaggerate! Speak, then."

"You know of my disgrace; I became a widow at twenty-five, after two years of marriage without the blessing of children."

"It would have been a greater disgrace if your widowhood had been accompanied with children. Life is full of painful surprises."

"A son or daughter would have compensated me for any disillusion. My heart would have found a sublime occupation; any sacrifice would have seemed a divine joy. The woman who doesn't become a mother is a wrong creature. In my husband I loved my children in advance."

"At twenty-five, you can still begin to love again. Faithfulness to the dead is absurd."

"Indeed. But on the point of deciding for a new bond in which all the aspirations of my heart would be satisfied, a very sad doubt holds me back. If I could only think of myself. . ."

"Of whom else should you think?"

"Of the children that I desire."

"Let them come, first."

"Do I have the right to compromise their happiness? To prepare for them a painful, unhappy life, just because my heart tells me: Marry the man you love and by whom you're loved?"

"I don't understand."

"What does science know about heredity?"

"Very little. Nature has mysteries that we have not yet managed to penetrate entirely."

"In the family of the man I would choose as my second husband, there have been cases of madness."

"Hereditary?"

—Conto su questa soprattutto. Voglio una parola di certezza, di certezza assoluta.

—Chi può sentirsi sicuro di essere in potere di darla?

—Ho letto un libro che mi ha sconvolta. Ignorare è una bella cosa! Non lo avevo mai capito prima di ora.

—Ha i suoi inconvenienti anche l'ignorare. Una colta signora come è lei sa che ogni faccenda di questo mondo può esser guardata da diversi punti di vista; così da uno si può veder bianco, e nero dall'altro, o grigio o rosso o giallo.

—Il mio caso è meno complicato: o bianco o nero. Il cuore mi fa vedere bianco; la mente, dopo quella malaugurata lettura, nero. A chi devo dar retta?

—Una donna deve dar retta sempre al suo cuore.

—Probabilmente non direbbe così, se sapesse….

—Appunto, non ci perdiamo in preamboli.

—Ha fretta?

—Soltanto per toglierla, se è possibile, dalla morale sofferenza che stimo acutissima, se non vedo sulle labbra di lei il dolce sorriso che la rende ordinariamente più bella. Non è un complimento, ma un'osservazione fatta appena l'ho veduta.

—Un'anima moribonda non può sorridere, dottore.

—Non esageri, via! Parli dunque.

—Ella sa la mia disgrazia; sono rimasta vedova a venticinque anni, dopo due anni di matrimonio non consolato da prole.

—Forse sarebbe stata disgrazia maggiore la vedovanza con prole. La vita è piena di dolorose sorprese.

—Un figlio o una figlia mi avrebbero compensata di ogni disillusione. Il mio cuore avrebbe trovato una sublime occupazione; qualunque sacrificio mi sarebbe parso gioia divina. La donna che non diventa madre è una creatura sbagliata. In mio marito io amavo anticipatamente i miei figli.

—A venticinque anni si può ricominciare ad amare un altr'uomo. La fedeltà ai morti è atto assurdo.

—Infatti. Ma sul punto di decidermi per un nuovo legame in cui sarebbero appagate tutte le aspirazioni del mio cuore, un tristissimo dubbio mi trattiene. Se potessi pensare soltanto a me….

—A chi altri?

—Alle mie creature, alle quali anelo.

—Le lasci prima venire.

—Ho io il diritto di compromettere la loro felicità? Preparare loro una vita dolorosa, disgraziata, unicamente perchè il cuore mi dice: Sposa l'uomo che tu ami e da cui sei riamata?

—Non capisco.

—Che cosa sa di certo la scienza sull'eredità?

—Molto e poco. La natura ha misteri che non siamo ancora riusciti a penetrare interamente.

—Nella famiglia di colui che dovrebbe essere il mio secondo marito sono avvenuti casi di pazzia.

—Ereditaria?

"Who knows? But his grandmother was crazy. His uncle was crazy. His brother was crazy!"

The doctor lowered his head, frowning, thoughtful. He was deeply impressed by the vibrant desolation in the voice of that woman in love who seemed to expect from him a sentence of life or death. And he didn't dare raise his eyes to her face for fear that his slight hesitation would irretrievably hurt that poor heart. He had seen her grow and flourish, and he loved her like a daughter. As a young girl, he had snatched her from the claws of death, and therefore she seemed to him somehow his own. He had been a witness at her wedding, as her closest family friend. He had seen her agonize over the great pain of losing her husband, taken from her suddenly by a devious *angina pectoris* on their second anniversary. He knew the man she had chosen among the many who now courted this beautiful, rich woman without relatives. He was surprised that her problem hadn't occurred to him before. As her doctor and her friend, it should have been his duty to warn her, even if not consulted, from the moment he realized that Marquis Attilio Volpes would likely become the second husband of Baroness Iole di Rivierasco, widow of Baron di Camposparto. Even now, after her revelation, he pretended ignorance. But her request for counsel saddened him and gave him a deep sense of remorse. All this went through his mind in a painful instant.

"Here it is," he said. "There are cases where science has no doubts. I met a family where all the children went crazy, for a year, as soon as they turned twenty. The madness suddenly broke out on a fixed day, a fixed hour, with incredible punctuality. Of the three males, the oldest presented with a sweet, idyllic madness, and would stay in bed in a room full of olive and oak branches prepared with his own hands, with the blanket covered with laurel leaves. The second had spent the painful year playing pipe and violin, which he learned how to play on his own during his madness; and his virtuosity only lasted until he regained his sanity. The third one believed himself to be a great captain, the holder of the most intimate secrets of the King and of the Pope, and continually quoted all the Latin texts studied in school, which he no longer remembered when the period of madness ended. But a son of the second son, in whom this temporary madness appeared, killed his brother. I don't know about the others. In cases like these, I repeat, the doctor's advice could not be uncertain. For alcoholics, for those born delinquent or deformed, the same thing applies. But we also have a lot of cases where madness is skipped, or inexplicably disappears, or even more inexplicably comes back. Germs, latent for two or three generations, develop suddenly. How? Why? Science doesn't know. Nor does it know how they propagate, nor can predict how and when. Certainly, since it's a kind of gambling, prudence would advise you not to play. But if there are other strong reasons for playing the game? A love like yours, for example, a love that means life, the happiness of two good creatures, for which a prohibition would be a great misfortune? Perhaps the day will come when science will be able to give infallible answers; and then legislation must intervene for the good of society, sacrificing the temporary good of the individual. But as of today. . ."

—Chi lo sa? Ma sono avvenuti. Pazza la nonna, pazzo uno zio, pazzo un fratello!—

Il dottore abbassò la testa, corrugando le sopracciglia, pensoso. Era profondamente impressionato della desolazione vibrante nella voce di quella donna innamorata che pareva attendesse da lui una sentenza di vita o di morte. E non osava alzarle gli occhi in viso per paura che la sua minima esitazione ferisse irrimediabilmente quel povero cuore. L'aveva vista crescere e fiorire, e le voleva bene come a una figlia. Da giovinetta, l'aveva strappata quasi a stento dagli artigli della morte, e perciò gli pareva cosa sua. Era stato testimone delle nozze di lei, come amico più intimo di famiglia. L'aveva vista agonizzare per il gran dolore della perdita del marito tòltole improvvisamente da una subdola *angina pectoris* proprio il giorno della festa del secondo anniversario delle loro nozze. Non ignorava chi fosse il prescelto tra tanti che ora aspiravano alla mano di lei, bella, ricca, orfana di parenti; e si meravigliava che lo scrupolo di lei non si fosse affacciato prima al suo pensiero di dottore e di amico. Sarebbe stato suo dovere metterla in guardia, quantunque non consultato, sin dal primo giorno in cui egli aveva acquistato la certezza che il marchese Attilio Volpes sarebbe divenuto, presto o tardi, il secondo marito della baronessa Iole di Rivierasco, vedova del barone di Camposparto. Per delicatezza, aveva finto d'ignorare, anche dopo la rivelazione della baronessa; e la richiesta del consulto lo contristava e gli dava la profonda sensazione di un rimorso.

Tutto questo gli era passato per la mente in un pauroso baleno.

—Ecco—egli disse.—Vi sono casi per i quali la scienza non può avere dubbio alcuno. Ho conosciuto una famiglia in cui tutti i figli ammattivano, per un anno, appena compiuti i vent'anni. La pazzia scoppiava improvvisamente a giorno fisso, a ora fissa, con puntualità incredibile. Dei tre maschi, il maggiore avea avuto una pazzia dolce, idilliaca, restando a letto in una camera tutta parata di rami di ulivo e di quercia preparati dalle sue mani, con la coperta cosparsa di foglie di alloro. Il secondo aveva passato l'anno doloroso suonando uno zufolo di canna e il violino, appresi a suonare da sè durante la pazzia; e la virtuosità perdurò quando egli ebbe riacquistato il senno. Il terzo si credeva un gran capitano, depositario dei più intimi segreti del Re e del Papa, e citava continuamente tutti i testi latini studiati nelle scuole e che non ricordò più quando l'accesso finì. Ma un figlio del secondogenito, nel quale si riprodusse la periodica pazzia, ammazzò un fratello. Degli altri non so. In casi come questi, ripeto, il consiglio del medico non potrebbe essere incerto. Per gli alcoolici, per i delinquenti nati, per i deformi, egualmente. Ma abbiamo anche moltissimi casi in cui avvengono salti, sparizioni inesplicabili, più inesplicabili riprese. Germi, latenti per due o tre generazioni, si sviluppano a un tratto. Come? Perchè? La scienza non ne sa nulla. Nè sa in che modo si propaghino, nè può prevedere come e quando. Certamente, trattandosi di una specie di gioco d'azzardo, la prudenza consiglierebbe di non giocare. Ma se vi sono altre e forti ragioni che consigliano il giuoco? Un amore come il suo, per esempio, un amore che è la vita, la felicità di due buone creature, per le quali una proibizione sarebbe una grandissima sventura? Verrà forse il giorno che la scienza potrà dare infallibilmente i suoi responsi su questo riguardo; e allora la legislazione dovrà intervenire pee il bene della società sacrificando quello, passeggero, dell'individuo. Ma oggi....

The baroness had listened anxiously, trembling, holding her breath, fixing her eyes on his to see if his words revealed all his thinking: and she had remained suspended, anxious, hearing those words, *But as of today*, that let a slit of light in the darkness of her heart.

"You know the family of Marquis Volpes, do you not?"

"Ah! Is it the Marquis, then?" exclaimed the doctor, simulating surprise. "His choice shows he has an excellent head on his shoulders. Should he lose it in the future, you would, no doubt bear some of the responsibility; but it is an absurd hypothesis."

"And?"

"Your scruple gives you credit."

"That is my friend speaking. What does the doctor recommend, what does he prescribe?"

"Nothing. I believe that the individual isn't obliged to sacrifice his short happiness to the eternal rights of the human species. What would you do if I told you not to marry him?"

"I would die! Perhaps I would kill myself because life would no longer have any attractiveness for me."

"That's a bit much. Life has always, as long as it lasts, new attractions to replace those destroyed by its own blind ferocity."

"Not always, Doctor!"

"Perhaps. Nobody, however, has the right to throw it away as a useless thing; religion and science agree on this point."

"Be explicit: Worry about truth, not about me."

"More explicit than that? It is imperative that science responds with a perhaps, and not with an affirmation that might be wrong. Be happy in your own way, let Nature take care of the rest. God, Fate, in short, that occult force that rules the Universe. To love and be loved are well worth playing the game."

The Baroness reflected for a moment, then said, "Thank you!"

The doctor left the living room with his heart in a tumult. Did he do the right thing? Did he do the wrong thing? Maybe he was wrong, but perhaps he might have been right.

Yet his skepticism as a scientist didn't reassure him fully.

"The human species and its need to propagate!" he mumbled, descending the stairs of the Rivierasco palace. "It should mind its own business! Is the human species and its need to propagate not what drives us to love that way? It really should mind its own business."

La baronessa lo aveva ascoltato ansiosa, tremante, trattenendo il respiro, tenendogli fissi gli occhi negli occhi per capire se le sue parole rivelavano tutto il pensiero di lui: ed era rimasta sospesa, ansimante sentendo quel *Ma oggi* che le faceva penetrare nel buio del cuore uno spiraglio di luce.

—Ella conosce la famiglia del marchese Volpes.

—Ah! si tratta del marchese?—esclamò il dottore simulando sorpresa.—La scelta è indizio di gran senno in lui. Se lo perdesse dopo, la colpa potrebbe essere un po' di lei; ma è un'ipotesi assurda.

—Dunque?

—Il suo scrupolo la onora.

—Questa è la parte dell'amico. Il dottore che cosa consiglia, che cosa impone?

—Niente. Io credo che l'individuo non è obbligato a immolare la sua breve felicità ai diritti eterni della Specie. Che farebbe lei se io le dicessi: Non lo sposi?

—Ne morrei! Forse, mi ammazzerei perchè la vita non avrebbe più nessuna attrattiva per me.

—È un po' troppo. La vita ha sempre, finchè dura, nuove attrattive da sostituire a quelle distrutte dalla sua stessa inconsapevole ferocia.

—Non sempre, dottore!

—Può darsi. Nessuno però ha diritto di buttarla via come cosa inutile; la religione e la scienza sono d'accordo su questo punto.

—Sia esplicito; si preoccupi della verità non di me.

—Più esplicito di così? È doveroso che la scienza risponda con un forse e non con un'affermazione che potrebbe risultare sbagliata. Sia felice, a modo suo, lasci che al resto pensi la Natura. Dio, il Caso, insomma quella Forza occulta che regola l'Universo. Amare ed essere amata valgon bene che si tenti il gioco.

La baronessa riflettè un momento, poi disse:

—Grazie!

Il dottore uscì dal salotto col cuore sconvolto. Aveva fatto bene? Aveva fatto male? Forse aveva fatto male; ma poteva anche darsi che avesse fatto bene.

Eppure il suo scetticismo di scienziato non lo rassicurava pienamente.

—La Specie!—brontolava, scendendo le scale del palazzo Rivierasco.—Pensi essa ai casi suoi! Non è essa che fa amare a quel modo?... Pensi essa ai casi suoi.

ALWAYS LATE!

TO JANE GREY

"Did you not love her?" Diego Punzi asked, with great amazement.

"A little," Falcini answered.

"A little. . . in what sense?"

"Not all women produce the famous *coup de foudre*, or love at first sight; many, most of them, in fact, slowly enter our heart, and they are the most dangerous."

"Don't pass yourself as a theorist, in the way of Stendhal!" Punzi interrupted.

"No; I simply want to explain to you. . ."

"So tell me, then. As for the explanation, I will give it to me myself."

"Are you interested?"

"You caused a great sorrow, at that time!"

"Ah!" Falcini exclaimed, looking firmly his friend in the eyes. And he added, "Unwillingly, however, and unknowingly. I'm sorry for you and for her."

"Who knows, maybe it was better this way?"

"People should think so when something doesn't happen, but it's not easy. Also. . . it's not always true. Now you, with this revelation, make me feel remorse."

"Don't worry. Fortunately, I was able to console myself."

"It doesn't matter. I believe that in this world the evil that is done without wanting it is much more than the one caused willingly.

"So?"

"So, you know, I found myself in an uncomfortable situation. I remember very well: It was a night in May. . . no, in June, with a marvelous full moon. Her father, her mother, her cousin, and the other two friends who accompanied them were climbing up Via Quattro Fontane on the sidewalk side, flooded by the moonlight; the two of us, on the other hand, were walking on the side in the shadow of the houses, which came almost to the middle of the road. Suddenly she said to me, 'In about ten days I'll leave.' 'For Lyon?' I asked. (She had a brother there, the director of a velvet factory.) 'For Kiel,' she replied. "How come?' . . . "I'll go to see a friend, who has in mind for me to help her in I don't know what project. . . It may be that I will never return to Rome. . . Oh! Give me some advice: Should I go? I entrust my future to your hands.' 'I would take a very serious responsibility by giving you any advice.'"

"She was walking with her head lowered, her eyes closed, and I could feel shaking her arm, holding mine. I looked at her; she was pale, and hearing my last words she had drawn her lips to a painful expression of disappointment. 'Look, Nelly,' I said. 'A little while ago, at Olgani's house, we joked and laughed too much. Your words right now are heavy and serious, if I understand their meaning. I can't answer you right away. I would like to say, *Stay*! But it would be a grave thoughtlessness on my part if I didn't think about it for a few days. Do you mind waiting until next Wednesday? We can meet again at Olgani's house. If you let me, I could even write to you.'

SEMPRE TARDI!

A JANE GREY

—Non l'amavi?—domandò, con gran maraviglia, Diego Punzi.

—Un po'—rispose Falcini.

—Un po'… in che senso?

—Non tutte le donne producono il famoso *coup de foudre*; molte, la maggior parte anzi, s'insinuano lentamente nel nostro cuore e sono le più pericolose.

—Non fare il teorico, alla Stendhal!—lo interruppe Punzi.

—No; voglio soltanto spiegarti….

—E allora raccontami. La spiegazione me la darò da solo.

—T'interessa?

—Mi hai causato un grande dolore in quel periodo!

—Ah!—esclamò Falcini guardando fissamente negli occhi il suo amico. E soggiunse:—Senza volerlo però e senza saperlo. Mi dispiace per te e per lei.

—Chissà, forse è stato meglio.

—Bisognerebbe pensare così quando una cosa non avviene; ma non è facile. E poi… non è sempre vero. Ora tu, con questa rivelazione, mi fai sentire rimorso.

—Non preoccuparti; fortunatamente sono riuscito a consolarmi.

—Non importa. Io credo che in questo mondo sia assai più il male che vien fatto senza volerlo, che non quello prodotto liberamente.

—Dunque?

—Dunque, capisci, mi trovai in imbarazzo. Ricordo benissimo: era una serata di maggio… no, di giugno, con un plenilunio maraviglioso. Il padre, la madre, la cugina e gli altri due amici che li accompagnavano salivano per Via Quattro Fontane sul lato del marciapiede inondato dal lume di luna; noi due, invece, dalla parte dell'ombra delle case, che tagliava quasi a mezzo la strada. Improvvisamente ella mi disse:—Tra una diecina di giorni parto.—Per Lione?—domandai (Aveva un fratello là, direttore d'una fabbrica di velluti).—Per Kiel—rispose.—Come mai?—Vado da un'amica…. che ha in mente per me non so quale progetto…. Potrebbe darsi che io non ritorni più a Roma….—Oh!…—Consigliatemi: devo andare? Affido il mio destino alle vostre mani.—Assumerei una gravissima responsabilità dandovi un consiglio qualunque.—

Ella saliva a capo chino, con gli occhi socchiusi, ed io sentivo tremare il suo braccio attaccato al mio. La guardai; era pallida, e alle mie ultime parole aveva atteggiato le labbra a una dolorosa espressione di delusione.—Sentite, Nelly,—le dissi.—Poco fa in casa Olgani abbiamo scherzato e riso troppo. Le vostre parole di questo momento sono serie e gravi, se io capisco il loro significato. Non posso rispondervi subito. Vorrei potervi dire: Restate! Ma sarebbe una gran leggerezza da parte mia, se non riflettessi qualche giorno. Vi dispiace attendere fino a mercoledì prossimo? Ci rivedremo in casa Olgani. Se me lo permettete, potrei anche scrivervi.

'No; give me your answer on Wednesday. Sincerely, I hope!' 'With the utmost sincerity!' 'Perhaps I was wrong to ask for your advice!' she exclaimed after a short pause. 'I am very grateful you did.' 'Let's join the others,' she concluded, smiling sadly.

"And as we crossed the street, I squeezed her hand, murmuring: 'You did the right thing: I thank you.'

"Meanwhile she had resumed her normal appearance. But I tried in vain not to look upset. And looking at her, I thought of the way women are better than us in concealing and mastering their emotions. In that short stretch of road, she had begun to talk about the subject of our laughs at Olgani's house, when a violinist had butchered I don't know what sonata of Saint-Saëns, and she seemed to have forgotten the serious things she had just told me.

"Returning home and walking along the road I had taken with Miss Nelly, it seemed to me to hear again, almost resounding over the air, the sound of her voice, and the uncertain tone with which she had asked me: 'Should I go?' I reproached myself of not having been honest. Why hadn't I told her immediately: 'You are free! I'm not in a position to give you a concrete answer.' And as I began to feel a kind of irritation against her for that inopportune question (I didn't think I had done anything to warrant it), I also felt a sweet pleasure that flattered my pride. I couldn't read clearly in my heart. I had spent that year like a butterfly among the many ladies who attended the Olgani house. Remember? We used to call those crowded Wednesday evenings the *Fair,* for Mrs. Olgani to arrange marriages. She thought especially of her daughter, whose beauty was already a bit fading, but she didn't want to show it. And therefore those evenings were a great appeal of moms and girls, filled with dances that should seem improvised, and music and singing academies. And, every night, new amusements. Poor lady! Money spent in vain. The bare bones of her daughter were left in her house, nobody had the courage to marry that skeleton, which also had a very decent dowry."

"Don't digress," Diego Punzi interrupted.

"Remember? Too many girls! No fewer than three in competition with each other for each bachelor. Pulled here, pulled there, none of us could stop. More than courting, we were courted. Good times! You too; don't deny it."

"Like the others; but. . ."

"I know. You seriously thought of marriage and wanted to choose well. I, convinced that in matters of marriage everything is left to chance, wanted to let the event, if ever had to happen, happen without me having to put neither salt nor pepper on it. After all, in the hubbub of those evenings, it seemed to me that not even the girls were taking things seriously. Miss Nelly and her cousin Jane were an exception. Jane, very beautiful, with her excessive British stiffness kept the suitors at a distance; in Miss Nelly, you could find little or nothing of the English traits; that is, only a simple and honest dignity that imposed respect. You could understand, approaching and conversing with her, that you were dealing with a lady to whom words meant exactly what they meant and nothing else. You could not use allusions nor lightly express feelings without substance, or compliments, or adulation, or mischievous teasing aimed at causing a reaction.

—No; mi darete la risposta mercoledì. Sinceramente, spero!—Sincerissimamente!—Ho, forse, fatto male a chiedervi un consiglio!—esclamò dopo una breve pausa.—Ve ne sono gratissimo.—Raggiungiamo gli altri—ella concluse, sorridendo tristemente.

E nell'attraversare la via, le strinsi forte una mano, mormorando:—Avete fatto bene; ve ne ringrazio.

Intanto ella riprendeva il suo aspetto normale; ma io mi sforzavo invano di non apparire turbato; e osservandola, pensavo quanto le donne siano superiori a noi nel dissimulare e nel padroneggiarsi. In quel breve tratto di strada, ella aveva cominciato a parlarmi del soggetto delle nostre risate in casa Olgani mentre un violinista rovinava non so quale sonata di Saint-Saëns; e pareva che avesse dimenticato le gravi cose che mi aveva detto poco prima.

Tornando a casa e rifacendo la strada fatta insieme con miss Nelly, mi sembrava di risentire, quasi ondulanti ancora per l'aria, il suono della voce e il tono incerto con cui ella mi aveva domandato:—Devo andare?—Mi rimproveravo di non essere stato sincero. Perchè non le avevo detto immediatamente:—Siete libera! Io non sono in una posizione da darvi una risposta concreta.—E mentre cominciavo a sentire una specie d'irritazione contro di lei per quella domanda inopportuna (non credevo di aver fatto niente che potesse autorizzarla a rivolgermela), provavo però anche un dolce compiacimento che lusingava il mio amor proprio. Non leggevo ben chiaro nel mio cuore. Quell'anno passavo come una farfalla fra le tante signorine che frequentavano casa Olgani. Ricordi? Noi chiamavamo la *Fiera* quei mercoledì affollatissimi, destinati dalla signora Olgani a combinare matrimoni. Ella pensava soprattutto a sua figlia già sullo sfiorire, ma non voleva farlo scorgere; e perciò gran richiamo di mamme e di ragazze, e balli che dovevano sembrare improvvisati, e accademie di musica e di canto; e, ogni sera, novità di divertimenti. Povera signora! Soldi spesi invano. Le quattro ossa spolpate della sua figliuola le sono rimaste in casa; nessuno ha avuto il coraggio di sposare quello scheletro che pure aveva una discretissima dote.

—Non divagare—lo interruppe Diego Punzi.

—Ricordi? Troppe ragazze! Per ogni scapolo, non meno di tre in concorrenza fra loro. Tirati in qua, tirati in là, nessuno di noi riusciva a fermarsi. Più che corteggiare, eravamo corteggiati. Bei tempi! Anche tu; non negarlo.

—Come gli altri; ma….

—Lo so; tu pensavi seriamente al matrimonio e volevi sceglier bene. Io, convinto che nel matrimonio tutto è caso, volevo lasciare che l'avvenimento, se mai, si compisse senza che dovessi metterci nè sale nè pepe. E poi, in quella baraonda di serate, mi sembrava che neppure le ragazze facessero sul serio. Miss Nelly e sua cugina Jane però erano un'eccezione tra la folla. Jane, bellissima, con la sua eccessiva rigidezza britannica teneva un po' a distanza i corteggiatori; in miss Nelly, invece, si scorgeva poco o niente d'inglese, cioè soltanto una dignità semplice e schietta che imponeva rispetto. Si capiva, avvicinandola e conversando con lei, che si aveva a che fare con una signorina per la quale le parole significavano precisamente quel che volevano dire e non altro. Non si potevano adoperare sottintesi o esprimere leggermente sentimenti senza sostanza, o complimenti, o adulazioni, o maliziose canzonature per provocare reazioni.

For that reason, Miss Nelly had soon become my favorite. I felt as if I was in unison with her, in everything. I especially liked her sweet gaiety of spirit. Sorry, I speak as if she were a person unknown to you."

"I was about to mention it. In short, what did you answer, that Wednesday?"

"I spent several days in a strange torpor, as if I wanted to avoid the difficulty of finding the answer at the bottom of my soul. Obviously I was not in love with her, and I was sorry I was not. Miss Nelly inspired me a great deal of sympathy, but she hadn't touched my heart so intensely as to give me the clear feeling that she was for me something more than a friend or a person I would like to spend together a few hours of the day. Also, I didn't find myself ready to tie myself to her for the rest of my life. On top of that, there were really family circumstances that would not allow me to make long-term commitments, not to mention that long engagements have always been odious to me. Yet I would have liked her to have waited longer, before putting me on the spot with that question and with the serious words 'I entrust my future to your hands!' In a few months' time, as things would mature, maybe, it would have been easy for me to make the decision she was looking for. . . But in those days, no. And I didn't want to lie. It is true, unfortunately, that often, a word, just *one* word inopportunely pronounced, affects without remedy the whole existence of a person. You consoled yourself easily."

"I didn't say easily."

"In any case, you consoled yourself. I, on the other hand, still regret what I lost. On that Wednesday, therefore, I was going to the house of Olgani without knowing exactly what I should have told Miss Nelly or at least not knowing how I could express myself. I didn't want to lie, but I didn't want to close the possibility of resuming that matter, in the case circumstances, one day, would allow me to say, 'Stay!' or any other equivalent word. As I entered the living room, I glanced around quickly and felt better: Miss Nelly was not there. *Maybe she won't come!* I thought. But at that very moment she appeared on the doorway, preceded by her cousin. I rushed to meet her, like a person who bravely faces an inevitable danger, and I told her, 'You are late!' She looked into my eyes, serious, almost amazed at hearing those words. And during the evening it seemed that she wanted to avoid me. Leaving Olgani's house, some people of the company suggested a walk to the Coliseum. We started. I offered her my arm. The evening was very beautiful; the lanes leading there were almost deserted. On the way, Jane had remained close to her cousin too obstinately, unlike she usually did: She seemed to do it on purpose, in agreement with her cousin. But I made sure to stay with her for a few moments. I had thought natural that Miss Nelly didn't look impatient to receive my answer. Now it was up to me to be impatient to give it. 'So,' I said, and you could see that I didn't know how to start the conversation, 'does your girlfriend have a project for you?' 'I am very grateful to you. Ah!' she exclaimed. 'Let's not talk about it. The other night I allowed myself to speak incoherent words. Forgive me. It's not worth going back over it.' 'Why?'

Per ciò miss Nelly era diventata presto la mia preferita; mi sembrava di sentirmi in ogni cosa all'unisono con lei. Mi piaceva soprattutto quella sua dolce gaiezza di spirito. Ma già, io te ne parlo come se si trattasse di una persona a te ignota.

—Stavo per dirtelo. Insomma, che cosa rispondesti quel mercoledì?

—Passai parecchi giorni in un torpore strano, quasi volessi evitarmi la fatica di ricercare in fondo all'animo la risposta da dare. Evidentemente non ero innamorato, e sentivo dispiacere di non esserlo. Miss Nelly mi ispirava una gran simpatia, ma non aveva ancora operato così intensamente sul mio cuore da darmi la chiara coscienza che ella fosse per me qualche cosa di più di una amica o di una persona con cui avrei voluto passare insieme alcune ore della giornata. Non mi trovavo pronto a legarmi con lei per tutta la vita. E poi, c'erano davvero circostanze di famiglia che non mi avrebbero permesso di prendere impegni a lungo termine, senza contare che i fidanzamenti lunghi mi sono sempre stati odiosissimi. Eppure avrei voluto ch'ella avesse atteso ancora prima di mettermi alle strette con quella domanda e con le gravi parole:—Affido il mio avvenire alle vostra mani!—Chissà? Tra qualche mese, lasciando maturare le cose, forse, mi sarebbe stato facile decidermi secondo quello che ella sembrava desiderasse…. Ma in quei giorni, no; e non volevo mentire. È vero, purtroppo, che spesso, una parola, una sola parola inopportunamente pronunziata influisce senza rimedio sulla intera esistenza di una persona. Tu ti sei consolato facilmente.

—Non ho detto facilmente.

—In ogni modo, ti sei consolato; io invece rimpiango ancora quello che ho perduto. Il mercoledì, dunque, mi avviavo verso casa Olgani senza sapere precisamente quel che avrei dovuto dire a miss Nelly, o almeno senza sapere in che modo avrei potuto formulare la mia risposta. Non volevo mentire e non volevo neppure chiudermi ogni strada per riprendere quell'argomento nel caso che le circostanze mi avessero, un giorno, permesso di dirle:—Restate!—o qualunque altra parola equivalente. Entrando nel salotto, una rapida occhiata in giro mi aveva consolato; miss Nelly non c'era.—Può darsi che non venga!—pensai. Ma proprio in quel momento ella apparse sull'uscio preceduta dalla cugina. Le corsi incontro, come chi affronta coraggiosamente un inevitabile pericolo, e le dissi:—Siete in ritardo!—Mi guardò negli occhi, seria, quasi maravigliata di udirsi dire quelle parole. E durante la serata mi sembrò che volesse evitarmi. Uscendo di casa Olgani, qualcuno della comitiva propose una passeggiata al Colosseo. Ci avviammo. Le offrii il braccio. La serata era bellissima; le viuzze che conducono là erano quasi deserte. Durante il tragitto, Jane era rimasta a fianco della cugina troppo ostinatamente, diversamente dal solito; pareva che lo facesse a posta, d'accordo con lei. Ma io feci in modo di restare solo con lei per alcuni istanti. Avevo riflettuto: È naturale che miss Nelly non si mostri impaziente di ricevere la mia risposta; ora spetta a me essere impaziente di darla.—Dunque—dissi, e si vedeva bene che non sapevo come cominciare a parlare—quella vostra amica ha un progetto per voi? Io vi sono gratissimo.—Ah!—ella esclamò.—Non ne parliamo. L'altra sera mi sono sfuggite parole incoerenti. Scusate. Non vale la pena di tornarci sopra.—Perchè?

'It's useless; I've decided to leave. The invitation is so affectionate, so pressing. . . And also, I need fresh air, a bit of countryside. My friend's villa is in the middle of a great forest.' She spoke slowly, harshly. I didn't dare to insist; I was mortified. Shortly thereafter, under the arches of the Coliseum, as soon as she got away from my arm, it seemed to me that something decisive had happened to me."

"That's all?"

"No. Three months later she had already come back. But during those three months, I had committed the idiocy of letting myself get entangled—mysteries of the heart! It doesn't matter that you know with whom, because it's all in the past, though it has left painful traces in my life. I had seen Miss Nelly again, fleetingly. I would make rare and short appearances at Olgani's house. Three nights before her mother's birthday, Miss Nelly reminded me that date: I couldn't have missed the party without being rude. You, too, were there that night."

"And it was then," interrupted Diego Punzi, "that I realized that in the heart of Miss Nelly there was no place for me. You had retired in the drawing room at the end of the hallway. . . I had seen you two disappear and I couldn't help the temptation of catching – I'm ashamed to confess it – a word or a gesture that would confirm my suspicions. You were seated in a corner. You didn't see me. . . It was a moment. . . You had your head lowered, and Miss Nelly was drying her eyes. . ."

"It's true. 'I need to talk to you,' she had told me. And on the pretext of showing me a Japanese statuette, a gift for her mother from her brother, that had arrived from Lyon the day before, she led me to the strange sitting room. Little colorful lamps spread a mystical light around the statue, sitting in a corner of a sort of altar. 'I have been too tough and rude to you,' she said. 'I wanted to apologize by letter from Kiel, but I lacked the courage.' 'Too much delicacy on your part,' I said. 'Let me talk,' she continued. 'You were right. When a woman tells a man what I have dared to say to you, she also deserves a worse response than you gave me. . . But I was deluding myself. I thought that my attitude was preventing you from opening up your soul, and I thought I would offer you a means to overcome the shyness that made you hesitate. I was expecting passion. . . Instead, you were glacial, utterly reserved. When, on the next Wednesday, you were about to speak. . . Oh, I had suffered so much in those days of waiting! I felt so mortified, so offended by your unexpected hesitation! And I interrupted you abruptly, with the wicked desire of taking revenge. Please forgive me; I was cruel. I regretted it almost instantly. Pride makes us commit so many misdeeds!' 'Not at all!' 'Yes, yes! Tell me that you have forgiven me, that you forgive me! I could not guess at the answer you were about to give me. If it was the one I had hoped to receive. . .' 'Ah, Nelly!' I interrupted her, taking her hands as she abandoned them in mine. 'It was unfortunate! My answer was not, perhaps, what I would have liked to give you and what you wanted, but it was not such to preclude a future for us; while today. . .' I didn't have the courage to continue. I saw those beautiful eyes filled with tears; she stared at me with great anxiety, and her lips, suddenly pale, stammered:

—È inutile; ho deciso di partire. L'invito è così affettuoso, così pressante…. E poi ho bisogno di aria nuova, di un po' di campagna. La villa della mia amica è in mezzo a una grande foresta.—Parlava lentamente, con tono severo. Non osai insistere, mortificatissimo. Poco dopo, sotto gli archi del Colosseo, appena ella si staccò dal mio braccio, mi parve che qualche cosa di decisivo fosse avvenuto per me.

—È tutto?

—No. Tre mesi dopo ella era già ritornata. Ma durante quei tre mesi, io avevo commesso la stupidaggine di lasciarmi adescare—misteri del cuore!—da…. Non importa che tu sappia da chi, perchè anche questo è un avvenimento ormai passato, sebbene abbia lasciato dolorose tracce nella mia vita. Avevo riveduto miss Nelly, fuggevolmente. Facevo rare e brevi apparizioni in casa Olgani. Tre sere prima dell'onomastico di sua madre, miss Nelly aveva avuto la precauzione di rammentarmi quella data; io non avrei potuto mancare alla festa senza mostrarmi scortese. C'eri anche tu quella sera.

—E appunto allora—lo interruppe Diego Punzi—io mi convinsi che nel cuore di miss Nelly non c'era più posto per me. Vi eravate rifugiati nel salottino in fondo… Vi avevo visti sparire e non avevo resistito al desiderio di sorprendere—ho vergogna di confessartelo—una parola, un gesto che potesse confermare il mio sospetto. Eravate seduti in un angolo. Non vi accorgeste di me…. Fu un istante…. Tu stavi a capo chino, e miss Nelly si asciugava gli occhi….

—È vero.—Ho bisogno di parlarle—mi aveva detto sotto voce. E con la scusa di mostrarmi una statuetta giapponese, regalo di suo fratello alla mamma, arrivata da Lione il giorno avanti, mi aveva condotto nello strano salottino, dove piccoli lumi colorati diffondevano fantastica luce attorno alla statua posata in un angolo su una specie d'altare.—Sono stata troppo dura e maleducata con voi—disse.—Volevo chiedervene scusa per lettera da Kiel; me n'è mancato il coraggio.—Eccesso di delicatezza da parte vostra—risposi.—Lasciatemi parlare—continuò.—Avevate ragione. Allorchè una donna dice a un uomo quel che io ho osato di dire a voi, merita anche una risposta peggiore di quella che voi mi deste…. Ma io mi illudevo; credevo che il mio contegno v'impedisse di aprirmi l'animo vostro, e pensai di offrirvi un mezzo per vincere la timidezza che vi faceva indugiare. Mi aspettavo un impeto… Invece, voi foste glaciale, riserbatissimo. Quando, il mercoledì dopo, stavate per parlare…. Oh, avevo sofferto tanto in quei giorni di intervallo! Mi ero sentita così avvilita, così offesa dalla vostra inattesa esitazione! E v'interruppi bruscamente, con la malvagia volontà di prendermi una rivincita. Vi prego di perdonarmi; sono stata perversa. Me ne pentii quasi subito. L'orgoglio ci fa commettere tante cattive azioni!—Ma niente affatto!…—Sì, sì! Ditemi che mi avete perdonato, che mi perdonate! Io non ho saputo indovinare quale sarebbe stata la risposta che stavate per darmi. Se fosse quella che mi ero illusa di ricevere….—Ah, Nelly!—la interruppi, prendendole le mani che ella abbandonò tra le mie.—È stata una disgrazia! La mia risposta non era, forse, quella che io avrei voluto darvi e che voi desideravate, ma non tale però da precluderci l'avvenire; mentre oggi….—Non mi resse l'animo di andare innanzi. Vidi riempirsi di lagrime quei begli occhi che mi fissavano con vivissima ansietà, e le sue labbra, improvvisamente impallidite, agitarsi per balbettare:

'So is it true what they told me?' 'I don't want to deceive you, I can't lie: It would be too cruel a pity, and unworthy of you and me.' She wept for a little, silently. Extremely moved, I begged her to stop. If anyone had walked in on us! 'The blame is mine! I must pay for it!' she said, wiping her eyes quickly, and trying to compose herself. I could barely master my emotions. At that moment I realized how an honest man can sometimes allow himself to commit an inexplicable infamy. I thought of the *other,* I had the heart, or rather, the senses possessed by *the other,* who had trust in my word as I trusted in hers, and I was very, very close to allow myself to be flattered by the possibility of playing a double match with her and with Miss Nelly. And see how strange life is! I would have done the right thing. By trying to act honestly, I have perhaps lost my chance at happiness!"

"And perhaps," Punzi added, "you made another lose his!"

"I still have the memory of that Japanese statuette that looked at us from that corner, with its enormously wide glass eyes, those pupils reflecting the colorful flames of the lamps, and I can't forget the last words of Miss Nelly, almost a sob: 'Always late!'"

"'Always late? Why?'

"It is the secret of that pained soul, and I didn't dare to ask her for an explanation. *Always late*! It could be the refrain for so many good men and women in this world. An explanatory refrain for thousands of dark tragedies of life, no less sad, indeed far more sad than those ending with poison or a gunshot; tragedies that torment their entire existence, and they don't even have the consolation of arousing interest and emotion around them."

"Sad consolation!" Putzi exclaimed.

"Afterward, when Miss Nelly had left town and I didn't know where to find her, I felt sprouting in my heart the hidden seed of an affection that would have given another direction to my life. And now that I know she died in Calcutta. . ."

"She's dead?"

"You didn't know? Now I seem to have in my heart something rotting, spreading in it a poisonous miasma."

"Oh, be reassured!" Punzi said. "*Vita mors est, et mors vita* (life is death, and death is life), someone said."

—È dunque vero quel che mi hanno detto?—Non voglio ingannarvi, non posso mentire; sarebbe pietà troppo crudele, e indegna di voi e di me.—Ella pianse un po' in silenzio. Estremamente commosso, io la pregavo di frenarsi. Se qualcuno fosse venuto a sorprenderci?—La colpa è stata mia! Debbo scontarne la pena!—ella disse, asciugandosi velocemente gli occhi, e facendo sforzi per rimettersi. Io potevo padroneggiarmi a stento. In quel momento ho capito come mai un'onesta persona possa talvolta lasciarsi indurre a commettere un'inesplicabile infamia. Pensavo all'*altra*, avevo il cuore, o meglio, i sensi invasati dall'*altra*, che aveva fiducia nella mia parola come io mi fidavo nella sua, e ci mancò poco, assai poco, che io non mi lasciassi lusingare dalla circostanza di giocare una partita doppia con lei e con miss Nelly. E, guarda la stranezza della vita! Avrei fatto bene. Per comportarmi onestamente, mi sono, forse, lasciato scappare di mano la felicità!

—E forse—soggiunse Punzi—l'hai fatta perdere a un altro!

—Mi è rimasta nella memoria la statuetta giapponese che ci guardava da quell'angolo con gli occhi di vetro enormemente spalancati, nelle cui pupille si riflettevano le fiammelle colorate dei lumi, e non ho potuto dimenticare le ultime parole di miss Nelly, quasi un singhiozzo:—Sempre tardi!—

—Sempre tardi? Perchè?

—È il segreto di quell'anima dolorosa, ed io non ho osato domandarle una spiegazione. Sempre tardi! Potrebbe essere il motto di tante buone creature di questo mondo. Motto esplicativo di mille oscure tragedie della vita, non meno triste, anzi assai più triste di quelle che finiscono con un veleno o con un colpo di pistola; tragedie che tormentano lunghe esistenze, e non hanno neppure il compenso di destare interesse e commozione attorno a loro.

—Magro compenso!—esclamò Punzi.

—Dopo, quando miss Nelly non era più qua ed io non sapevo dove poter rintracciarla, ho sentito schiudersi nel mio cuore il germe nascosto di un affetto che avrebbe dato certamente un altro indirizzo alla mia vita. Ed ora che la so morta a Calcutta....

—È morta?

—Lo ignoravi? Ora mi par di avere qualche cosa che mi si imputridisce nel cuore e vi spande miasmi deleteri.

—Oh, rassicùrati!—fece Punzi.—*Vita mors est, et mors vita*, ha detto qualcuno.

THE NAMELESS SORROW

TO SALVATORE LI GRECI

The woman seemed unable to rid herself of the oppressing shell of the clay that shaped her. Only her head stood up fiercely, pulling violently upward, the mass of hair sloping over her naked shoulders and her arched back, mixing with her flesh due to a lack of molding. And since the sculptor's stick had not yet opened her eyes, her beautiful oval face had an expression of such a desperate anguish that it hurt to look at her.

What he wanted to represent with her, the young sculptor Vittorio D'Arèba didn't know.

That sorrowful attitude had flashed into his imagination with such precision of detail that he had thought he would be able to finish the piece in two or three days. Instead, several weeks had passed, and the tormented female figure who had appeared to him, suddenly leaping out of nowhere and with all the harmonious perfection of the sculptural form, never managed to conquer the hesitation of his hand.

He had applied quick strokes with his thumb and stick, had set clay pieces nervously sprawled or rounded between his fingers, and then, with angry discontent, had taken away others recognized as superfluous by his severe judgment. He stood motionless in front of the *bozzetto*, the rough clay study of the masterwork he hoped to create. The beautiful, frustrating study, perpetually unable to display the spontaneity, the vigor, and the life of what his imagination had marvelously presented to him.

All he had to do was to copy that vision, as a schoolboy copies the chalk drawing presented by the teacher. But as soon as his hand approached the clay roughly piled and posed in the idealized figure that had inspired so much enthusiasm and given him so many happy moments of artistic creation, he encountered a strange, invincible resistance, as if the thumb and the stick refused to obey the intellect.

It was a completely new experience for Vittorio D'Arèba, who was aware he possessed the gift of a rare ease of improvisation.

Even newer, however, was the feeling of deep sadness that he felt, day after day, struggling against that incredible helplessness that held him obstinately locked in his studio from eight in the morning until six in the evening, and that made him avoid the cheerful meetings with friends and fellow artists that he frequented to rest from the day-to-day work and to renew his creative juices by way of enthusiastic discussions.

Some of his most intimate friends came several times to knock at the door of his studio, in his solitary home in the countryside, off Via Flaminia. But the door had remained inexorably shut to the blighters, whose interruptions irritated him, and who seemed to arrive just to make him lose his inspiration at the very moment when it was about to burst, uncontainable.

DOLORE SENZA NOME

A SALVATORE LI GRECI

Quella figura di donna sembrava non riuscisse a liberarsi dall'opprimente involucro della creta che le dava forma. Soltanto la testa si ergeva con fierezza, quasi tirasse violentemente in su la massa dei capelli spioventi su le spalle ignude e la schiena arcuata, ma che si confondevano con le carni per mancanza di modellatura. E siccome la stecca dello scultore non le aveva ancora aperto gli occhi, così il bellissimo volto ovale aveva un'espressione di tale disperata angoscia da far proprio male a guardarlo.

Che cosa volesse rappresentare con essa il giovane scultore Vittorio D'Arèba non avrebbe saputo dirlo neppur lui.

Quel doloroso atteggiamento gli era balenato nella fantasia con tanta precisione di particolari, ch'egli si era illuso di poter terminare il bozzetto in due o tre giorni. Invece erano trascorse parecchie settimane, e la tormentata figura femminile che gli era apparsa davanti, come balzata a un tratto fuori dal nulla e con tutta l'armoniosa perfezione della forma scultoria, non arrivava mai a vincere le esitazioni della sua mano.

Dati qua e là rapidi colpi di pollice e di stecca, impostati i pezzettini di creta nervosamente spiacciati o arrotondati tra le dita, e tòlti, con rabbiosa scontentezza, altri riconosciuti superflui dal severo giudizio dell'occhio, egli rimaneva in piedi, immobile, davanti al bozzetto che gli pareva non acquistasse nelle linee e nella fattura la spontaneità, il vigore e la vita di quello che l'immaginazione gli aveva presentato in modo meraviglioso.

Non avrebbe dovuto fare altro che copiarlo, come uno scolaro copia il gesso indicatogli dal professore; ma appena la mano si accostava alla creta accumulata in fretta sul cavalletto e rozzamente atteggiata a quel modello ideale che lo aveva tanto entusiasmato e gli aveva dato i felici momenti di creazione artistica, egli incontrava una strana invincibile resistenza, quasi il pollice e la stecca si rifiutassero di obbedire all'intelletto che voleva adoprarli.

Caso completamente nuovo per Vittorio D'Arèba, che sapeva di possedere il dono d'una rara facilità di improvvisazione.

Più nuovo assai però era il sentimento di profonda tristezza da cui si sentiva invadere di giorno in giorno nella lotta contro quell'incredibile impotenza che lo teneva ostinatamente chiuso nello studio dalle otto di mattina alle sei di sera, e che gli faceva sfuggire gli allegri ritrovi di amici e colleghi artisti da lui frequentati per riposarsi dall'assiduo lavoro giornaliero e per prendervi anche alimento di forze produttive tra le calorose discussioni.

Alcuni dei più intimi amici eran venuti a picchiare più volte alla porta del suo studio nella solitaria casa, in piena campagna, in una traversa di Via Flaminia; ma la porta era rimasta inesorabilmente chiusa davanti ai seccatori che lo irritavano con quelle interruzioni e che pareva venissero apposta per fargli smarrire l'ispirazione di esecuzione proprio quando stava per prorompere trionfante.

So he would drop, exhausted, on his old sofa, his arms worn by inexplicable tiredness, his head abandoned on his chest, and he did not dare look at the damn figure that twisted, just sketched, with her proud gesture aiming to pull violently upward from the sloping mass of her hair.

And as the figure, still unshaped, seemed horribly pained by the useless effort against the inflexible fate that kept her entangled in the damp block of clay, where the curves of her breast, belly, and hips had barely been shaped, he now was suffering as he had never suffered before. It was as if his spirit was also struggling against inner constraints, and he couldn't freely transfer himself into his work, which now held the fascination of the forbidden or unattainable things, that are nevertheless wanted and chased with indomitable ardor.

His astonishment was immense the morning when he realized that the feeling of deep sadness that had tortured him for a week did not concern him and his inability to obtain the right shape in his work of art, but was rather caused by a vivid participation in the desperate sorrow of that figure who began to appear to him as a living person. Yes, a living person. Perhaps – he tried to explain to himself this phenomenon – because of the intense and long contemplation that made him see in his unfinished work the human expression that he had imagined in his mind, and should have given it a life, if only he had succeeded in modeling it.

"But I will never succeed!" he sighed.

It seemed to him that he had already committed a crime, condemning this beautiful creature – Where had he seen her? How did he meet her? – to the indescribable torture from which he no longer felt able to free her. And this idea, which at first seemed to him silly or crazy, insinuated itself in him more every day. It gave him a sense of remorse, which was mixed with a hint of pleasure, because a situation such as this could not happen to just anybody, and it had to indicate a force, an extremely intelligent power in the person who had come, even if unknowingly, to that artistic attempt.

And so he kept locking himself in his studio at dawn, coming out of it only late in the evening. But if one could have observed him standing in front of his clay study, with his eyes fixed on it, eyes that looked but didn't see, distracted as they were by some obscure fascination that stopped the flow of impressions between the senses and the spirit; if one could have observed him, especially in those last few days, when, stretching his hand toward the figure with a small lump of clay on the tip of the finger, he would stop, hesitating with a trembling arm, almost afraid of desecrating the naked body of the woman by placing that small lump on it; if one, finally, could have observed him, during the long intervals of inactivity, as he laid on the sofa, with his contracted face, with his hands gripping its cloth, tearing it off, one would never have imagined how that young artist had lost the joyful spirit that was so welcome among his friends and relations. His failure to complete this artistic creation had given him the crazy idea that, in his work, a human being was suffering.

Where had he seen her? How had he met her? He asked himself this often, and in vain.

Allora egli si lasciava cadere, sfinito, sul vecchio sofà addossato al muro, con le braccia rotte da inesplicabile stanchezza, la testa abbandonata sul petto, e non osava guardare la maledetta figura che si contorceva, appena abbozzata, col fiero gesto di tirar violentemente in su la massa spiovente dei capelli.

E come quella figura ancora informe sembrava soffrire orrendamente per l'inutile sforzo contro l'inesorabile fatalità che la teneva impigliata nell'umido blocco di creta dove si disegnavano appena le curve del seno, del ventre e delle anche, così egli sentiva, ora, di soffrire quanto non aveva mai sofferto; come se anche il suo spirito si dibattesse impacciato da nodi interiori e non potesse liberamente trasferirsi in quell'opera, che ormai aveva il fascino delle cose vietate o stimate irraggiungibili e, ciò nonostante, desiderate e rincorse con indomabile ardore.

Immenso fu poi il suo stupore la mattina in cui si accorse che il sentimento di profonda tristezza dal quale veniva torturato da una settimana, non riguardava se stesso e la sua incapacità di raggiungere la giusta forma della sua opera d'arte, ma fosse invece vivissima partecipazione al disperato dolore di quella figura che cominciava a sembrargli persona viva, forse—egli aveva voluto darsi una spiegazione del fenomeno—per l'intensa e lunga contemplazione che gli faceva scorgere nell'opera non finita l'espressione che lui aveva in mente e che avrebbe dovuto animarla se egli fosse riuscito a modellarla.

—Ma non ci riuscirò!—sospirava.

Gli sembrava anzi di aver già commesso un delitto, condannando la bellissima creatura—Dove l'aveva vista? Come l'aveva conosciuta?—all'ineffabile tortura di quell'atteggiamento da cui egli più non si sentiva capace di liberarla. E quest'idea, che all'inizio gli parve sciocca o pazza, lo penetrava ogni giorno più, gli dava un senso di rimorso, che però non era senza un misto di compiacimento, giacchè non a tutti poteva accadere un caso uguale; ed esso indicava una forza, un potere intelligentissimo in colui che era arrivato, sia pure inconsapevolmente, a quel tentativo.

E perciò egli tornava a chiudersi nello studio di buon'ora e ne usciva a sera tarda. Ma chi avesse potuto osservarlo ritto davanti al bozzetto, con gli occhi fissi in esso, e che guardavano e non vedevano, distratti da qualche oscuro fascino dal quale veniva interrotta la corrente di impressioni tra i sensi e lo spirito; chi avesse potuto osservarlo, specie in quegli ultimi giorni, quando, stesa la mano verso la figura con un briciolo di creta su la punta dell'indice, egli si arrestava esitante con un tremito nel braccio, quasi temesse di compire una profanazione posando quel briciolo sul nudo corpo della donna; chi lo avesse, finalmente, osservato nei lunghi intervalli di sosta, buttato sul sofà, col viso contratto, con le mani che ne afferravano la stoffa strappandola, non avrebbe mai immaginato che il giovane artista avesse perduto il suo spirito gioioso, con cui riusciva gradito nei ritrovi e nelle relazioni sociali, unicamente perchè la mancata creazione artistica gli dava la pazza convinzione che nella sua opera soffrisse una creatura umana.

—Dove l'aveva vista? Come l'aveva conosciuta?—se lo domandava spesso e inutilmente.

One morning, on his way to the studio, he had lingered in front of a showcase of modern etchings and photographic reproductions of painting masterpieces.

"Ah! Are you alive?" He felt his friend's hand grabbing his arm. "What are you doing? Do you work at least, or are you lost chasing some skirt, like that imbecile Dorini?"

"Leave me alone!" Vittorio D'Arèba replied.

"Are you discouraged, then? Just as well. Only fools are happy with themselves."

"If only you knew what's been happening to me!"

"The same thing that happens to everyone—that each of us supposes to be a special, exceptional case. Let's hear!"

Giulio Nolli used to talk this way, in a tone halfway between authoritative and mocking, which left those who didn't know him as a cultured and immensely witty art critic uncertain whether he was a respected intellectual or a pompous twit.

Vittorio D'Arena, who greatly appreciated Giulio Nolli's opinions and advice, regained his wits, regretting having let pass his lips the beginning of a confidence which he could not now retract without being very rude.

"Perhaps," he answered. "You may not believe it, since, like so many others, you don't think ease of execution to be among the inferior qualities of the artistic talent, and you were often pleased to rejoice about it with me. You will not believe that for a month and a half, I cannot seem to complete. . . a small work of art. . . a female figure. It appeared like this before my eyes, it is fixed like this in front of my eyes, better than a real model. . . but even so. . ."

"Who knows what concept, who knows what symbol you set yourself out to express! Because now you sculptors want to contribute to social well-being, civilization, the emancipation of the people! And, with the pretext of the concept and the symbol, you create nasty, painful to look at statuettes, or you are utterly incapable of creating anything at all, even something ugly."

"Nothing of the sort, my dear sir. I saw, or rather, I fantasized, or, better yet, it suddenly came to my imagination, this figure that. . . that I can't tell you what she wants to express with her sorrowful attitude. And I immediately, anxiously set out to create her. I thought I could do it in two or three days, but I've been trying for a month and a half, and I don't even know how to sketch it out! Such strange thing has upset me so much that sometimes – don't roll your eyes! – I feel like I'm going crazy."

"Oh, come on!"

"Because my imagination makes me see so much life in that woman's figure. There's an acute sense of pity, almost as if. . . – I said, *don't roll your eyes*! – almost as if I wasn't in front of an unfinished work of art, but I was watching, unable to assist, the suffering of a human creature who remains trapped in the clay because of me."

"Oh! I really must see this miracle!

"This infamy, you should say. I'm ashamed of myself. I'm a fool! My mind is going!"

"The first case is more likely."

Quella mattina, dirigendosi allo studio, aveva indugiato davanti a una vetrina di acqueforti moderne e di riproduzioni fotografiche di capolavori di pittura.

—Ah! Sei vivo?

E sentì afferrarsi un braccio dalla mano dell'amico che lo apostrofava con quelle parole.

—Che fai? Lavori almeno, o ti sei perduto anche tu dietro qualche gonna, come l'imbecille di Dorini?

—Lasciami stare!—rispose Vittorio D'Arèba.

—Sei scoraggiato dunque? Tanto meglio. Soltanto gli sciocchi sono contenti di loro stessi.

—Se tu sapessi quel che mi accade!

—Quel che accade a tutti e che ognuno di noi suppone caso speciale, eccezionale. Sentiamo!

Giulio Nolli soleva parlare così, con aria tra autorevole e beffarda, che lasciava incerti coloro che non ne conoscevano la vasta cultura e il fine ingegno di critico d'arte, s'egli fosse un gran pedante o un pallone gonfiato.

Vittorio D'Arèba, che ne apprezzava moltissimo i giudizi e i consigli, a quel *Sentiamo!* si scosse, pentito di essersi lasciato scappar di bocca un'inizio di confidenza che sarebbe stato assai scortese interrompere.

—Può darsi—rispose.—Tu forse non lo crederai, tu che non credi, come tanti altri, che la facilità d'esecuzione sia tra le qualità inferiori dell'ingegno artistico (e spesso ti sei compiaciuto di rallegrartene con me). Tu non crederai che io da un mese e mezzo non riesco a portare avanti … una cosina da niente… una figura di donna. Mi è apparsa così davanti agli occhi, mi sta fissa così davanti agli occhi, meglio di un modello reale… e intanto….

—Chissà che concetto, chissà che simbolo ti sei messo in testa di esprimere! Perchè ormai anche voi scultori volete contribuire al benessere sociale, alla civiltà, all'emancipazione del popolo! E, col pretesto del concetto e del simbolo, fate brutte statue inguardabili o non riuscite a farne neppure brutte.

—Niente affatto, caro mio. Ho veduto, o meglio, ho fantasticato, o, meglio ancora, mi si è presentata improvvisamente all'immaginazione questa figura che…. che non so dirti che cosa voglia esprimere con quel suo doloroso atteggiamento; e mi son messo subito ansiosamente a eseguirla. Credevo di riuscirci in due o tre giorni; e ci provo da un mese e mezzo, non so neppure come finire di abbozzarla soltanto! Questo stranissimo fatto mi ha talmente impressionato, che in certi momenti—non alzare gli occhi!—mi pare d'impazzire.

—Eh! Eh!

—Perchè l'immaginazione mi fa vedere tanta vita in quella figura di donna, da darmi un pungentissimo senso di pena, quasi….—non alzare gli occhi!—quasi io non mi trovi davanti a un'incompiuta opera d'arte, ma assista, impotente di soccorrerla, al martirio di una creatura umana attratta in un agguato per colpa mia.

—Eh! Eh! Bisogna vedere questo miracolo!

—Quest'infamia, dovresti dire. Mi vergogno di me. Sono incretinito! Sto per smarrire la ragione!

—Il primo caso è più probabile.

But the affectionate pressure on his arm made Vittorio D'Arèba understand that his friend was joking.

The young sculptor sought, for a while, to resist the insistent art critic who demanded to go directly with him to the studio. In the end, he surrendered.

"You will tell me what to do."

"There will be no need for that."

Giulio Nolli stopped, frowning, at the sight of the clay study, and, to great amazement of the artist, remained in contemplation of it for a long time, looking at it from all sides, ignoring the anxiety with which his friend was waiting for his response.

"Oh! It's a portent!" Nolli exclaimed at last. "You created your masterpiece. You won't create anything better in the future, I assure you."

"Are you teasing me?"

"You are really a fool, if you don't understand the value of this work, which has only one irreparable defect," added Nolli, still enthralled. "It will have to remain what it is, a study. No artist will possess the ability to translate it into marble while retaining the freshness of its incompleteness. Don't you dare to work on it any longer. You would ruin this vividness of expression, and that is exactly what your artistic instinct has kept you from altering, by giving it more finishing touches."

Vittorio D'Arèba was moved, his eyes full of tears.

Meanwhile, the critic, continuing to express his praise and explaining the concept behind that tormented figure, asked the artist, "So you didn't think of any of this?"

"No!"

"Very well. The living forces of Nature thus create, with mysterious serendipity. And artistic genius, which is one of the many natural forces, cannot act otherwise. Set your study in bronze right away. You will see what a success it will be at your next showing!"

"But. . .?" D'Arèba said with a trembling, questioning gesture.

"What should you call it? I have it: *Nameless Sorrow!*"

"Thank you! That's exactly it!" stammered the sculptor.

And he felt within himself all the anguish of that unnamed sorrow suddenly becoming – oh, the miracle of art! – an infinite sweetness.

Ma un'affettuosa stretta di mano fece capire a Vittorio D'Arèba che il suo amico scherzava.

Il giovane scultore cercò per un pezzo di lottare contro le insistenze del critico d'arte che voleva accompagnarlo a ogni costo allo studio; alla fine si arrese.

—Mi saprai consigliare.

—Non occorrerà.

Giulio Nolli si fermò, increspando le sopracciglia, alla vista del bozzetto e, con grande stupore dell'artista, rimase lungamente assorto a contemplarlo da tutti i lati, senza curarsi dell'ansietà con cui l'amico stava aspettando il suo responso.

—Oh! È un portento!—esclamò all'ultimo il Nolli.—Hai fatto il tuo capolavoro. Non farai niente di meglio in avvenire, te lo dico io.

—Ti beffi di me?

—E sei davvero incretinito, se non comprendi il valore di quest'opera, che ha un solo irrimediabile difetto—soggiunse il Nolli non ancora sazio di ammirare:—dovrà rimanere quel che è, un bozzetto. Nessuna abilità di esecutore potrà tradurlo in marmo conservandone la freschezza del tocco, l'incompleto. Non osare lavorarci ancora; sciuperesti questa terribilità di espressione che risulta appunto da quel che il tuo istinto d'artista ti ha preservato di alterare dando maggiore finitezza alla modellatura.

Vittorio D'Arèba era commosso, con gli occhi pieni di lagrime.

Intanto il critico, continuato a profondersi in elogi, a sviluppare ampiamente il concetto risultante da quella tormentata figura, domandava all'artista:

—Tu dunque non hai pensato niente di tutto questo?

—Niente!

—Benissimo. Le vive forze della Natura creano così, con misteriosa inconsapevolezza; e l'ingegno artistico, che è una delle tante forze naturali, non può agire altrimenti. Fai formare subito e poi fondere in bronzo il tuo bozzetto. Vedrai che successo alla prossima mostra!

—Mah…?—fece il D'Arèba con trepidante gesto interrogativo.

—Come battezzarlo? Ecco: *Dolore senza nome!*

—Grazie! È proprio così! balbettò lo scultore.

E sentiva dentro di sè tutta l'angoscia di quel dolore senza nome, che intanto gli si trasformava—prodigio dell'arte!—in infinita dolcezza.

THE NAÏVETY OF DON ROCCO

TO GRAZIA DELEDDA

Since that year when they made him suspect that the issue of the *Barbanera* almanac he bought had been falsified – and even Don Rocco Aragona had to admit it was inaccurate since, of all the many predictions of war, disasters on land and sea, deaths of kings, earthquakes, etc., not even one had come to pass – he had taken the precaution of having the almanac sent to him directly from the publisher in Fuligno by registered mail. The day when the postman delivered the pretty volume with its blue cover was an absolute joy for Don Rocco, who immediately would begin reading the *predictions* – the only thing that interested him.

The *Barbanera* usually arrived around the beginning of November, and he was in a state of anxious expectation until about March, reading over and over the terrible pages, announcing all the troubles expected for that year, month by month. Troubles that, according to him, never failed to occur.

His faith in the astrologer whose picture appeared on the front page of the publication was extraordinary.

Whenever his brother, Don Lucio, during lunch or dinner, told him of a piece of news he had read in the newspaper, Don Rocco would exclaim, "An earthquake? Barbanera predicted it!"

"But he didn't say where," Don Lucio would answer, laughing sarcastically. "If that's the way it's done, I'm an astrologer too!"

"Disasters at sea? Barbanera predicted them!"

"I can well believe it! It's the season."

And so the *Barbanera* had become yet another of the many opportunities for disagreement between the two brothers, as if any more were required, beginning with the disagreements that Mother Nature herself had been pleased to introduce.

Don Lucio was well over six feet tall. Don Rocco was decidedly not.

Skinny, always dressed in black, with a great overcoat a dozen years old, miraculously appearing almost new thanks to meticulous brushing and care, and with a top hat bought new every three years, and a long stick to match his stature, Don Lucio possessed a severity of appearance and behavior that would fool those who saw him for the first time at least before they heard him speak. The illusion would shatter as soon as he opened his mouth. "Your foolishness exceeds even your stature!" Dr. Lepiro often told him, in the *Gobbo* pharmacy. And he wasn't wrong.

Short, plump, with a rosy complexion, a belly protruding on slightly curved legs like those of a horseman, with vacant, blue eyes, and a forehead covered with thick, stubbly hair, Don Rocco's appearance telegraphed precisely just how few brain cells he had inside that little pear-shaped head of his. But, unlike his brother, he had the savvy to talk little and then only about agricultural matters.

L'INGENUITÀ DI DON ROCCO

A GRAZIA DELEDDA

Dall'anno in cui gli avevano fatto nascere il dubbio che l'edizione del *Barbanera* da lui comprata era falsa—e don Rocco Aragona aveva dovuto convincersene perchè di tante predizioni di guerre, di disastri di terra e di mare, di morti di regnanti, terremoti ecc., non se n'era avverata neppur una!—egli aveva usato la precauzione di farsi spedire l'almanacco dall'editore di Fuligno, per posta raccomandata: e il giorno che il postino gli recava a casa il grazioso volumetto con la copertina azzurra, era proprio una festa per don Rocco, che si metteva subito a leggere le *predizioni,* unica cosa di cui s'interessasse.
Il *Barbanera* gli arrivava di solito verso i primi di novembre, ed egli stava in ansiosa aspettativa fino ai primi mesi dell'anno nuovo, leggendo e rileggendo le terribili pagine che annunziavano tutti i guai dell'annata, mese per mese, e che, secondo lui, non mancavano mai di avverarsi.
La sua fede nell'astrologo disegnato sul frontispizio era straordinaria.
Ogni volta che suo fratello don Lucio, a pranzo o a cena, gli riferiva la notizia letta sul giornale, don Rocco scattava:
—Barbanera lo aveva predetto!… Terremoto?
—Ma non dice dove—rispondeva don Lucio ridendo sarcasticamente.—A questo modo faccio l'astrologo anche io!
—Barbanera li aveva predetti!… Disastri in mare?
—Lo credo! È la stagione.
E così quella pubblicazione era divenuta tra i due fratelli una delle tante occasioni di dissensi, quasi ne mancassero tra loro, a cominciare dalle discordanze che si era compiaciuta di produrre tra essi madre Natura.
Don Lucio superava i due metri di altezza: don Rocco era un tappo.
Magro, vestito sempre di nero, con il gran cappotto miracolosamente conservato quasi nuovo, da una dozzina di anni, a furia di spazzole e di cure meticolose, con il cappello a cilindro cambiato ogni tre anni, e il grosso bastone corrispondente alla statura, don Lucio aveva una gravità di aspetto e di modi da ingannare chi lo vedeva la prima volta ancora prima di sentirlo parlare. L'illusione spariva appena egli apriva bocca. Siete più bestia di quanto siete lungo!—gli diceva spesso il dottor Lepiro nella farmacia del *Gobbo.* E non aveva torto. Basso, tondo, roseo di carnagione, con la pancia sporgente sulle gambette un po' curve come quelle di un cavallerizzo, con gli occhi azzurri ma stupidi e la fronte coperta da capelli folti ed irsuti, don Rocco faceva capire subito quanto poco cervello dovesse essere dentro quella testa piccola a forma di pera; esso aveva la furbizia di parlar poco e di parlare soltanto di cose di campagna.

While Don Lucio split his time between the club and the *Gobbo* pharmacy, speaking nonsense about politics and municipal issues, he looked after the sowing and the harvesting of wheat and olive trees in the two small estates that formed the brothers' joint estate. He had no time to occupy himself with the poppycock that interested his brother and made him look so ridiculous.

But Don Rocco was the administrator and kept his brother on a short allowance. Don Lucio was not too careful with money and, on the occasions when he felt like spending a few *lire* to indulge himself in some sweets, he would place an order with the nuns of the local convent, famous for their baking. Don Rocco considered those few *lire* a great waste: He well knew how hard it was to earn them. And so the bitterness of a fight at the table always ruined Don Lucio's pleasure in eating his sweets, not to mention Don Rocco's sulking, which normally lasted for several days.

That year the *Barbanera* almanac had arrived just after one of these quarrels and during the sulking period. Don Rocco, who would typically discuss these predictions with his brother at length, was in such a mood that he hid his almanac under lock and key to prevent Don Lucio from reading it in his absence.

Don Lucio, who was also in a spiteful mood, had asked him, "So, what does The Astrologer say about the New Year? Will the world be ending on January 2nd?"

Don Rocco gave him a look of deep condescension and did not respond.

A few weeks later, Don Lucio was astonished to see one of the infamous desserts he liked so much, and the cause of so many fights and so much sulking, gracing their dinner table.

"Ehh? What's this? Have you finally cracked?"

"It was given to me by the Mother Abbess, to thank me for a favor."

Don Rocco took only a thin slice and let his brother eat all the rest.

The next week, another dessert appeared.

"What's this? Is this also a gift?"

"Eat it, and the rest doesn't concern you."

Don Lucio didn't wait to be asked again and didn't realize that his brother had neglected to even taste it.

He observed, with astonishment, this change of behavior and was desperate to discover a reason for it. Don Rocco now no longer contradicted him, but, instead, anticipated his desires. And since his great weakness was sweets, he no longer dared to ask "What's this?" in the face of this gustatory benevolence. He ate them silently, but also a little pensively. Could it be that his brother was near death? Perhaps that would explain why he had changed so much and so suddenly!

For a month and a half, there were no fights and not a hint of a sulk. Don Lucio realized that he was being observed with a kind of compassionate tenderness, and he was, in turn, moved to pity. He had even discussed it in the *Gobbo* pharmacy, "My brother will die soon. I don't even recognize him any more!"

And now, almost every day, finding a new dessert on the table, though his gluttony was irresistible, he ate it with a sense of remorse that ruined his enjoyment.

"And you? Don't you want some? Why not?"

Mentre don Lucio se la spassava tra il *Casino* e la farmacia del *Gobbo*, spropositando di politica e di cose municipali, egli badava alle seminagioni, alla raccolta del grano e degli ulivi dei due piccoli possedimenti che formavano il loro comune patrimonio, e non aveva tempo di occuparsi delle sciocchezze di cui s'interessava tanto suo fratello e che lo rendevano ridicolo.

Don Rocco però era l'amministratore e teneva a stecchetto il fratello che non guardava molto per il sottile nello spendere qualche paio di lire, di tanto in tanto, per certe leccornie ch'egli ordinava alle monache del Monastero famose per i dolci. A don Rocco quelle poche lire sembravano un grande spreco: egli solo sapeva quel che ci volesse per guadagnarle. E così al dolce si mescolava sempre per don Lucio l'amaro di una lite a tavola, e il broncio di don Rocco che durava parecchi giorni.

Quell'anno l'almanacco del *Barbanera* era arrivato appunto dopo una di queste liti, in giorni di broncio, e don Rocco, che soleva comunicare al fratello le predizioni, aveva spinto la dimostrazione del suo malumore fino a nascondere sotto chiave l'almanacco, perchè don Lucio non potesse leggerle neppure nell'assenza di lui.

Don Lucio, che era anche caparbio, gli aveva domandato:

—Che cosa predica l'Astrologo per l'anno nuovo? La prossima fine del mondo?

Don Rocco, guardatolo compassionevolmente, non gli aveva risposto nulla.

Qualche settimana dopo, don Lucio si stupiva di veder in tavola uno di quei famosi dolci, causa di liti e di bronci tra loro.

—Come mai? Sei ammattito?

—Me l'ha regalato la Badessa, per ringraziarmi di un servizio.

Don Rocco ne prese appena una fettina e lasciò che il fratello mangiasse golosamente tutto il resto.

La settimana appresso, nuovo dolce.

—Come mai? Regalo anche questo?

—Mangialo, e non badare ad altro.

Don Lucio non se l'era fatto dire due volte e non si era accorto che il fratello avea dimenticato di gustarne un pezzettino.

Egli osservava, con meraviglia, quel mutamento di comportamento e avrebbe voluto trovarne la ragione. Don Rocco ora non lo contraddiceva più, anzi preveniva i suoi desideri; e siccome il gran debole di lui erano i dolci, egli non osava, ogni volta che ne trovava uno in tavola, domandare al solito:—Come mai?—Lo mangiava zitto zitto, ma un po' impensierito. Suo fratello doveva essere vicino alla morte, se si mostrava cambiato tanto e quasi tutt'a un tratto!

Da un mese e mezzo, nessuna lite, nessun'ombra di broncio tra loro. Don Lucio si vedeva guardato con una specie di tenerezza compassionevole e s'inteneriva a sua volta. Ne aveva persino parlato nella farmacia del *Gobbo*, ripetendo:—Mio fratello morirà presto, non lo riconosco più!—

E trovando ora, quasi ogni giorno, un nuovo piatto dolce in tavola, pur lasciandosi vincere dalla gola, lo mangiava con un senso di rimorso che gliene guastava il sapore.

—E tu? Tu non ne mangi? Perchè?

Two tears swelled in Don Rocco's eyes and slid down his rosy and chubby cheeks.

"What's happening to you? What are you doing?"

"Nothing!"

And Don Rocco got up from the table and locked himself in his room.

Don Lucio was immensely puzzled.

Before dinner, his brother had asked him several times, "How do you feel?"

But why? He felt very well. In fact, he had never felt better. So what did that question mean? Was he sick and didn't realize it? He must know.

"You have asked me many times now, 'How do you feel?' Why are you asking me this? What are you thinking?"

Instead of answering, Don Rocco asked in his turn, "You don't feel anything wrong?"

"Why should I feel something's wrong? You're scaring me."

"Ignore me. I must be mistaken. I thought. . ."

The next day, two things surprised Don Lucio: Two sweet dishes instead of one and the presence at lunch of Dr. Lopiro.

The doctor had whispered in his ear before going to the table, "Your brother must really be about to kick the bucket! Invitations for lunch as well as sweets! Perhaps he's just hit his head."

Don Rocco now wore such a strange, funereal expression that his brother could no longer stand the strain and cried out, "What's wrong with you? For God's sake, tell us!"

"Me? What's wrong with *me*? Is today the fifteen of the month?"

"Yes. And so?" asked the doctor.

"Doctor, no more questions! Eat in peace. Two desserts! I'll eat some myself, although I don't like sweets very much. . ."

But they could see very well that he made a great effort to appear cheerful. He kept his eyes on his brother, as if expecting something extraordinary to occur from one moment to the next, and, at the same time, wondering why it wasn't happening. Toward the end of lunch, the parish priest, Stella, arrived.

"You insisted I come for coffee. What's the news? An imminent wedding?"

Don Rocco seemed stunned, and Don Lucio, even more so. While pouring the coffee, Don Rocco's hand trembled.

"Have you heard?" said the parish priest. "Bismarck died. The French will be happy. Yes, lots of sugar, otherwise coffee doesn't agree with me. And you, Don Rocco, you must be happy, too."

"Me? Why?" Don Rocco said.

"Your *Barbanera* guessed right, for once. *Death of a man of great stature!* Predicted for the first two weeks of this month.

"Was he tall? Taller than Lucio?" Don Rocco stammered.

"Very tall, they say. But that's not it. A man of *great stature* doesn't only mean a tall man, it means an important man: men of *great stature* are kings, the pope, certain ministers. . ."

Due lagrime spuntarono negli occhi di don Rocco e gli scivolarono su per le gote rosee e paffute.

—Che hai? Che cosa è stato?

—Niente!

E don Rocco si alzò da tavola per andare a chiudersi nella sua camera.

Don Lucio rimase interdetto.

Prima di mettersi a tavola, suo fratello gli aveva domandato più volte:

—Come ti senti?

Perchè? Egli si sentiva benissimo, non si era anzi mai sentito così bene come allora. Che cosa significava dunque quella domanda? Era malato e non se n'accorgeva? E volle saperlo.

—Mi hai domandato più volte: Come ti senti? Perchè? Che ti pare?

Invece di rispondere alla domanda, don Rocco avea domandato alla sua volta:

—Non ti senti proprio niente?

—Che cosa dovrei sentirmi? Mi metti paura.

—Non badarmi. Mi sono ingannato. Credevo....

Il giorno dopo, don Lucio fu stupito di due cose; della vista di due piatti dolci invece di uno e della presenza del dottor Lopiro straordinariamente invitato a pranzo.

Il dottore, prima di mettersi a tavola, gli avea sussurrato in un orecchio:

—Vostro fratello vuol proprio morire! Inviti a pranzo, dolci! Oppure ammattisce, come voi dite.

Don Rocco aveva un viso così strano, così funebre che suo fratello proruppe:

—Ma che hai? Si può sapere?

—Che ho? Che ho? Oggi è il quindici del mese?

—Ebbene?—fece il dottore.

—Dottore, non mi chiedete altro! E tu mangia tranquillo. Due dolci! Voglio mangiarne anche io, sebbene mi piacciano poco....

Ma si vedeva benissimo che faceva un grande sforzo per apparire allegro. Teneva fissi gli occhi in viso al fratello, quasi si aspettasse da un istante all'altro qualcosa di straordinario, e nello stesso tempo si meravigliasse di non vederlo accadere. Verso la fine del pranzo arrivava il parroco Stella.

—Avete voluto che venissi a prendere il caffè da voi. Che belle notizie ci sono? Nozze in arrivo?

Don Rocco sembrava istupidito, e don Lucio peggio di lui. Nel versare il caffè al parroco la mano di don Rocco tremava.

—Avete sentito?—disse il parroco.—È morto *Bismarco*. I francesi saranno contenti. Sì, molto zucchero, altrimenti il caffè non mi fa digerire. E anche voi, don Rocco.

—Io? Chi lo conosce costui?—rispose don Rocco.

—Il vostro *Barbanera* ha indovinato. *Morte di un alto personaggio!* annunziava per la prima quindicina di questo mese.

—Era alto! Più alto di Lucio?—balbettò don Rocco.

—Un omaccione, dicono. Ma non si tratta di questo. *Alto* significa: importante: *alti personaggi* sono i re, il papa, certi ministri....

The look on Don Rocco's face on hearing this explanation was so comical that both the priest, Stella, and Dr. Lopiro burst into laughter. Stella began coughing and spraying coffee about the room.

"What on earth had you imagined? Ha ha ha!"

Don Rocco began crying for joy. Yes, he had imagined – he naively confessed to it – that *Barbanera* had meant. . . and he didn't want to say anything to his poor brother and make his final days a misery. Instead he had done everything he could to let him die a happy man. A man of great stature! Oh! He had spent two months of hell, living in fear of seeing him drop dead in front of him from a stroke or a heart attack! He had not realized that *great stature* also meant. . .

Only Don Lucio did not laugh. He was thinking that his brother would make him pay for all those desserts he had eaten over the last two months.

And in fact. . .

E vedendo il viso che faceva don Rocco nell'udire questa spiegazione, il parroco Stella e il dottor Lopiro scoppiarono in una gran risata. Il parroco, preso da un colpo di tosse, spruzzava il caffè che stava per sorbire.

—Che vi eravate immaginato? Ah! Ah! Ah!

Don Rocco piangeva dalla contentezza. Sì, si era immaginato—lo confessava ingenuamente—che il *Barbanera* indicasse.... E non avea voluto dir niente al suo povero fratello, e aveva cercato di farlo morire sazio di piatti dolci, almeno! Un alto personaggio! Oh! Egli aveva passato due mesi d'inferno, con la gran paura di vederselo cascar davanti, morto di un colpo! Non lo sapeva lui che *alto* volesse anche dire...

Solo don Lucio non rideva, pensando che il fratello ora gli avrebbe fatto scontare tutti quei piatti dolci datigli a mangiare in due mesi!

E infatti....

THE SILENCE

TO DR. MARIANO SALLUZZO

Why did she never answer? Why, since my recriminations were unjust, did she not rebel, with a word, a gesture, or at least a look? She was silent! And from her white face nothing transpired, of what she certainly *had* to feel at the bottom of her saddened soul.

Now that I understand how cruel I have been, I can't forgive her, even now that she is dead. And if sometimes I think that perhaps she has commiserated and forgiven me, the deep rancor against her makes me almost crazy. Her revenge is terrible!

I was jealous, yes, stupidly jealous, unreasonably jealous. But she had to have known that my jealousy came from excessive love.

Did she understand it, and is that the reason of her silence? No, my friend. I would have understood that. That soul of hers remains a dark mystery to me.

I always see her in front of me, white, slim, with clear, luminous blue eyes that looked like a patch of smiling sky; with her slightly pink lips, which preserved their freshness to the last, similar to that of a dewy flower; with her expression of the sweetest grace, which gave her person the appearance of an artistic creation, rather than earthly reality. And I always seem to hear the sound of her voice, the inflections of her words that would create a delightful melody, and would move and unsettle me like a spiritual caress even in the most ruthless moments of my jealous rages. And I feel as if I am losing my sanity at the idea that she could resign herself to withstand the tortures I inflicted on her for two years, hour by hour, day by day, incessantly, doubling my ferocity the more I saw her docile, resigned to that torture, never knowing what feelings she was concealing under such incredible docility, under such inexplicable resignation. I feel hatred for Gemma, now that she is no more, at least as much as I loved and worshiped her when she was alive.

Do you think it is possible for a woman to remain unmoved in the face of an unexpected and almost sudden change in the soul of the one who promised her happiness, but instead gave her hell?

Do not say to me: "And why not?" You are trying in vain to deceive and console me. I don't want to be consoled. My disgrace is now irreparable.

She chose to leave me without giving me the satisfaction of an answer, any answer. She let herself die, impenetrable, like the Sphinx that opens its unseeing eyes to the travelers in the sands surrounding the Egyptian pyramids, and for thousands of years has neither asked questions nor given any answers. She did the same.

I have almost lost, thinking about it over and over, the notion of time. I have been questioning her for four years. But it seems like an eternity that this mysterious Sphinx has been alive before me and is now dead before me. Now that she is dead, she will not answer my insistent questions, just as she never did when she was alive.

OH, QUEL SILENZIO!

AL DOTTOR MARIANO SALLUZZO

Perchè non rispondeva mai? Perchè, visto che le mie recriminazioni erano ingiuste, lei non si ribellava, con la parola, col gesto, con lo sguardo almeno? Taceva! E dal suo bianco volto non traspariva niente di quel che doveva certamente sentire in fondo alla sua anima contristata.

Ora io capisco quanto sono stato crudele, e perciò non so perdonarla neppure ora che è morta. E se talvolta penso che forse ella mi ha compatito e mi ha perdonato, il profondo rancore contro di lei, mi rende quasi pazzo. La sua vendetta è terribile!

Ero geloso, sì, stupidamente geloso, irragionevolmente geloso; ma non doveva ella intendere che la mia gelosia proveniva da eccesso di amore?

Lo ha compreso e per questo taceva? No, amico mio; lo avrei indovinato. Quella sua anima è rimasta un tetro mistero per me.

Me la vedo sempre davanti, bianca, esile, con gli occhi azzurri limpidi e luminosi che sembravano un lembo di cielo sorridente; con le labbra leggermente rosee, che conservarono fino all'ultimo la loro freschezza simile a quella di un fiore umido di rugiada; con l'espressione di dolcissima grazia, che dava alla sua persona l'apparenza di una creazione d'arte più che di terrena realtà. Ed ho sempre nell'orecchio il suono della sua voce, le inflessioni della sua parola che si modulavano in deliziosa melodia, e mi commovevano e mi turbavano come una carezza spirituale anche nei momenti più spietati delle mie gelose irruzioni. E sento vacillare la ragione all'idea che ella ha potuto sopportare rassegnatamente le torture che le ho inflitto per due anni, ora per ora, giorno per giorno, incessantemente, raddoppiando tanto più la mia ferocia quanto più la vedevo docile, rassegnata a quella tortura, e senza che io abbia mai potuto scoprire quali sentimenti si nascondessero sotto così incredibile docilità, sotto così inesplicabile rassegnazione. E sento di odiar Gemma, ora che non c'è più, per lo meno quanto l'ho amata ed adorata da viva.

Ti sembra forse possibile che una donna rimanga la stessa, di fronte a un'inattesa e quasi improvvisa mutazione dell'animo di colui che le avea promesso la felicità e le dava l'inferno?

Non dirmi: Perchè no? Tenti invano d'illudermi e di consolarmi. Non voglio essere consolato. La mia sciagura è ormai irreparabile.

Ella ha voluto andar via, senza darmi la sodisfazione di una risposta qualunque. Si è lasciata morire, impenetrabile come quelle Sfingi che spalancano gli occhi privi di sguardo in faccia ai viaggiatori tra le sabbie che circondano le Piramidi egiziane, e non interrogano nè rispondono da mille e mille anni. Così lei.

Ho quasi perduto, a furia di pensarci su, la nozione del tempo. La interrogo da quattro anni, o da un'infinità di anni questa misteriosa Sfinge che mi è stata davanti prima viva e mi sta egualmente davanti morta, e che da morta non risponde alle mie insistenti interrogazioni, come non rispose mai, mai, da viva!

It seems that all my life has been spent in constant questioning, in the exquisite expectation of a response, in this desperate hopelessness of one day receiving it.

She wanted revenge in this way, and she couldn't have found one more agonizing or more cruel.

In her last few moments, staring at me with her blue eyes veiled in agony and whispering to me, "I can't see your face. A fog surrounds me!," had she been truly resigned, she ought, at least, to have left me with a word of explanation, even a single word. But no, nothing!

Had it even been a word of contempt, of hate, a curse, I would have been satisfied. At least I would have had some clarity at last! But no, she wanted to leave silent, closed, without a glance, a gesture, a syllable revealing the secret of her heart, her spirit. She! She who once upon a time, when I loved her and I was not jealous, seemed to me transparent as crystal, clear as a pure diamond. At that time, it was sufficient for me to look into her eyes to discover the slightest hues of feeling in the depths of her heart, to grasp the quickest thoughts that brightened her mind like lightning, behind that wide forehead of hers, that underneath her black, wavy hair, looked like fine ivory!

As soon as the monster that is jealousy plunged its claws into my heart, as soon as the first gestures of impatience, suspicion, and reproach made her understand the devouring passion that had begun to consume me, she suddenly appeared to me as another person. Her heart closed up, and I could no longer read anything in it. Her forehead became opaque, as if that beautiful living creature had turned into a statue with no soul, only artistic beauty—the physical expression of the artist's concept, but incapable of pervading the wood, the clay, or the marble with which it is made.

I knew that inside that statue were heart and soul and spirit. But between them and me stood, obstinate, that silence like a bronze door on which I knocked in vain. And for all my hammering, it made no sound, so solid it was. My hands almost felt its coldness. At times the image I had conjured of this bronze door became, in my altered imagination, a real thing.

And when my jealous rage, provoked by a trifle (as I now see) would explode in disagreeable words, in screams, in violent gestures, and Gemma stood motionless in front of me, without a glimmer of indignation or pity in her eyes, without her lustrous lips trembling under the injury of the accusations, suspicions, and insults that rolled over her, I was tempted to physically strike her heart, where the impenetrable bronze door stood. In these moments, I was not afraid of committing murder!

No, she did not have pity on me! If she had, she would have defended herself, protested, cried. She would have responded to accusations with other accusations, suspicions with other suspicions, insults with other insults, wrong or right, it didn't matter. No, no, I tell you, she didn't have pity on me! She avenged herself with that terrible silence, with that horrible resignation, without showing, even by the slightest gesture, that she considered herself the innocent victim of my insane jealousy!

Mi sembra che tutta la mia vita sia trascorsa in questo atteggiamento di continua interrogazione, in quest'ansiosa aspettativa di una risposta, in questa desolata disperazione di riceverla, un giorno!

Ella ha voluto vendicarsi in questo modo, e non poteva trovarne un altro più straziante e più crudele.

Se fosse stata rassegnata davvero, negli ultimi istanti, quando mi fissava in viso gli azzurri occhi già velati dall'agonia, dicendomi con un fil di voce:—Non ti vedo più! Una nebbia mi circonda!—in quegli ultimi momenti almeno ella avrebbe dovuto dirmi una parola rivelatrice, una sola parola.... Niente!

Fosse anche stata una parola di disprezzo, di odio, di maledizione, ne sarei stato sodisfatto; almeno avrei saputo qualche cosa, all'ultimo!... Ma no, ha voluto andarsene muta, chiusa, senza uno sguardo, nè un gesto, nè una sillaba che mi rivelasse il segreto del suo cuore, del suo spirito. Ella! Ella che, prima, quando l'amavo e non ero ancora geloso, mi sembrava trasparente come un cristallo, limpida come un purissimo diamante. Allora mi bastava guardarla negli occhi per scoprire le più lievi sfumature di sentimento nel fondo del suo cuore, per afferrare i più rapidi pensieri che le illuminavano come lampi la mente, dietro quell'ampia fronte che sotto i neri capelli ondulati sembrava di finissimo avorio!

E appena gli artigli del *mostro dagli occhi verdi* mi si conficcarono nel cuore, appena le prime mie ruvide mosse d'impazienza, di sospetto, di rimprovero le fecero intendere la divoratrice passione che cominciava ad invasarmi, ella mi apparve un'altra tutt'a un tratto. Il suo cuore si ottenebrò, ed io non potei più leggervi nulla; la sua fronte diventò opaca, quasi la bella creatura vivente si fosse mutata in statua che non ha anima, ma soltanto linee e rilievo di bellezza, espressione esteriore che fa comprendere il concetto voluto significare dall'artista, ma che non penetra, non pervade il legno la creta o il marmo di cui essa è formata.

Ma invece io sapevo che dentro quella statua c'erano e il cuore e l'anima e lo spirito; e intanto, tra essi e me si opponeva, insuperabile, quel silenzio che pareva mi tenesse chiusa in faccia una porta di bronzo a cui invano picchiavo; di cui le mie mani, battendo, quasi sentivano il freddo; e che non risonava neppure, tanto era solida. L'immagine di questa bronzea porta, in certi momenti, si mutava nella mia alterata immaginazione in una cosa reale.

E mentre il mio geloso furore provocato da un nonnulla (ora lo capisco) prorompeva in parole sconnesse, in urli, in gesticolazioni da pazzo, e Gemma mi stava immobile davanti, senza mutar di colore, senza che nei bei occhi le si accendesse un baleno d'indignazione o di pietà, senza che le sue rosee labbra s'increspassero lievemente sotto l'offesa di accuse, di sospetti, di insulti che la investiva, io ero tentato di percuoterla al petto, dove mi sembrava fosse quella inespugnabile porta di bronzo.... E non mi spaventava l'idea di commettere anche un delitto!

No, ella non ha avuto nessuna pietà di me! Se ne avesse avuta, si sarebbe difesa, avrebbe protestato, avrebbe pianto; avrebbe risposto alle accuse con altre accuse, ai sospetti con altri sospetti, agli insulti con altri insulti, a torto o a ragione, non voleva dir nulla. No, no, ti ripeto, non ha avuto nessuna pietà di me! Si è vendicata con quel terribile silenzio, con quell'orrida rassegnazione, e senza mostrare, neppur con un cenno, che si stimasse vittima innocente della mia stolta gelosia!

And she did worse, much worse. She concealed her illness from me, she let herself die little by little. And only a few days before the catastrophe, when all her energy was finally exhausted, only then did she announce to me, softly but firmly, "Dino, I think I am dying!"

And I, unhappy man, didn't believe her! And the day I could no longer doubt it, you know what thought horrified me, what thought filled my eyes with angry tears? "She will escape me! She will escape me! She is leaving without telling me her secret!" And so it was! So it was!

And you dare to say, "She was a saint!" A saint without pity? Without charity? Oh, no!

Forgiveness is not silent.

Fece peggio! Mi nascose il suo male, si lasciò struggere a poco a poco; e soltanto pochi giorni prima della catastrofe, quando ogni sua energia era finalmente esaurita, soltanto allora mi annunziò con voce esile ma ferma:

—Dino, mi sento morire!

Ed io, sciagurato, non lo credetti! E il giorno che non potei più dubitare, sai tu quale fu il pensiero che mi sconvolse, che mi riempì gli occhi di infocate lagrime di rabbia?—Ella mi sfugge! Ella mi sfugge! Ella se ne va senza dirmi il suo segreto!—Ed è stato così! Così!

E tu dici: Era una santa!—Una santa senza pietà? Senza carità? Oh no!

Il perdono non è muto.

THE ARIA

TO BRUNA

"Among the memories of my childhood," Forcelli said, "there is a gentle figure. . ."

"Depraved since you were a child!" Miozzi interrupted him, laughing.

". . .a kind old woman," continued Forcelli, ignoring Miozzi, "who comes to my mind every time I hear some melody of the last century. She was my father's cousin, and she lived all alone in a lodge older than she, where everything was old like she was, and from where everything disappeared with her many, many years ago. From such ruin was saved – and I don't know how – only a spinet, wobbling on three feet, already worm-eaten, with yellowed, twisted keys, and a broken pedal haphazardly fixed with twine. I purposely left it as it was, and I keep it in the corner of my studio to remember the woman who brought me the sweetest musical impressions of my life. I said sweeter, not more intense, dear master," he added, turning to the other who shook his head, protesting and almost commiserating with him, fanatical admirer of Wagner that he was.

"I was going to say!" he commented.

"I often went to visit my cousin, as we all called her in the family, because she had a great predilection for me. I was the living portrait of my grandfather, according to her, and in fact she had given me the nickname of *Nonnino*, little Grandfather. I confess that I exploited this, allowing myself to commit in her house all sorts of mischief that my father and mother would not have allowed.

"Ah, Nonnino! Nonnino!' she scolded me, threatening with her finger. But she always laughed at once.

Now, one of my favorite entertainments was banging my hands, almost with my fists, on the keys of that poor spinet, which shook and creaked with all its copper strings, and seemed to cry out for help against the suffering I inflicted upon it.

My cousin would come running from wherever she happened to be in the house, all bent over, shuffling on her slippers, yelling at me from afar: "Ah, Nonnino! Nonnino! No, no—the spinet, no! Do not touch that!"

And in fact, I have not touched it since the day my cousin, in an effort to induce me to leave her dear instrument in peace, told me: "When you want, I'll play the spinet and I'll sing you a nice little song that you can learn by heart."

"And will you teach me to play it?"

"I wouldn't know how, my dear Nonnino!"

So I had to content myself with the song, accompanied by the clear chirping of those strings, which today, compared with the sound of a piano, sounds like a mosquito's buzz.

UN'ARIA DI CIMAROSA

A BRUNA

Tra i ricordi della mia fanciullezza—disse Forcelli—c'è una gentile figura….

—Vizioso fin da bambino!—lo interruppe Miozzi, ridendo.

—…. una gentile figura di vecchina—continuò Forcelli senza badargli—che mi torna alla memoria ogni volta che sento qualche melodia del secolo scorso. Era cugina di mio padre e viveva, sola sola, in una casetta più vecchia di lei, dove tutto era vecchio come lei e da dove tutto è sparito con lei, molti e molti anni fa. Si è salvata dal disastro—e non so come—soltanto una spinetta barcollante sui tre piedi, con la cassa tarlata anche allora, coi tasti ingialliti e sconnessi e col pedale rotto e aggiustato alla meglio con spago. Ho voluto lasciarla com'era, e la tengo in un angolo del mio studio per ricordo di colei che mi ha fatto godere le più dolci impressioni musicali di vita mia. Ho detto più dolci, non più intense, caro maestro—egli soggiunse, rivolgendosi a colui che scoteva la testa protestando e quasi commiserandolo, da quel rabbioso wagnerista che era.

—Volevo ben dire!—rispose questi.

—Andavo spesso dalla cugina, come tutti la chiamavamo in famiglia, perchè ella mostrava una grande predilezione per me. Ero il vivente ritratto del nonno, secondo lei; e infatti ella mi aveva imposto il soprannome di Nonnino. Confesso che abusavo volentieri di questo privilegio, permettendomi in casa sua tante monellerie vhr il babbo e la mamma non avrebbero tollerato.

—Ah, Nonnino! Nonnino!—ella mi sgridava, minacciando con l'indice della mano destra.

Ma subito rideva.

Ora, uno dei miei più piacevoli divertimenti consisteva, in principio, appunto nel tempestare con le mani, quasi coi pugni, sui tasti di quella misera spinetta, che fremeva e strideva con tutte le corde di rame e sembrava chiedere aiuto contro lo strazio che le infliggevo.

La cugina accorreva da qualunque punto della casa, curva, strascicando le ciabatte, sgridandomi da lontano:

—Ah, Nonnino! Nonnino! No, no; la spinetta, no! Questa non si tocca.

E infatti non la toccai più dal giorno in cui la cugina, per indurmi a lasciare in pace il suo caro strumento, mi disse:

—Quando vuoi, suono io la spinetta e ti canto anche una bella canzonetta che potrai imparare a memoria.

—E a suonare m'insegnerai?

—Non saprei insegnarti, Nonnino mio!

Così mi contentai della canzonetta, accompagnata dall'argentino frinire di quelle corde, che oggi, a confronto del suono di un pianoforte, sembrerebbe ronzìo di zanzara.

Oh, she was not a good player, nor a decent singer! She knew only how to play a few chords and always repeated the same cheerful, cheeky song, which somehow assumed a melancholic expression because of her trembling voice. Even the chords were shaky, because the old woman had lost all agility in her fingers. To me, the song and chords seemed a marvelous thing, and I wanted to listen to them over and over again when I went to visit.

"What is this song about?" I asked her one day.

"A secret marriage."

"And who wrote it?"

"*Maestro* Cimarosa."

"Do you know him?"

"No."

"How, then, did you learn it?"

"My mother taught it to me."

"What does 'secret marriage' mean?"

"It means that they have married in secret."

"Why?"

"Maybe their relatives were opposed to the marriage."

"Did you yourself marry in secret?"

"I never married!"

"Why not?"

Oh, the inopportune and inevitable questions of children!

My cousin tried to smile, but stroking my hair and stammering a little, she said, "Because. . ." She had tears in her eyes.

She had been dead for a while when, coming back from the university, I saw the spinet that was so dear to her in my house. That forgotten scene immediately came to my mind, and I was moved by the sad drama that one could imagine, listening to Cimarosa's aria – or song, as she called it.

I haven't seen the performance of the *Secret Marriage* by the great musician from Aversa, nor do I ever want to hear again from another voice the song whose words and the tune I forgot, while retaining the indefinite feeling of the happy melody, to which the trembling voice of my cousin also lent a sense of gentle sadness. It would have seemed to me to desecrate something sacred, superimposing on that childlike and delicate sensation a recent feeling that, perhaps, could have made it fade or vanish.

And for that reason, I keep in my studio the worm-eaten spinet, of which several wires have already broken and twisted, and whose keys are, more than ever, separated, the pedal broken and fixed with twine.

Often, while smoking a cigarette, lying in an armchair, I enjoy imagining the mysterious tragedy that beset my old cousin's heart. And it seems to me that the little song by Cimarosa had to be, for her, an ineffable consolation in the long sadness of her solitary life.

Oh, non era una sonatrice e nemmeno un'abile cantante! Sapeva fare pochi accordi e replicava sempre quell'unica canzonetta allegra, spigliata, che assumeva nello stesso tempo un'espressione malinconica per il suono tremulo della voce. Anche gli accordi tremolavano, perchè le dita della vecchierella avevano perduto ogni agilità. A me, canzonetta ed accordi sembravano cosa maravigliosa, e volevo riudirli più di una volta, di sèguito, quando andavo dalla cugina.

—Come si chiama questa canzonetta?—le domandai un giorno.

—Il matrimonio segreto.

—E chi l'ha fatta?

—Il maestro Cimarosa.

—Lo conosci?

—No.

—Dunque, come l'hai appresa?

—Me l'ha insegnata mia madre.

—Che vuol dire: matrimonio segreto?

—Vuol dire che si sono maritati di nascosto.

—Perchè?

—I parenti forse non volevano.

—Ti sei maritata di nascosto tu?

—Non mi sono maritata mai!

—Perchè?

Oh, gli importuni e inevitabili perchè dei bambini!

La cugina, quella volta, tentò di sorridere: ma, accarezzandomi i capelli e balbettando:—Perchè…. Perchè….—aveva le lacrime agli occhi.

Ella era morta da un pezzo quando, tornato dall'Università, rividi in casa nostra la spinetta a lei così cara. Mi venne subito alla mente quella scena dimenticata, e fui commosso per il triste dramma che l'aria o la canzonetta (come ella diceva) di Cimarosa lasciava immaginare.

Io non ho visto rappresentare il *Matrimonio segreto* del gran musicista d'Aversa, o non ho mai voluto riudire da altra voce la canzonetta della quale ho dimenticato le parole e il motivo, pur conservando la indefinita sensazione dell'allegra melodia, a cui la tremula voce della cugina comunicava anche un senso di dolce tristezza. Mi sarebbe parso di profanare qualche cosa di sacro, sovrapponendo all'infantile e delicata sensazione una sensazione recente che, forse, avrebbe potuto affievolirla o farla sparire.

E, per ciò, conservo nel mio studio la tarlata spinetta, di cui parecchie corde sono già rotte e attorcigliate e i tasti più sconnessi di una volta e il pedale guasto e accomodato con spago.

Spesso, fumando una sigaretta, sdraiato su una poltrona, mi diverto a immaginare la misteriosa tragedia del cuore della vecchia cugina, e penso che la canzonetta di Cimarosa ha dovuto essere per lei un'ineffabile consolazione nella lunga tristezza della solitaria sua vita.

THE CHOICE

TO GIUSEPPE COSTANZO

"I don't believe in fate," said Oddo Remossi, "at least not in the way that is generally understood. As much as we want to expand the action and the influence of external and hereditary circumstances, there always remains a wide margin where individual freedom can find a place. The fact is that we don't sufficiently oppose the hostile forces that surround us. Often, unfortunately, we neither have the time nor the ability to do so. Life rushes on. The same civilization that should make us more independent and free, enslaves our acts and thoughts even though we are unaware it is so. Today, none of us would have the courage to blow his nose with his fingers, like the great knight of La Mancha did, and still, on rare occasions, some of our modern farmers do. Does the slavery of the handkerchief seem of no consequence to you? Do you laugh? Well, many of these slaveries of ideas are no less ridiculous. Think about it a little, and you'll realize it is so."

"What does this have to do with fate?" Mazzani asked.

"It does," Remossi answered, "because we are accustomed to define *fate* as those events for which we can't see the series of links and logic."

"Too much philosophy, and it seems to me, philosophy wasted on such a petty and common occurrence as that which we are discussing!"

Gramoglia spoke without taking his mouth off the cigar he was enjoying blissfully, lying down on the armchair that he called *his* because every time he came to Remossi's studio, Gramoglia wanted it for himself, preferring to remain standing if it was already occupied by another person.

"In your opinion," he added, continuing to smoke, "I should rebel against the slavery of *my* chair that I consider so comfortable and sweet. Why?"

"It's impossible to reason with you!" Remossi said. "Do you want proof? I will tell you a story. It is a true story; I didn't invent it to make a point. I already know how you will judge it, and this will be the confirmation of my thesis.

"Fine. But let's not leave the sphere of fatally predestined husbands. There are several categories of these. Those who have no eyes to see, nor ears to hear; those who see and feel, but resign themselves to their destiny; those who rebel in vain, because a fact is a fact and nothing can change it after it has happened. A husband who kills his unfaithful wife or her lover. . ."

"It is pointless that you quote Balzac to me. I read *The Physiology of Marriage*, too. What do I want to prove to you? That we have become slaves of a prejudice, or of a feeling reduced to that. There are no *predestined* people in a marriage, but only silly, careless, heedless, nervous, unreasonable, criminal husbands. . ."

NON PREDESTINATO?

A GIUSEPPE COSTANZO

—Io non credo alla fatalità—disse Oddo Remossi—almeno nel modo in cui generalmente s'intende. Per quanto si voglia ingrandire l'azione e l'influenza delle circostanze esteriori ed ereditarie, resta sempre un largo margine dove può trovar posto la libertà individuale. Solamente avviene che noi non ci opponiamo abbastanza a quelle forze, diciamo, nemiche che ci stanno attorno. Spesso, purtroppo, non ne abbiamo il tempo, nè il modo. La vita c'incalza; la stessa civiltà che dovrebbe renderci più indipendenti e più liberi, ci costringe a una schiavitù di atti e di pensieri di cui non ci rendiamo mai conto. Oggi nessuno di noi avrebbe il coraggio di soffiarsi il naso con le dita, come il gran Cavaliere della Mancia e qualche raro contadino attuale. La schiavitù del fazzoletto vi sembra poca cosa? Ne ridete? Ebbene, tante altre schiavitù di idee non sono meno ridicole di essa. Rifletteteci un po', e ve ne accorgerete.

—Che c'entra tutto questo con la fatalità?—disse Mazzani.

—C'entra—rispose Remossi—perchè noi siamo soliti chiamare *fatali* quei fatti dei quali non riusciamo a scorgere la concatenazione e la logica.

—Troppa filosofia e, mi sembra, sprecata a proposito di un avvenimento così meschino e comune come quello di cui parliamo!

Gramoglia aveva parlato senza togliersi di bocca il sigaro gustato beatamente, stando sdraiato sulla poltrona, sulla *sua* poltrona, da lui chiamata così perchè ogni volta che si trovava nello studio dell'amico Remossi la voleva per sè, o preferiva restare in piedi se era già occupata da un'altra persona.

—Secondo te—soggiunse continuando a fumare—io dovrei ribellarmi alla schiavitù della *mia* poltrona che stimo tanto comoda e tanto dolce. Perchè?

—Con voi è impossibile ragionare!—esclamò Remossi.—Ne volete la prova? Vi racconterò un fatto. È autentico, autenticissimo; non lo invento per comodità. So già, anticipatamente, il giudizio che ne darete, e sarà la conferma di quel che sostengo.

—Non usciamo però dalla sfera dei mariti fatalmente predestinati…. Ce ne sono parecchie categorie. Quella di coloro che non hanno occhi per vedere, nè orecchie per sentire; quella di coloro che vedono e sentono e si rassegnano al loro destino; quella di coloro che si ribellano inutilmente, perchè un fatto è un fatto e niente può annullarlo dopo che è avvenuto. Un marito che ammazza la moglie infedele o l'amante….

—È superfluo che tu mi citi Balzac: la *Fisiologia del matrimonio* l'ho letta anch'io. Che cosa voglio provarvi? Che noi ci siamo appunto resi schiavi di un pregiudizio, o di un sentimento ridotto tale. Non ci sono *predestinati* nel matrimonio, ma, invece, mariti sciocchi, imprevidenti, incuranti, mariti nervosi, irragionevoli, delinquenti….

"Six of one, half-a-dozen of another," interrupted Mazzani. "But tell me about this wonderful example. We can resume our discussion later."

"Here it is," Remossi said. "With the three usual characters: *She, He,* and *the Other.* I won't use names, though there would be nothing wrong if I did. But these are intimate facts, that I happen to know by accident, and human wickedness being what it is, it is possible things have gone differently from the way I learned them."

"You're not absolutely sure of this, then!" Gramoglia said.

"Absolutely certain. I never knew a wiser man than. . . of course, I must name my characters to avoid confusion so let's call him Roberto Cagli. Nature and circumstances had uniquely endowed him. He was almost rich, from an excellent family, and a handsome man on top of that. He had studied a lot, without taking up a profession. He considered professions tyrannical, and he wanted to enjoy the lucky circumstances that allowed him to remain independent of everything and everyone. He used to say, 'The perfect man is the one who can keep himself savage in the midst of civilization.' For him *savage* was synonymous with *free.* At thirty-five, he married the woman his heart had chosen, beautiful and moderately educated. Because Miss Balestri could only bring him a modest dowry, it was a true-love marriage. The first years of their marriage were happy, and their happiness, evidently, caused admiration and envy. No one, however, would have dreamed of disturbing their blissful state. Mrs. Cagli was considered to be one of those women who, by nature, remain immune to any pitfall. But while her husband shared that view, he, nevertheless, kept an eye on her, surreptitiously observing her while leaving her great freedom. Here enters *the Other,* the third party, the tempting serpent. What else would you call someone who, in the critical, decisive moment, abandons his role as the husband's most trusted and intimate friend? Similarity of feelings and ideas, in addition to the circumstances of the two families, had linked Roberto Cagli to Adolfo Gissi with a strong friendship from the early years of their youth. They had studied together, and made mischief together. The marriage of one, which seemingly should have acted as a brake on their intimacy, had somehow strengthened it. Gissi was a handsome man, too, with a sunny disposition, and easy and colorful speech, which was a bit of contrast with his friend's more serious and reserved character.

"Mrs. Cagli was almost intimidated by Gissi's relentless cheerfulness whenever he came to see them or was invited to lunch, something that happened once a week on a fixed day, a habit from Cagli's bachelor days. And then. . .

"One morning, I do not remember why, Roberto Cagli had gone to visit his friend, and had surprised him in the midst of preparing his luggage.

"'Are you leaving?'"

"'Yes, for a long journey.'

"'And where are you going?'

"'I don't know. Far away.'

"'Why didn't you tell me?'

"'I was planning on coming to you this evening, to say goodbye.'

—Se non è zuppa è pan bagnato—lo interruppe Mazzani.—Ma è meglio che tu racconti il fatto. Riprenderemo a discutere dopo.

—Eccolo—fece Remossi—coi tre soliti personaggi *Lei, Lui, L'altro*. Permettetemi di non dire i nomi, quantunque non ci sarebbe niente di male se io li rivelassi. Ma si tratta di un fatto intimo, saputo per caso, e la malvagità umana è tale da poter sospettare che le cose siano andate diversamente da come io le ho apprese.

—Non sei assolutamente certo, dunque!—disse Gramoglia.

—Certissimo. Non ho conosciuto un uomo più saggio di…. (Mi accorgo che bisogna ribattezzare i miei personaggi per evitare confusione) di Roberto Cagli. La natura e le circostanze lo avevano singolarmente dotato. Era quasi ricco, di eccellente famiglia, e bell'uomo per giunta. Aveva studiato molto, senza prendere una professione. Le professioni le considerava tiranne, e voleva godersi le fortunate circostanze che gli permettevano di restare indipendente da tutto e da tutti. Soleva dire:—Uomo perfetto è colui che può conservarsi selvaggio in mezzo alla civiltà.—Per lui selvaggio era sinonimo di libero. A trentacinque anni aveva sposato la donna scelta dal suo cuore, bella e abbastanza colta. Vero matrimonio di amore, perchè la signorina… Balestri poteva portargli una dote modesta. I primi anni del loro matrimonio erano trascorsi felici, e la felicità, evidentissima, dei due sposi destava ammirazione ed invidia. Nessuno però osava pensare d'intorbidirla. La signora Cagli veniva stimata una di quelle donne che, anche per indole, rimangono superiori a ogni insidia. Ma, pur non essendo diversa la convinzione di suo marito, egli non tralasciava di tenerla d'occhio, di osservarla senza averne l'aria e lasciandole amplissima libertà. Qui entra in scena *l'altro*, il terzo, il serpente tentatore, secondo la leggenda, se può dirsi tale uno chead un certo momento, nel momento più pericoloso e quasi decisivo, rinunziava alla sua parte: era, naturalmente, il più intimo amico del marito. Somiglianza di sentimenti e di idee, oltre a circostanze delle due famiglie, avevano legato Roberto Cagli ad Adolfo Gissi con un'amicizia più che fraterna sin dai primi anni della loro giovinezza. Avevano studiato insieme, e fatto insieme qualche piccola stravaganza. Il matrimonio dell'uno, che sembrava avesse dovuto rallentare la loro intimità, l'aveva anzi rafforzata. Era un bell'uomo anche Gissi, di carattere gioviale però, e di parola facile e colorita, che formava un po' di contrasto col carattere più serio e riservato del suo amico.

La signora Cagli, da principio, si sentiva quasi intimidita davanti a quell'espansione di allegria che il Gissi metteva nella conversazione ogni volta che veniva a trovarli o che era invitato a pranzo, cosa che accadeva una volta la settimana, in un giorno fisso. (Cagli aveva voluto mantenere quella sua abitudine di scapolo). Poi….

Una mattina, non ricordo per quale circostanza, Roberto Cagli era andato dal suo amico, e lo aveva sorpreso occupatissimo a preparare le valige.

—Parti?

—Intraprendo un lungo viaggio.

—E dove vai?

—Non lo so; lontano.

—Come mai non me n'hai detto niente?

—Sarei venuto ad accomiatarmi questa sera.

"'What mystery is this? It seems you keep secrets from me while I never kept any from you.'

"Gissi stared at his friend who returned his look just as intently.

"'What's happened to you?' Cagli said. 'Our friendship gives me the right to ask you this with the certainty of getting a sincere answer.'

"'Perhaps you do not need *me* to give you the answer, Gissi.'

"'I don't understand. Why can't you speak plainly?'

"'There are things in this world that you neither can nor should confide, even to your most intimate friend.'

"'To any intimate friend, I agree; to me, no.'

"And both of them were amazed to find themselves speaking to each other with such unusual severity.

"'You're right!' Gissi exclaimed, after a moment of hesitation.

"He passed his hand two or three times over his forehead, as if trying to hold back the words he was about to speak, then he blurted out, 'I am leaving because. . . because. . . I love your wife!'

"'Does she know that?'' Cagli asked quietly.

"'Yes,' said Gissi, lowering his forehead as if in pain.

"'Is there anything else?'

"'Oh! I am a gentleman, and above all a friend. You should not doubt that for a single moment.'

"'I didn't doubt it, and I don't doubt it now. I had realized that my wife was beginning to love you. She is a noble and honest soul, too. What are you both afraid of?'

"'Of our weakness. How can you not understand?'

"'Your departure, in any case, would not remedy anything, but would, rather, worsen the situation. Are you a man?'

"'Need you ask? Another. . .'"

"'Precisely because you are not another man, you have to stay. If you insisted on leaving, I would be right to suppose that a late remorse is forcing you to do so.'

"'No, I swear to you!'

"'You don't need to swear it to me.'

"'If I remained, I could not come to your house anymore. What would people say?'

"'I have never cared for what people think or say about me and my personal affairs. They will not have to think or say anything, because you will continue as before, you *must* continue to attend my home as you have always done. You are a man. Your duty is to conquer yourself. Give me your word of honor that you will do as I wish.'

"Although Gissi knew his friend's soul, he was nevertheless amazed, hearing him speak so. For a moment he suspected that his apparent tranquility concealed a trap. *No man is a hero in every circumstance, even when he is endowed with all the qualities that produce heroism*, he thought. But his suspicions vanished with his friend's final words.

"'I give you my word of honor! But I beg you, consider what you are doing.'

—Che mistero è questo? Hai tu dunque dei segreti per me che per te non ne ho avuti mai?

Gissi lo guardò negli occhi; anche il suo amico lo guardava intentamente; pareva volessero scrutarsi a vicenda.

—Che ti accade?—disse Cagli.—La nostra amicizia mi dà il diritto di farti questa domanda con la certezza di ottenere una schietta e sincera risposta.

—Forse non hai bisogno che te la dia—rispose Gissi.

—Non capisco. Commetteresti una indegna azione se non mi dicessi la verità.

—Vi sono cose in questo mondo che non si possono nè si devono confidare neppure al più intimo amico.

—A un intimo amico qualunque, sì; non a me.

E tutti e due rimasero stupiti di parlarsi con tanta insolita severità.

—Hai ragione!—esclamò Gissi dopo un istante di esitazione.

Si passò due o tre volte una mano sulla fronte, fece qualche sforzo quasi per trattenere le parole che stavano per uscirgli dalle labbra, poi, prorompendo, disse:

—Parto perchè... amo tua moglie!

—Ella lo sa?—domandò tranquillamente Cagli.

—Sì—rispose Gissi, chinando dolorosamente la fronte.

—Non c'è altro?

—Oh! Sono gentiluomo e sopratutto amico; non dovresti dubitarne un solo momento.

—Non ne ho dubitato, e non ne dubito. Mi ero accorto che mia moglie cominciava ad amarti. È un'anima nobile ed onesta anche lei. Di che cosa avete paura tutti e due?

—Della nostra fragilità. Come puoi non capire?

—La tua partenza, in ogni caso, non rimedierebbe a nulla. Peggiorerebbe la situazione. Sei un uomo?

—Lo vedi. Un altro....

—Precisamente perchè non sei quest'altro tu devi restare. Se ti ostinassi a partire, io avrei ragione di supporre che cedi a un tardivo rimorso.

—No, te lo giuro!

—Non occorreva giurarmelo.

—Restando non potrei più frequentare la casa tua. Che direbbe la gente?

—Non mi sono mai curato di quel che la gente può pensare o dire di me e dei fatti miei; intanto non avrà da pensare e da dir niente, perchè tu continuerai, tu devi continuare a frequentare la mia casa come hai fatto finora. Sei un uomo? Il tuo dovere è di vincere te stesso. Dammi la tua parola di onore che farai come io voglio.

Per quanto Gissi conoscesse l'animo del suo amico, non rinveniva dallo stupore di sentirlo parlare a quel modo. Gli era balenato il sospetto che quella tranquillità apparente nascondesse un tranello; *l'uomo non è sempre un eroe, in ogni circostanza, anche quando è dotato di tutte le qualità che producono l'eroismo,* egli pensava. Ma il rapido sospetto era sparito dopo le ultime parole del suo amico.

—Ti dò la mia parola di onore! Rifletti però... te ne prego.

"'For her sake, perhaps? Listen to me. I predict a miracle. I don't believe in all-powerful passions, in the *coup de foudre* of Stendhal. We commit bad deeds because we tell ourselves we aren't able to stop ourselves. I mean especially bad deeds caused by passion. If you look well inside yourself, you will see that you have invited and evoked, and not unknowingly, feelings that you could have easily suffocated when they began. Your righteousness of mind has now suggested to you a violent means that, like all violence, can produce, indeed, *will* certainly produce effects that are the opposite of the ones you foresee. If you want your, my, and her tranquility. . .'

"In short Gissi had to surrender to such incredible mildness.

"That same day, a strange scene occurred that, nonetheless, achieved the desired goal. Gissi did not expect it. He had gone to his friend's house for what, under other circumstances, would have been his usual visit. Mrs. Cagli was in the living room with her husband, who had begged her to play while he was finishing a cigar after lunch.

"'Continue!' he told his wife, who had stopped playing at the unexpected arrival.

"She knew that Gissi intended to leave without seeing her again, after a moment of weakness in which they had confessed their mutual secret, or rather after Gissi's imprudence had extorted a confession from her that had made her cry, indignant at them both.

"To hide her turmoil, she had begun to play again. She stopped after a few notes.

"'So,' said Roberto Cagli, 'The two of you are falling in love?'

"Gissi got to his feet, pale, desperate, his hand on his head. The lady bowed her forehead to the music sheet holder on the piano, half fainting.

"'Don't you think you are being ridiculous?' Cagli added. 'Would you really become two vulgar adulterers? Oh, come, come!'

"It was done.

"Gissi and the lady found themselves making an involuntary move, facing one another, looking into each other's eyes, ridiculous just as he had said, nothing but ridiculous, and both of them red in the face, from the shame of recognizing their absurdity, even though in recent days they had believed themselves in the unbreakable grip of a tragic fate.

"And it all ended then and there!"

"Dear Remossi," said Gramoglia mischievously, "can we really believe you? It all ended then and there?"

"I believe you," said Mazzani. "You've told the story with so much sincerity and too many details to leave any doubt about the truthfulness of the matter. But it doesn't disprove at all that some people are doomed by fate. Your friend Roberto Cagli was not one of them, that's all."

—Per lei, forse? Senti: io sono sicuro di vedere un prodigio. Non credo alle passioni fulminanti, al *coup de foudre* dello Stendal. Noi commettiamo cattive azioni, perchè ci diciamo che non sapremmo non commetterle, intendo parlare specialmente delle cattive azioni passionali. Se guardi bene dentro te stesso, vedrai che tu hai lusingato, accarezzato, e non inconsapevolmente, sensazioni che avresti potuto con facilità soffocare nel momento che cominciavano a determinarsi. La tua rettitudine di animo ti ha ora suggerito un mezzo violento che, come tutte le violenze, può produrre, anzi, produrrà certamente effetti contrari a quelli preveduti. Se vuoi la tua, la mia e la tranquillità di lei....

Insomma Gissi dovette arrendersi davanti a così incredibile mitezza.

Avvenne, lo stesso giorno, una scena che può sembrarvi strana ma che raggiunse lo scopo voluto. Gissi non se l'aspettava. Era andato, come per una solita visita, in casa del suo amico. La signora Cagli si trovava in salotto col marito che l'avea pregata di suonare mentre egli finiva un sigaro dopo la colazione.

—Continua!—disse alla moglie che cessava di suonare all'inattesa apparizione.

Ella sapeva che Gissi doveva partire senza più rivederla, dopo che in un istante di debolezza si erano lasciati sfuggir di bocca il loro reciproco segreto, o piuttosto dopo che l'imprudenza di Gissi le aveva strappato una confessione che l'aveva fatta piangere, indignata contro lui e sè stessa.

E soltanto per nascondere il suo turbamento, riprese a suonare; smise dopo poche battute.

—Dunque—disse Roberto Cagli—voi due vi amate o state per amarvi?

Gissi scattò in piedi, pallido, portando disperatamente le mani alla testa; la signora chinò la fronte sul leggìo del pianoforte mezza svenuta.

—Non vi sembra di essere ridicoli?—soggiunse Cagli.—Vorreste diventare due volgari adulteri? Eh, via! Eh, via!

Il colpo era fatto.

Gissi e la signora si trovarono, con una mossa involontaria, l'una di faccia all'altro, l'una con gli occhi in quelli dell'altro, ridicoli come quegli aveva detto, nient'altro che ridicoli, e rossi tutti e due dalla vergogna di riconoscersi tali, mentre nei giorni scorsi si erano creduti sopraffatti da fiero tragico destino.

E tutto finì là!

—Caro Remossi—disse maliziosamente Gramoglia—dobbiamo proprio crederti? Tutto finì là?

—Io ti credo—soggiunse il Mazzani.—Hai raccontato con troppa calorosa sincerità e con troppi particolari, da non lasciar nessun dubbio sulla veridicità del fatto. Ma esso non prova niente contro la teoria dei *predestinati*. Il tuo amico Roberto Cagli non faceva parte di quel numero; ecco tutto.

THE CIPHER

TO FANNY ZAMPINI-SALAZAR

Was he skeptical and selfish? Or was he merely pleased to show himself so because of his vanity?

I loved him, despite his great defects; probably because of them. There are bad qualities that attract us in an extraordinary way, perhaps because they give us the illusion of concealing, under their wicked appearance, counterbalancing qualities worthy of admiration. The fascination inspired by certain criminals, by certain wicked women, can be explained this way.

Federico Toacci was shameless in his actions, and this sometimes made one suspect that he exaggerated in recounting them.

He used to say, "I don't believe in denial and sacrifice because I consider them inhuman virtues, and therefore I don't practice them.

"Everyone's duty is to procure for themselves, by whatever means, that which can satisfy his needs and his desires, and make him happy.

"Someone invented morality because they wanted to prevent others from achieving a good thing and reserve it for himself alone.

"The moral code is the most valuable code in the world because it teaches us how to harm others while avoiding harm to oneself.

"Love is not worth the time, effort, and money that people waste buying it. You have to take it as it comes, when it comes, from anyone it comes from, without being too picky. It is a very foolish thing that we put love at the center of our lives, perhaps to prove that life is worth nothing better."

And if someone pointed out to him that his actions often contradicted his solemnly repeated aphorisms, he would reply, "The ability to do the opposite of what you think and feel is the best evidence one can give himself of the absolute independence and freedom that he possesses."

He once told me, "Bad day today! I had to do a good deed, with only the hope that it will cause many future bad ones."

"What did you do?"

"I lent a thousand lire to a man who didn't dare ask to borrow it, because he was certain – he said –that he would not be able to return it to me."

"So what?"

"You don't understand that, if it was true, he would have been extremely forward in asking me for it?"

"He will return it to you, then."

"No, because now he knows I am not counting on him to do so."

"Why did you lend him the money?"

"To avoid the temptation of believing that there might be an honest person in this world."

CHI SA?

A FANNY ZAMPINI-SALAZAR

Era scettico ed egoista? O si compiaceva, per vanità, di mostrarsi tale?

Io gli volevo bene, nonostante i suoi grandi difetti; probabilmente per essi. Vi sono cattive qualità che attraggono in modo straordinario; forse perchè dànno l'illusione di nascondere, sotto la loro malvagia apparenza, qualità opposte, degne di ammirazione e che servono da compenso. Il fascino di certi delinquenti, di certe malefiche donne può spiegarsi così.

Federico Toacci era spudorato nelle sue azioni, e questo faceva qualche volta sospettare ch'egli esagerasse raccontandole.

Soleva dire:

—Io non credo all'abnegazione e al sacrificio perchè le stimo virtù inumane; e per ciò non li pratico.

Il dovere di ogni individuo consiste nel procurarsi, con qualunque mezzo, quel che può soddisfare i suoi bisogni, i suoi desideri, e renderlo felice.

La morale è stata inventata da colui che voleva impedire agli altri il conseguimento di un bene creduto degno di esser riservato a lui solo.

Il codice è il libro più prezioso del mondo perchè indicacome nuocere agli altri, evitando di nuocere a sè stessi.

L'amore non vale il tempo, le forze e i quattrini che si sciupano per acquistarlo. Bisogna prenderlo come viene, quando viene, da chiunque viene, senza guardar molto per il sottile. Tanto, esso è una sciocchissima cosa, di cui abbiamo fatto il perno della vita forse per dimostrare che la vita non vale niente di meglio.—

E se qualcuno gli faceva notare che parecchie sue azioni contraddicevano gli aforismi da lui solennemente e ripetutamente proclamati, egli rispondeva:

—Il poter fare il contrario di quel che si pensa e si sente è la miglior prova che uno possa dare a sè stesso della propria assoluta indipendenza e della libertà che possiede.

Una volta mi disse:

—Brutta giornata oggi! Ho dovuto fare una buona azione, con la semplice illusione che essa ne faccia commettere parecchie cattive.

—Che cosa hai fatto?

—Ho prestato mille lire a un tale che non osava chiedermele perchè era certo— diceva—di non potere restituirmele.

—Ebbene?

—Non capisci che se fosse stato vero, me le avrebbe invece insistentemente richieste?

—Te le restituirà dunque.

—No, giacchè ora sa che io non conto più sulla sua restituzione.

—Perchè gliel'hai date?

—Per togliermi la tentazione di credere che vi sia una persona onesta in questo mondo.

"And if, contrary to what you suspect, he does eventually return the thousand lire?"

"I'll be convinced he will soon ask me for ten thousand, an even bigger score. Honesty is a financial calculation that typically assumes an interest rate of one thousand percent. . ."

"Oh!"

". . . in this, or in the other world, for those who have faith."

"Yet, you do so many things—obeying morality, laws, and social conventions!"

"Man is not perfect. It means I am honest, too, at intervals, at great intervals, fortunately."

Yes, it was true: Federico Toacci enjoyed an unscrupulous life, without restraints. Just like so many others, who, however, take great pains not to express the rules of their own conduct in the form of ruthless aphorisms.

Left free of any family supervision at the age of twenty-two, he had been educated away from home, far away, in Paris and London, because his parents had split up almost immediately after his birth, and his father didn't want the inconvenience of keeping Toacci with him even though he was required to do so by law. Nor did his mother remember, in her chaotic existence, that she had a son. He was good-looking, extremely rich, and he had matured precociously in environments in which it was difficult to have a clear idea of good and evil. So he had made up a flexible experimental philosophy of life, and in all his actions and decisions, he had conformed to it.

I often suspect he was actually quite sentimental but disguised himself as a selfish skeptic. He was certainly a proud man who didn't want to be deceived by anyone. His fear of being laughed at for his natural goodness of spirit and his good faith, forced him, as I said, to exaggerate his bad side.

I recall, in this regard, two incidents.

The first was a grand lunch he organized at his home. The invitation read: *To celebrate a sad event. Attire: Informal.*

The table was scattered with white chrysanthemums. The tablecloth and napkins were bordered in black. The massive fruit-bearing silver platters were covered with black veils.

None of the guests had wondered at the extravagance, but we were all curious to know the reason for it.

When the moment came for a toast, he stood up with a glass full of champagne in one hand, and said in a cheerful voice, "A humble girl has committed suicide for my sake. This is the first time that has happened to me. I have let a tear drop in my glass, and I now drink in honor of this event, which has either really happened, or not. Friends, I beg of you, do the same!"

None of us dared to drink.

He drained his glass, looked at us ironically and exclaimed, "I'm pleased to learn that I still have something to teach my friends."

I said, "You're only afraid to show emotion in front of people who would pity you."

"Commiseration! Yes, that's all I was missing!"

—E se, contrariamente a quel che tu sospetti, costui verrà a restituirti, presto o tardi, le mille lire?

—Penserò che, tra qualche tempo, vorrà chiedermene dieci mila, per fare un colpo più grosso. L'onestà è un calcolo profondo; è l'impiego di un capitale ideale con gli interessi al mille per cento....

—Oh!...

—.... in questo, o nell'altro mondo, per coloro che credono.

—Eppure tu fai tante cose in ossequio alla morale, alle leggi, alle convenienze sociali!

—L'uomo non è perfetto. Vuol dire che sono un onesto anche io, a intervalli, a grandi intervalli per fortuna.

Sì, era vero: Federico Toacci godeva la vita senza scrupoli, senza ritegni, al pari di tanti altri, che però si guardano bene dal formulare in ispietati aforismi le norme della loro condotta.

Rimasto libero a ventidue anni da ogni soggezione di famiglia, era stato educato fuori di casa, lontano, a Parigi e a Londra, perchè i suoi genitori si erano divisi quasi subito dopo la sua nascita e il padre non avea voluto fastidi tenendolo presso di sè come gli era stato accordato dalla legge, nè la madre si era più ricordata, nel disordine della sua esistenza, di avere un figliuolo. Era bello, straricco, cresciuto precocemente in ambienti dov eera difficile farsi una ben chiara idea del bene e del male: si era creato una particolare filosofia sperimentale e aveva conformato ad essa tutti gli atti della sua vita.

Spesso mi viene il sospetto ch'egli fosse un sentimentale camuffato da scettico e da egoista. Era certamente un orgoglioso che non voleva essere ingannato da nessuno, e che per il timore di far ridere della sua bontà naturale e della sua buona fede, si obbligava, come ho detto, ad esagerare le apparenze dal lato cattivo.

Ricordo, a questo proposito, due fatti.

Primo, un gran pranzo dato da lui. La lettera d'invito diceva: *Per celebrare un mesto avvenimento. N. B. In abito chiaro.*

La tavola era sparsa di crisantemi bianchi. La tovaglia e i tovaglioli orlati a lutto. Le massicce fruttiere d'argento, velate di crespo nero.

Nessuno degli invitati si era meravigliato di quella stravaganza, ma tutti eravamo curiosissimi di saperne la ragione.

Allo champagne, rizzatosi in piedi e tenendo con una mano la coppa ricolma, egli disse con tono scherzevole:

—Un'umile ragazza si è suicidata... per me. È il primo caso che mi capita. Lascio cascare una lagrima nella mia coppa, e bevo in onore di quest'avvenimento, che può essere una verità o una menzogna. Amici, fate altrettanto!

Nessuno di noi osò bere.

Egli vuotò la coppa, ci guardò sorridendo ironicamente ed esclamò:

—Mi compiaccio di apprendere che ho ancora qualcosa da insegnare ai miei amici.

Io gli dissi:

—Tu hai paura di sembrare commosso a chi fai pena.

—Mi mancava soltanto la commiserazione di qualcuno!

He lit a cigarette with an indifferent attitude and the lunch ended on a cold note.

Two years later, I was taking a friend from out-of-town to visit a famous monument in the cemetery, I don't recall which.

On that October evening, a bit humid and cold, with a mostly cloudy sky, the city of the dead was deserted. So I was amazed to see, at the end of the path, a man kneeling in front of a monument I had not noticed before but which seemed beautiful even from afar. On a dark marble pedestal, a bronze angel was spreading its wings and lifting its open arms upwards as if it was about to fly off into the sunset.

We approached the monument.

"You!" I exclaimed, recognizing Federico Toacci. And I bent to read the inscription. It read:

TO A POOR GIRL DEAD FOR LOVE.

I shot Federico a long, meaningful look.

"I know what you're thinking, and you're mistaken." he said with his usual mocking tone, pulling me aside. "This monument has served me well over the years. I asked a beautiful lady to meet me here, one who expects to be deeply moved before betraying her husband. The human heart knows so many tricks! Unfortunately, she's late. I had wanted her to find me kneeling here in distress. Could you and your friend please make yourselves scarce? Here she comes now." he added, pointing towards a woman dressed in dark clothing who was coming down the path.

But it was an old, not-particularly attractive English lady who passed in front of us, paused for a moment to look with her monocle at the angel spreading its wings, and turned to the right at the end of the row.

I spent the rest of my time at the cemetery covertly maneuvering in such a way as to ascertain, without being seen, if Federico Toacci had really been waiting for a woman or if he had been lying.

After a long time, I saw him leave, looking around cautiously. No lady had come to surprise him, kneeling before the monument he had erected to the poor girl who had killed herself for love.

So I now suspect that there are all kind of hypocrites in the world, even those preaching skepticism and selfishness. My friend was one of them.

He died of typhus at thirty-five. No one ever knew for sure whether he really was skeptical and selfish or whether he was merely pleased to show himself so because of his vanity.

E accese con indifferenza una sigaretta.

Il pranzo finì freddamente.

Due anni dopo, accompagnavo un amico di provincia che voleva osservare non ricordo più qual monumento al cimitero.

In quella sera di ottobre, con il cielo coperto di nuvole, un po' umida e fredda, la città dei morti era deserta. Perciò fui stupito di scoprire, in fondo a un viale, un uomo inginocchiato davanti a un monumento che non avevo avuto occasione di vedere prima e che sembrava bello anche da lontano. Su un piedistallo di marmo scuro, un angelo di bronzo spiegava le ali levando in alto le braccia aperte, quasi stesse per spiccare il volo verso il cielo.

Ci accostammo.

—Tu!—esclamai maravigliato, riconoscendo Federico Toacci.

E mi chinai a leggere l'iscrizione. Essa diceva:

A UN'UMILE MORTA PER AMORE

Guardai Federico con una lunga occhiata significativa.

—Ti sbagli—egli disse col solito ironico accento, tirandomi da parte.—Questo monumento mi è servito bene con le altre donne. Ho dato appuntamento qui a una bellissima signora che vuol essere commossa prima di tradire il marito. Ha tante furberie il cuore umano! Mi rincresce che ella sia in ritardo. Volevo farmi sorprendere ginocchioni davanti a questo monumento. Fammi il piacere di allontanarti con il tuo amico. Eccola—soggiunse, indicandomi una signora vestita di scuro che s'inoltrava per il viale.

Invece, quella signora, brutta e vecchia inglese, ci passò davanti, si fermò un istante ad osservare con l'occhialino l'angelo che spiegava le ali, e svoltò a destra infilando un altro viale.

Io feci in modo da accertarmi, non visto, se Federico Toacci si fosse sbagliato, e mi avesse detto la verità.

Lo vidi andar via dopo molto tempo, guardando cautamente attorno, senza che nessuna signora fosse venuta a sorprenderlo ginocchioni davanti al monumento da lui eretto all'umile suicida per amore.

Così mi è nato il sospetto che ci siano al mondo anche gl'ipocriti dello scetticismo e dell'egoismo, e che il mio amico fosse di questi.

È morto di tifo a trentacinque anni, e nessuno ha potuto sapere con certezza se egli sia stato proprio scettico ed egoista, e se si sia compiaciuto, per vanità, di mostrarsi sempre tale.

THE SUMMONER

TO CORDELIA

"Come now! Do you really believe in ghosts, as children do?"

"Why are you surprised? There are many great scientists, like Crookes, Wallace, and others, who do."

"Failed scientists! So-called scientists!"

"You are a fool, dear friend," replied Dr. Maggioli, "for summarily dismissing the discoverer of fluorescence and Darwin's rival. As far as I'm concerned, I am as modest as it is wise to be for those who have not dealt with these types of studies, which became fashionable only after I became too old to engage in them. I didn't say, first of all, that *I* believe in ghosts. But I would consider myself presumptuous if I dared to say that I could never believe in them. I have no reason to express a judgment of this sort. I am seventy years old and, soon enough, I will have personal knowledge of these matters and how things are in the other world. I am greatly curious, I confess."

"My apologies, but I don't follow."

"Perhaps I didn't make myself clear. In short, I declare that there is no solid argument for scientifically affirming or denying the existence of ghosts. But the only time I was tempted to try to see them myself, the result was negative."

"Quelle surprise."

"But though that effort failed, I don't feel entitled to say that Crookes, Wallace, and many other good-faith investigators deceived themselves or were deceived."

"But science. . ."

"Science is made by scientists and passes through many mistaken assumptions. Yesterday's science is not today's. And tomorrow's science will be different yet again. No sooner is one problem solved than new and more complicated ones present themselves. Sometimes scientists are annoyed to see them pop up, and close their eyes and ears in order to live in peace for a bit. However, this doesn't make the new problems disappear. Eventually, some scientists, more curious or more daring than others, open their eyes slightly and look, timidly at first, so as not to scandalize their colleagues. Then their love of truth conquers their personal pride, and science takes another step, and the absurdity of today becomes the received wisdom of tomorrow."

"But of course, Doctor! With regard to ghosts, however, there are no facts that can be seen with our eyes or observed with the microscope. They are fantasies of weak minds, hallucinations of sickly senses, old wives' tales, remnants of ancient traditions from the days when primitive man gave himself superficial explanations for natural phenomena and believed his shadow a duplicate of his person. If science were to take account of such nonsense, where would we be?"

L'EVOCATRICE

A CORDELIA

—Andiamo! Voi credete agli Spiriti, come le donnicciole?

—Che maraviglia? Ci credono tanti grandi scienziati, il Crookes, il Vallace, ecc.

—Scienziati falliti! Scienziati per modo di dire!

—Siete temerario, caro amico—riprese il dottor Maggioli—giudicando così sommariamente lo scopritore della materia radiante e l'emulo del Darwin. In quanto a me, sono modesto come si conviene a chi non si è occupato di questo genere di studi venuti in voga quando l'età non mi consentiva più di sperimentare. Non ho detto, intanto, che credo agli Spiriti; ma mi considererei presuntuoso, se osassi affermare che non posso crederci affatto. Non ho nessuna ragione per esprimere un giudizio di questa sorta. Ho settant'anni, e tra poco mi sarà dato conoscere *de visu* come stanno le cose dell'altro mondo. Ne ho una grande curiosità, ve lo confesso.

—Non capisco, mi scusi.

—Forse mi sono spiegato male. Insomma io dichiaro di non avere nessun solido argomento per affermare o negare scientificamente l'esistenza degli Spiriti. Ma l'unica volta che mi son lasciato indurre a tentare di vederli, la prova è riuscita negativa.

—Lo credo bene!

—Io però, da quella prova non riuscita, non mi sento autorizzato a dire che il Crookes, il Vallace e tanti altri sperimentatori di buona fede si siano ingannati o siano stati ingannati.

—Ma la Scienza....

—La Scienza la fanno gli scienziati a furia di sbagliare. Quella di ieri non è più questa di oggi; e quella di domani sarà un'altra cosa. Risolto un problema, se ne presentano nuovi e più complicati e più astrusi. Certe volte gli scienziati si seccano di vederseli affacciare davanti, e chiudono gli occhi e gli orecchi per vivere un po' in pace e non guardare nè udire. Ma non per questo i nuovi problemi scompaiono. Allora qualche scienziato, più curioso o più ardito degli altri, socchiude gli occhi e osserva, timidamente dapprima, per non scandalizzare i colleghi; poi l'amore della verità vince l'orgoglio personale; e così la Scienza fa un altro passo, e l'assurdo di oggi diventa la conquista assodata del giorno dopo.

—Lo sappiamo, dottore! Ma, riguardo agli Spiriti, non si tratta di fatti che possono cadere sotto gli occhi, da osservarsi con il microscopio. Fantasie di menti deboli, allucinazioni di sensi malati, credenze di femminucce, resti di tradizioni primitive, quando l'uomo ancora selvaggio si dava una spiegazione superficiale dei fenomeni della natura e credeva l'ombra un duplicato della sua persona.... Se la scienza dovesse tener conto di tali sciocchezze, starebbe fresca!

"Everything must be taken into account. Therefore I, who am a scientist, of a sort, having studied and practiced the most practical of sciences, medicine, am not ashamed to tell you that I, too, made the effort the day a friend came and asked me: 'Would you like to see ghosts? I have abandoned the experiment once, out of fear.' That friend of mine, a serious, well-educated man, a bit of an artist, a philosopher in the best sense of the word, with an intelligence open to all sorts of beliefs, is interested in great contemporary, political, economic, religious, and scientific problems. He's read all sorts of things, deepening his knowledge of everything with indomitable enthusiasm. He has nothing else to do: His large fortune allows him this intellectual luxury without requiring him to overlook the practical aspects of life. Recently, therefore, he became passionate about spiritual studies, and he was convinced that ghosts were a reality, just like any other; a reality of a superior order, perhaps, but something that couldn't be doubted. And when I told him, 'We may never know for sure!' he would get impatient at my hesitation in the face of the evidence. There was much more evidence for ghosts, he would say, than there was for so many facts that have now entered the domain of history and are fully accepted by everyone. I actually didn't deny the phenomena or the facts. I merely doubted their explanation. At my age, one doesn't embark, not even in one's mind, on explorations of unknown regions, and one always slightly distrusts the reports of the travelers who have visited them for the first time.

"But the day he came to me and asked, 'Would you like to see ghosts? I have abandoned the experiment once, out of fear.' I let my curiosity take over. Why not trust a man such as he?

"'What does one need to do to see them?' I asked after a moment of reflection.

"'Come to my house tomorrow. I will alert the *summoner.*'

"'You mean the *medium.*'

"'No. The person I am speaking of does not fall into a *trance*: that is, she doesn't fall asleep. She summons the ghosts, through a mysterious power, in full daylight, simply by using a magic formula of hers.'

"'So she is a witch, it seems.'

"'She is a poor woman—skinny, pale, sickly, badly clothed, who lives, I think, on alms.'

"'And on doing odd-jobs as a witch,' I interrupted him, laughing.

"'Not at all. She only asks for specific things that are indispensable to the summoning: a little salt, a little oil, a blessed candle, one of those used during Holy Week.'

"'I see.' I said, shrugging.

"'Probably not even salt, oil, and a blessed candle are needed. Perhaps they serve more than anything to stimulate her imagination.'

"'You have an answer for everything, it seems!'

"'I said *probably*. When you see her at work, my hypothesis will not seem strange to you.'

"'Why were you afraid?'

—Di tutto deve tener conto. Perciò io, che sono piuttosto scienziato per aver studiato e praticato la più materiale tra le scienze, la medicina, non arrossisco di far sapere che ho tentato anche di *vedere* gli Spiriti il giorno che un amico venne a dirmi:—Vuoi vederli? Io ho avuto paura e ho interrotto a metà l'esperimento.—Quel mio amico, uomo serio, coltissimo, un po' artista, un po' filosofo nel miglior senso di questa parola, intelligenza aperta ai quattro venti del pensiero, s'interessava dei grandi problemi contemporanei, politici, economici, religiosi, scientifici, leggendo tutto, approfondendo tutto con ardore indomabile. Non aveva altro da fare; il suo largo patrimonio gli permetteva questo lusso intellettuale senza fargli trascurare il resto. Ultimamente dunque si era entusiasmato degli studi spiritici, e si era convinto che gli Spiriti sono una realtà come un'altra, d'ordine superiore, forse, ma qualcosa di cui non si poteva dubitare. E siccome io gli rispondevo:—Bisogna attendere ancora!—egli si spazientiva delle mie esitazioni nonostante le tante e tante prove, quante forse— soggiungeva—non ne hanno parecchi fatti ormai entrati nel dominio della storia e considerati certi da tutti. Io veramente non negavo i fenomeni, i fatti; dubitavo della spiegazione di essi. Alla mia età non s'intraprendono neppur con la mente esplorazioni in regioni ignote, e si diffida sempre un po' delle relazioni dei viaggiatori che le hanno visitate la prima volta.

Il giorno però ch'egli venne a dirmi:—Vuoi vedere gli Spiriti? Io ho avuto paura e ho interrotto a metà l'esperimento—mi lasciai vincere dalla curiosità. Perchè non aver fiducia in un uomo come lui?

—Che cosa bisogna fare per vederli?—gli domandai dopo qualche istante di riflessione.

—Venire domani a casa mia. Io avviserò la *evocatrice*.

—La *medium* vuoi dire.

—No. La persona di cui ti parlo non cade in *tranche*, cioè: non si addormenta, non entra in catalessi; èvoca gli soiriti, con potere misterioso, in pieno giorno, semplicemente, usando certi suoi scongiuri.

—È una maga, a quel che pare.

—È una povera donna, secca, pallida, malaticcia, vestita sciattamente, che vive, credo, di elemosina....

—E col mestiere di fattucchiera,—lo interruppi, ridendo.

—Niente affatto. Chiede soltanto cose strane che dice indispensabili all'evocazione: un po' di sale, un po' di olio, una candela benedetta, di quelle che si usano nella settimana santa.

—Uh!—feci, alzando le spalle.

—Probabilmente nemmeno il sale, l'olio e la candela benedetta sono necessari; forse servono più che altro a stimolare la sua fantasia.

—Tu spieghi tutto!

—Ho detto probabilmente; e quando la vedrai operare, la mia ipotesi non ti parrà strana.

—Perché hai avuto paura?

"'Well, we were in my study, she and I, with the door open to the hallway. She began to mumble her summoning, kneeling behind a balcony curtain, in front of the little oil-filled pitcher, the lit candle, and the saucer with salt. From time to time, she took a pinch of salt and threw it into the pitcher. I was positioned so I could watch the operation, peeping from one side of the curtain. I was relaxed, very expectant, yes, but also a bit skeptical. It seemed impossible to me that that poor woman, that ghost of a woman, I should say, could possess such high powers.'

"'So what happened?'

"'Bear in mind that this all took place during the middle of the day. Without warning, the hallway lit up with light brighter than sunlight. There was the sudden sound of footsteps and the rustle of cloth. I don't mind telling you, I was afraid! I began shouting, 'No! No! Stop this!' I rubbed my eyes with my hands. I was in a cold sweat and trembling like a child.'

"'She simply relied on your imagination; she had manipulated you with those strange incantations!'

"'You're wrong. That's what I thought too, at first. But then, thinking it over. . . Well, you and I together, we'll be better able to resist. Shall we try?'

"'Yes. Let's!'"

Dr. Maggioli paused to look around the living room, and stared quizzically at some of the ladies who had been listening to his story with obvious signs of fear.

"Have you no respect for my health? I shall not sleep a wink tonight!" exclaimed Baroness Lanari.

"On the contrary. I wish to know if I should continue my story or not. . ."

"Oh very well! Why not?" said the baroness. "After all, you said that the experiment failed. . ."

"I no longer recall," replied the doctor, "who it was who wrote 'If they came to tell me that someone had stolen the Coliseum, before answering, 'It's impossible,' I would go and check.' Well, whoever it was, I agree. The scientist, in my opinion, should behave this way. I was punctual, arriving at the appointed time. The woman arrived shortly afterward. My friend's study has two balconies, one facing east, the other facing south, and the study was bathed in sunshine at that time of day. 'I had great difficulty getting permission for this,' said the summoner. 'From whom?' I asked. 'From my superiors,' she replied. 'This gentleman is a skeptic,' she added, addressing my friend. 'Ghosts don't willingly show themselves to those who don't believe. 'I want to believe,' I said, 'That's why I'm here.' Well, well, I thought, someone is hedging her bets! I watched her carefully as she arranged the little pitcher with the oil, the lit candle, and the saucer with the salt behind the balcony curtain. Her face held no signs of trickery, only a great weariness, the weariness of poverty. 'Who taught you?' I asked. 'My mother,' she said, as she hid herself behind the curtain. 'Now pay attention. The ghosts will not enter this room; they will cross the hallway, passing in front of the door.' She spoke with such confidence, that I thought, 'Maybe you really are going to see a miracle!' My friend and I stood so that we had a clear view of the door and the hallway. Suddenly, my friend grabbed my hand and began squeezing it, hard. But I did not let my attention waver from the hallway, even though I realized that he was deeply afraid. I, however, felt very calm, trustful. We spent ten minutes in intense anticipation. . .

—Ecco: eravamo nel mio studio, io e lei, con l'uscio aperto sul corridoio. Ella cominciò a brontolare le sue evocazioni inginocchiata dietro una tenda del balcone, con davanti l'orciolino pieno di olio, la candela accesa e il piattino col sale. Di quando in quando, prendeva un pizzico di sale e lo buttava nell'orciolino. Mi ero situato in maniera da poter seguire, sbirciando da un lato della tenda, l'operazione. Ero tranquillo, in grande aspettativa, sì, ma anche un po' incredulo. Mi pareva impossibile che quella povera donna, quel fantasma di donna dovrei dire, possedesse così alto potere....

—E allora....

—Allora, tienlo a mente, di pieno giorno, all'improvviso, vedo il corridoio illuminarsi con luce più splendida del sole e sento subito un fruscio di passi e di stoffa.... Ho avuto paura!... Mi son messo a gridare:—No! No!... Basta!—coprendomi gli occhi con le mani. Tremavo come un bambino, sudavo freddo.

—Quella donna aveva contato sulla tua immaginazione, l'aveva eccitata con queli strani riti....

—Ti sbagli. Ho pensato così di primo acchito; ma poi, riflettendo bene.... In due, saremo più forti. Vuoi provare?

—Proviamo!

Il dottor Maggioli s'interruppe per guardare attorno, nel salotto, e interrogare le signore che erano state ad ascoltare con evidenti segni di paura.

—Non vuol farci dormire questa notte!—disse la baronessa Lanari.

—Appunto, volevo sapere da lei se devo o no proseguire....

—Ormai!—fece la baronessa.—E poi ha detto che la prova è fallita....

—Non ricordo più—rispose il dottore—chi abbia scritto: «Se venissero a riferirmi che un tale ha portato via il Colosseo, prima di rispondere:—È impossibile—andrei a vedere.» Io la penso come costui; e gli scienziati, secondo me, dovrebbero comportarsi così. Fui puntuale, all'ora fissata; la donna arrivò poco dopo. Lo studio del mio amico aveva due balconi, uno a levante, l'altro a mezzogiorno, e una larga ondata di sole lo invadeva in quel punto.—Ho avuto a stento il permesso—disse la evocatrice.—Da chi?—domandai.—Dai miei superiori—rispose semplicemente.—Questo signore è un incredulo—soggiunse rivolta al mio amico.—E gli spiriti non si mostrano volentieri a chi non crede.—Voglio credere—dissi.—Sono qui per questo. Costei—pensavo intanto—mette le mani avanti! E la osservai attentamente mentre si accingeva a disporre dietro la tenda del balcone l'orciolo con l'olio, la candela accesa e il piattino col sale. Nessun indizio di furberia su quel viso, ma una grande stanchezza, la stanchezza della miseria.—E chi vi ha insegnato?—le domandai.—Mia madre—rispose. Stiano attenti. Gli spiriti non entreranno qui; attraverseranno il corridoio, passando davanti all'uscio.—E si nascose dietro la tenda. Parlava con tale sicurezza, da spingermi a pensare: Tu forse stai per vedere un prodigio! Eravamo, il mio amico ed io, in piedi, in faccia all'uscio. A un tratto, il mio amico mi afferra una mano, e comincia a stringermela forte. Non mi distolsi dal guardare verso il corridoio, pur comprendendo che quegli aveva paura. Io mi sentivo tranquillissimo, senza diffidenza.... Dieci minuti di intensa aspettazione....

Then the woman came out from behind the curtain.

"'Did you see them?' she said.

"'No.'

"'You didn't see them?' My friend asked, almost stuttering and pale as a dead man.

"'Seven,' he added. 'I counted them. Four women and three men. They looked like they were made of fog, with long white tunics. . . They passed slowly. I squeezed your hand hard in that terrible moment. And that light!'

"'I saw nothing!'

"'He doesn't believe!' said the woman. 'To be able to see, you need to have the gift.'

"Perhaps it is so. You have to have the gift, as she said, that is, a natural disposition, a special power. What do we really know of these things? And my friend remained so convinced that he was not the victim of a hallucination, that he died still wondering about my good faith. He believed that I had refused to admit seeing anything, out of a materialistic physician's stubbornness. But that's not the case."

e la donna uscì fuori dalla tenda.

—Ha veduto?—disse.

—No.

—Non li hai veduti?—esclamò il mio amico quasi balbettando.

Era pallido come un morto.

—Sette—soggiunse.—Li ho contati; quattro donne e tre uomini.... come fatti di nebbia, con lunghe tuniche bianche.... Sono passati lentamente.... Ti ho stretto forte la mano nel terribile momento. E quella gran luce?

—Non ho visto nulla!

—Non crede!—disse la donna.—Per vedere bisogna avere la grazia....

Forse è così: bisogna avere la grazia, come ella si esprimeva, cioè una disposizione naturale, una facoltà speciale. Che ne sappiamo? E il mio amico è rimasto talmente convinto di non essere stato vittima di un'allucinazione, che è morto sospettando sempre della mia buona fede. Ha creduto che io abbia negato di aver visto per cocciutaggine di medico materialista. E non è vero.

THE SUGGESTION

TO L. ANTONIO VILLARI

At Efisio Chiardi's answer, Bedini made a gesture of disbelief.

"And not only," added Chiardi, "am I not in love with that lady, but I actively can't stand her! I find her unpleasant. . . I can't stand her!"

"Now you are exaggerating," he said. "I understand, to a certain extent, your wish for privacy. But from this, to want me to believe that you find her unpleasant, that you can't stand her. . . please!"

"Wish for privacy? With you, my dear Bedini? Oh, no!"

"And if I told you where I heard this?"

"I would convince you in two words that it's an unreliable source."

"Well. . . I heard it from someone's mother!"

"Yours?"

"No, hers."

"From Lady Carlotta?. . . I am flabbergasted!"

Indeed, two days before, having met Lady Carlotta Nerucci in Piazza di Spagna with a large bunch of white chrysanthemums in her hand, Bedini had stopped to inquire about her husband's health, who, on the last Thursday — the Neruccis received friends at home each Thursday night — had not come in the card room for the usual game of *scopa*, a great favorite of his.

"Still sick?"

"Gone quail hunting in Fiumicino! I never worry about him when he says he doesn't feel well. He's made of steel. But I am worried about. . . Ah, these blessed daughters!"

"Miss Amelia? She appears to be in remarkable health!"

"Don't pretend you don't know! How well you do it!"

Of course he pretended well! He didn't know anything.

"But. . .! Is it possible?"

Lady Carlotta was very surprised.

Bedini was absolutely mortified to ignore what, according to Lady Carlotta, *everyone* already knew. And perhaps to charitably save him from that incredible feeling of inferiority in which he found himself in front of that *everyone*, she had told him, taking his arm while they were walking up Salita San Sebastiano, all the details of the painful story. That same story that now stupefied Efisio Chiardi, who, in turn, had heard what *everyone* knew, repeated almost word for word from Bedini.

"In short," Bedini concluded, "is it true or is it not true that you discreetly courted Miss Amelia?"

"I? I ran from that house, rather, and never went back, as soon as I suspected that certain readings, imposed on me by the young lady and that I suffered through for an excess of politeness, could have been misunderstood. . ."

"Ah, reading together! Well, well! You should have imagined where this kind of thing would lead."

"It was, for me, a bit of practice in a foreign language. . . and nothing else."

SUGGESTIONE

A L. ANTONIO VILLARI

Alla risposta di Efisio Chiardi, Bedini fece una mossa d'incredulità.

—E non solamente—soggiunse Chiardi—non sono innamorato di quella signorina, ma non la posso sopportare! Mi è antipatica…. Non la posso sopportare!

—Ora esageri!—disse lui.—Capisco, fino a un certo punto, la tua riserbatezza. Ma da questo al volermi dare a intendere che ti è antipatica, che non la puoi soffrire… scusa….

—Riserbatezza?… Con te, caro Bedini? Ma no!

—E se ti rivelassi da quale fonte ho potuto attingere la notizia?

—Ti convincerei con due parole che è fonte inquinata.

—Ebbene… L'ho saputo dalla mamma!

—Tua?

—No, di lei.

—Dalla signora Carlotta?… Casco dalle nuvole!

Infatti, due giorni prima, incontrata in piazza di Spagna la signora Carlotta Nerucci con un gran mazzo di crisantemi bianchi in mano, Bedini l'aveva fermata per chiederle notizie sulla salute del marito che, l'ultimo giovedì—i Nerucci ricevevano gli amici ogni giovedì sera—non era comparso nella stanza da gioco per la immancabile partita a scopa, suo grande divertimento.

—Ancora malato?

—A caccia di quaglie, a Fiumicino! Io non mi preoccupo mai per lui, quando dice di non sentirsi bene. È di acciaio. Mi impensierisce invece… Ah queste benedette figliuole!

—La signorina Amelia? Eppure sembra in ottima salute!

—Non faccia l'ignaro! Come sa fingere bene!

Lo credo che fingeva bene! Non sapeva niente.

—Ma…! È possibile?

La signora Carlotta era molto sorpresa.

Bedini era proprio mortificato di ignorare quello che, come diceva la signora Carlotta, già sapevano tutti. E forse per farlo caritatevolmente uscire da quell'incredibile stato di inferiorità in cui si trovava di fronte a *tutti*, prendendolo per un braccio, verso la salita di San Sebastiano, lei gli aveva raccontato per filo e per segno la dolorosa istoria che faceva ora stupire Efisio Chiardi udendola ripetere, quasi con le stesse parole, da lui.

—Insomma—conchiuse Bedini—è vero o non è vero che tu hai fatto discretamente la corte alla signorina Amelia?

—Io? Io, invece, sono scappato via da quella casa, e non vi sono più ritornato, appunto quando sospettai che certe letture insieme, impostemi dalla signorina e da me sopportate per eccesso di cortesia, potevano far supporre…

—Ah, le letture insieme!… Dovevi immaginare dove saresti andato a finire.

—Si trattava, per me, di un po' di esercizio di inglese… e di nient'altro.

"Is it true or is it not true that Lady Carlotta, a serious and thoughtful mother, one evening made an appearance in the living room in lieu of her daughter, and told you that those readings could cause a scandal, and that, if you had good and honest intentions. . .?"

"I didn't let her finish. I answered, 'My dear Lady, I have no intentions of any sort, neither good nor bad; and even if I had them, and very honest ones, my financial condition would prevent me from expressing them. I know my duty, as a gentleman.' What should I have told her? 'Your daughter is ugly and unpleasant, and I don't come to your house on Thursday evenings for her, but to meet someone else?'"

"I can only imagine what a sad countenance you must have assumed during your little speech! Lady Carlotta said you barely restrained your tears. . ."

"Tears of laughter, perhaps."

"She was deeply moved, too, and she said to her daughter, 'Poor man! You must resign yourself to waiting. He left here as if he had nothing left to live for!'"

"Right! I was whistling, going down the stairs! They're both crazy, the pair of them!"

"And Miss Amelia is now tormented, for her own sake and yours, more for yours than for hers; she even fears that one of these days you might commit some foolish act out of despair! . . . Each day, she is more consumed by sorrow, grateful for your discretion, for your heroic sincerity. She will be yours, or no one else's! And her mother, in order not to contradict her and make things worse, endorses her decision, 'Yes, his, or no one else's!'"

"Crazy, I tell you, mother and daughter!"

"Listen: You must feel some remorse. You probably didn't imagine that a little courting could produce such serious consequences."

"Nothing! Nothing! I swear. And since that night I made myself scarce. If I meet them in the street, I hide; I avoid going to gatherings where I suspect that I might run into them. . ."

"Too much caution! They are right to imagine you are inconsolable."

"But there is no way to convince them of their error!"

"So you already knew. . .?"

"Yes, I knew something. I couldn't imagine, however, that their nonsense had come to this point."

"Really! To me, you seem proud of having caused such a serious feeling in a girl's heart."

"If she were at least beautiful!"

"She is young."

"Affected, pretentious, and ridiculously sentimental!"

"And yet I think she wouldn't be a bad wife, despite the ugliness, which after all isn't so bad. At a first glance, yes, I don't disagree. . ."

"Then you marry her!"

"Alas, no. 'Yours or no one else's,'" Bedini said comically. "When some girls get an idea in their head. . . they are terrible! I think yours is capable of dying for it!"

"She's not mine! But I feel sorry for her."

—È vero o non è vero, inoltre, che la signora Carlotta, da mamma seria e oculata, una sera si fece trovare lei in salotto, invece della figlia, e ti disse che quelle letture potevano essere male interpretate dalle persone, e che, se tu avevi buone e oneste intenzioni…?

—Non la lasciai finire; risposi:—Signora mia, non ho intenzioni di nessuna sorta, nè buone nè cattive; e anche se le avessi, e onestissime, le mie condizioni finanziarie mi impedirebbero di manifestarle; so il mio dovere di galantuomo.—Che cosa dovevo dirle? Sua figlia è brutta, antipatica, ed io non frequento i suoi giovedì per lei, ma per un'altra persona?

—Chissà che aria triste hai preso parlando! La signora Carlotta ti ha visto frenare a stento le lagrime….

—Le risa, semmai.

—Era profondamente commossa anche lei; e per ciò disse alla figlia:—Poverino! Bisogna rassegnarsi ad attendere; è andato via più morto che vivo!—

—Fischiettando per le scale! Sono matte, madre e figlia!

—E la signorina Amelia ora si tormenta per lei e per te, più per te che per lei; ha persino paura che un giorno o l'altro tu non commetta qualche pazzia per la disperazione!… Si consuma a vista d'occhio, gratissima del tuo riserbo, della tua eroica sincerità. Sarà tua, o di nessun altro! E la mamma, per non contrariarla e non far peggio, l'approva, la asseconda:—Sì, sua, o di nessun altro!—

—Sono matte, madre e figlia!

—Senti: qualche rimorso devi averlo. Probabilmente non ti immaginavi che un po' di corte poteva produrre così gravi conseguenze.

—Niente! Niente! Te lo giuro. E da quella sera in poi non mi sono più fatto vivo. Se le incontro per via, mi nascondo; evito di andare nelle riunioni dove sospetto che potrei imbattermi in loro….

—Troppe cautele! Hanno ragione di immaginare che non sai come consolarti.

—Ma se non c'è verso di disingannarle!

—Dunque già sapevi….

—Sì, qualche cosa sapevo; non potevo però immaginare che la loro sciocchezza fosse arrivata fino al punto che tu mi dici.

—Ma dai! Mi sembri già orgoglioso di aver prodotto così grave guasto nel cuore di una ragazza.

—Fosse bella almeno!

—È giovane.

—Leziosa, pretenziosa, ridicolmente sentimentale!

—Eppure io credo che non sarebbe una cattiva moglie, nonostante la bruttezza, che non è poi tanta. A prima vista, sì, non dico di no….

—Spòsala!

—O tua o di nessun altro!—esclamò comicamente Bedini.—Quando certe ragazze si mettono in testa un'idea… sono tremende! Quella, vedi, è capace di morirne!

—La compiango.

Bedini began noticing that, from that day on, whenever they were together, Efisio Chiardi, on some pretext or other, brought the topic of the conversation around to Miss Nerucci's fixation, as he called it.

"It seems to me that people are making a concerted effort to make her appear even more annoying in my eyes!" he would say. "Everyone talks about her, about her great passion; and several people have already made me understand that they consider me, if not exactly dishonest, certainly not very sensitive. . . It makes me so angry!"

"Let them talk. Is your conscience clear?"

"Extremely."

"I can tell you, however, that mother and daughter have not only a great deal of esteem for you, but they are deeply concerned about your welfare. They are convinced that you suffer, that you have no peace, that you can't sleep any more, can't laugh any more, and you have an unhealthy fixation. . .!"

"Really! It's an aberration!"

***

A month later, Efisio Chiardi, walking with Bedini on the great avenue of the Pincio, nearly deserted because of the late hour, had told him, "I feel pity for Miss Amelia. She deluded herself; it is excusable. Perhaps no one before had shown himself as attentive to her as I did. But her mother is unforgivable. She, a woman of age and experience, should have understood the true meaning of my words and my conduct. Instead, what did she do? She nurtured and strengthened the illusion in her daughter, perhaps because of the absurd vanity of making everyone believe her daughter was capable of inspiring a great passion. . . How else can one otherwise explain her mania for telling people her daughter is unhappy and that there is another person (me!) unhappy as well? The funniest thing of all is that the more I protest that I'm *not* unhappy, the more they convince themselves that I say so only to hide the serious state of my heart from the young lady, in the hope that she, at least, might forget me, since I can't forget her!"

And a few weeks later, picking up the subject again, on the pretext of the wedding of a mutual friend who had the fortitude to marry a girl with a slight hump – or perhaps a limp, I don't remember exactly – but very rich, anyway, Efisio Chiardi declared: "Well, I can understand that someone could marry an ugly woman, or at least a not beautiful one – often ugliness and beauty in a woman are in the eyes of the beholder – provided that he does so for love, for passion. That I can understand. Love is a great excuse, especially if it is mutual – because often someone only marries a woman to try and forget another; it may seem absurd, but it happens. But to marry, as Sarti did, some kind of monster because she has a rich dowry, it's unworthy of an honest man. It may be a business like any other, a successful speculation; but it also means selling your name, alienating your freedom. . . I myself, you see, would consider myself inexcusable if I arrived to think, in my case: 'You are loved; then marry her, even if you don't love her. Perhaps love will come later on.'"

"And you wouldn't be wrong," Bedini interrupted.

"On the contrary, I would be very wrong. I would allow myself to suffer an offense."

"An offense?"

Aveva notato che da quel giorno in poi, ogni volta che si trovavano insieme, Efisio Chiardi, con questo o con quel pretesto, faceva cadere il discorso intorno alla fissazione, come la chiamava, della signorina Nerucci.

—Sembra che la gente si sia messa d'accordo per rendermela più noiosa!—esclamava.—Tutti mi parlano di lei, della sua gran passione; e parecchi mi hanno già fatto capire che mi considerano, se non disonesto a dirittura, certamente poco delicato…. Mi fa infuriare!

—Lasciali ciarlare. La tua coscienza è tranquilla?

—Tranquillissima.

—Io però posso dirti che madre e figlia hanno non solamente grandissima stima di te, ma si affliggono profondamente della tua sorte. Sono convinte che tu soffri, che non hai pace, che non dormi più, che non ridi più, cou un pensiero fisso…!

—È un'aberrazione, addirittura!

***

Un mese dopo, Efisio Chiardi, passeggiando con lui pei il gran viale del Pincio, che in quell'ora era quasi deserto, gli diceva:

—La signorina Amelia mi fa pietà. Si è potuta illudere; è scusabile. Forse nessuno si era mostrato con lei così compiacente come me. Imperdonabile però è la sua mamma. Avrebbe dovuto capire lei, donna di età e di esperienza, il vero significato delle mie parole e della mia condotta. Invece, che cosa ha fatto? Ha alimentato, ha rafforzato l'illusione della figlia, forse per la stupida vanità di far credere che ha potuto ispirare una gran passione…. Come spiegare altrimenti la manìa di raccontare alla gente che sua figlia è infelice e che c'è un'altra persona—io—infelice altrettanto? Il bello è che più io protesto di non sentirmi affatto infelice, e più esse si incaponiscono a credere che parli così per nascondere alla signorina il grave stato del mio cuore, perchè mi dimentichi almeno lei, non potendo dimenticarla io!—

E qualche settimana dopo, riprendendo lo stesso argomento a proposito delle nozze di un comune amico che aveva avuto il coraggio di sposare una ragazza un po' gobba,—o un po' sciancata, non ricordo bene—ma molto ricca, Efisio Chiardi dichiarava:

—Ecco, io capisco che uno sposi anche una brutta o una non bella—spesso la bruttezza e la bellezza della donna sono modi di vedere di chi guarda—purchè lo faccia per amore, per passione; lo capisco. L'amore è una grande scusa, specialmente se reciproco—perchè spesso qualcuno sposa unicamente per levarsi una donna dal cuore; pare assurdo, ed è vero.—Ma sposare, come ha fatto Sarti, una specie di mostro perchè fornita di ricca dote, è cosa indegna di uomo onesto. Sarà un affare come un altro, una speculazione ben riuscita; ma è pure un vendere il proprio nome, un alienare la propria libertà… Io stesso, vedi, mi considererei inescusabile se arrivassi a fare questo ragionamento nel caso mio:—Sei amato; spòsala dunque, anche se tu non l'ami. Può anche darsi che in te l'amore nasca dopo.—

—E non ragioneresti male—lo interruppe Bedini.

—Malissimo. Mi piegherei a subire un sopruso.

—Quale?

"Someone else's passion. I confess to you that the more I think about it, the more I feel indignant."

"Why do you think about it at all?"

"Because it seems to me that all of you have agreed not to let me think of anything else. I can't approach a friend, an acquaintance, even someone who doesn't attend Nerucci's Thursdays at home, without having them say to me, 'So, then?. . . When is this wedding going to happen?. . . Decide, once and for all!' They might as well grab me by the neck and shake me. And they make that poor girl appear even more hateful to me, that girl who after all – as a woman – is perhaps not ideal, but is a good, virtuous, rare homemaker, and probably would, I agree with you, make an excellent wife. . ."

"Certainly," Bedini said.

"But what can I tell you?" Chiardi continued. "The way she imposes herself on me! Her insistence on making people believe I'm madly in love and madly loved! You must admit, it is simply too much. If I let myself be flattered, if in a moment of weakness. . . Oh! Afterward, I would come to hate myself. I have only one pride, that of my freedom. I would twist her mother's neck. The girl – I have to be fair – I don't consider her guilty. She is deluded, but sincere. Yesterday, in fact, I thought I would write her a long letter to make her understand her error, to put an end to her state of tormented excitement. . . I pity her, I've told you many times. I'm sorry to be the involuntary cause. . . very involuntary, I swear. . . I wouldn't lie to you. If I had the slightest shadow of guilt, if by lightness or even inadvertence, I felt I had contributed to making her think. . . Nothing! I swear to you. That's why I feel sorry for her. Shall I tell you something? If I look at her from a distance, with the eyes of imagination, I could almost think that, perhaps, she is not quite as ugly as she seemed at first. In fact, she has an excellent body. It isn't unimportant. . . And she does have a certain grace. . . And that sentimentality of hers, on second thought, is not a serious defect. . . Yesterday, as I said, I thought of writing her a long letter. I was already halfway through; but then I thought, 'What's the point? She won't believe you. She'll just assume that it's something concocted with her relatives, or another heroic act of yours. . .' It seems that she believes me capable of any heroism. . . And, so, I tore it up. . . Oh! I'm annoyed, annoyed, annoyed!"

"So I gather. That's why I no longer bring it up. You, however. . ."

"I vent to you because you know me better than the others, you understand, and, unlike the rest of them, you are not so silly as to ask, 'This wedding, when?'"

Bedini had observed how much the language of Efisio Chiardi had changed since the first time he had mentioned Miss Nerucci to him: 'She is unpleasant; I can't stand her. She's ugly, affected, pretentious, ridiculously sentimental!' Now, instead, he was close to finding her beautiful in the right light. . . He recognized in her a certain grace, and he no longer found her sentimentality reproachable. . . What did these changes mean? He had no explanation.

Especially in matters of the heart, Efisio Chiardi loved being mysterious. It was only by chance that Bedini had discovered some of his friend's female relationships. And Bedini appreciated such privacy very much, though he was very curious – and he didn't try to hide it – about other people's business.

—La passione altrui. Ti confesso che più ci ripenso su e più mi indigno.

—Perchè ci ripensi?

—Perchè pare che tutti vi siate messi d'accordo per non farmi pensare ad altro. Non posso avvicinare un amico, un conoscente anche di quelli che non frequentano i giovedì di casa Nerucci, senza sentirmi dire:—Dunque?... Queste nozze quando?... Si decida una buona volta!—Vogliono prendermi pel collo, violentarmi; e mi rendono maggiormente odiosa quella povera ragazza, che infine poi—come donna—non è forse un ideale, ma è buona, virtuosa, rara donna di casa, e probabilmente sarebbe, sono di accordo con te, ottima moglie...

—Certamente—soggiunse Bedini.

—Ma che vuoi?—riprese Chiardi.—Con questo modo d'imporsi! Con questo voler far credere che io sia innamorato pazzo e pazzamente amato! Devi ammetterlo, è troppo. Se mi lasciassi lusingare, se in un momento di debolezza... Oh! Dopo, arriverei a sentire orrore di me stesso. Ho un solo orgoglio, quello della mia libertà. Io torcerei il collo a quella mamma. La ragazza—sono giusto—non la considero colpevole. È illusa, ma sincera. Ieri, appunto, pensavo di scriverle una lunga lettera per disingannarla, per far cessare quel suo stato di tormentoso eccitamento... Mi fa pietà, te l'ho detto più volte. Mi dispiace di essere involontaria causa... Involontarissima, te lo giuro... con te non farei misteri. Se avessi una minima ombra di colpa, se per leggerezza, o anche per inavvertenza, sentissi di aver contribuito a farle sospettare... Niente! Te lo giuro. Per questo m'ispira pietà. Debbo confessartelo? Quasi quasi, ora, guardata da lontano con gli occhi dell'immaginazione, non la giudico più tanto brutta quanto mi è parsa sempre. Ha un bel corpo. Non è poco... E una certa grazia di modi... E quella stessa sua sentimentalità, riflettendoci bene, non è un grave difetto... Ieri, dunque, pensavo di scriverle una lunga lettera; l'avevo anzi scritta a metà; ma poi mi son detto:—A che serve? Non ti crederà. Potrà supporre che sia una cosa combinata con i parenti, oppure un altro tuo atto eroico...—A quel che pare mi crede capace di ogni eroismo...—Ed ho stracciato il foglio... Oh! Sono seccato, seccato, seccato!

—Me ne accorgo; per questo non te ne ho riparlato più. Sei tu ora...

—Mi sfogo con te che mi conosci meglio degli altri, che comprendi, e non sei sciocco da ripetermi come gli altri:—Queste nozze, quando?—

Bedini intanto osservava quanto mutato era il linguaggio di Efisio Chiardi dalla prima volta che gli aveva accennato della signorina Nerucci:—Mi è antipatica; non la posso soffrire. È brutta, leziosa, pretensiosa, ridicolmente sentimentale!—Ora, invece, per poco non la diceva bella... Le riconosceva certa grazia di modi, e più non ne trovava biasimevole la sentimentalità... Che cosa voleva dire questo cangiamento? Non riusciva a spiegarselo.

In fatto di amori specialmente, Efisio Chiardi amava il mistero. Soltanto per caso Bedini aveva scoperto qualche relazione femminile del suo amico; e tanta circospezione gli piaceva, anche se era molto curioso—non lo nascondeva—dei fatti altrui.

He was interested in it, he enjoyed it, maybe because he was an idler and he had no better way to employ his time. You could say he had the instincts of a police inspector. . . Well, yes! He didn't blush in confessing that he had occasionally followed, for weeks, for months, a love affair between people he barely knew, merely because a gesture, a glance, had made him realize that under apparent indifference they were concocting something that deserved to be uncovered. And he couldn't rest until he did.

That unexpected change in language had peaked his interest, and he was curious. Was Efisio simply pulling his leg? Were the Nerucci ladies, mother and daughter, actually correct? It seemed to him that his friend had involuntarily betrayed himself. The contradiction between his words on that first day and his latest declaration was evident. As always, he wanted to be mysterious. But even with him? To what purpose? And his investigative instincts saw, hiding in the shadows, the possibility of a great enterprise. He would pull the thread Chiardi had put into his hands by means of that involuntary contradiction and penetrate, guided by it, into the labyrinth of the facts and his heart. And then, at last, tell him with a smile: "Why were you not honest with me? I was unconvinced. And now I know as much, and perhaps more, than you know yourself. I see how things are!" It would be a great satisfaction, an excellent revenge!

***

But just then, Bedini had to leave Rome, and, in the three months he was away, his curiosity was further whetted by the letters that Efisio Chiardi wrote to him every week. Two-page letters at first, then four, then eight, and they would have reached the length of a book, if Bedini's sojourn at the National Library of Florence had not finally ended.

On the pretext of keeping him informed on Roman gossip, especially regarding their circle of friends, Efisio Chiardi wrote to him only of Miss Nerucci, who was evoking in him a growing and ever deeper pity.

"You know, this is an interesting case! I don't want to deal with her at all, and instead I'm forced to deal with nothing else. Her witch of a mother travels about Rome with the express purpose of letting everyone know about my misfortune. She talks more about me than she does about her daughter and I am the object of her commiseration. It makes me look ridiculous. Now, when I meet someone, not a minute passes before whoever it is, brimming with compassion, tells me, 'Have courage! Let it go. She isn't the only girl in the world!' I protest, I get angry and it only makes things worse. No one will believe me. Regardless of what I say or do, I remain the unhappy lover in everyone's eyes!"

And a few days later:

"I'm furious. I met Babolani, that great gossip; remember him? That long, thin man with a crooked nose, who some time ago had tried to be a newspaper reporter, and now he is the publicist for I don't know what company. I hadn't seen him in ages. He pestered me for two eternal hours! Can you believe it? Now even her father appears on stage! Babolani says that Mr. Nerucci talked to him about me, praising, as usual, my delicacy of feeling. As for my financial condition, Babolani says that I am exaggerating, that I should have more confidence in myself. And after all, her family could easily help me find a job, if necessary! They have so many contacts! I would be worshiped in that house. Her parents would make any sacrifice to see their daughter happy.

Lo interessavano, lo divertivano, forse perchè era uno sfaccendato e non sapeva come impiegar meglio il suo tempo. Direte che aveva istinti polizieschi... Ebbene, sì! Non arrossiva di confessare che qualche volta aveva seguito, per settimane, per mesi, un intrigo amoroso di persone che conosceva appena di vista, unicamente perchè un gesto, un'occhiata gli avevano fatto scorgere che sotto l'apparente indifferenza esse tramavano chi sa che cosa meritevole di essere scoperta. Nè si era mai dato pace fino a che non l'aveva scoperta.

Quell'inatteso cambiamento di linguaggio gli aveva fatto rizzare le orecchie, e lo aveva incuriosito. Che l'amico Efisio volesse farsi giuoco di lui? Che le signore Nerucci, madre e figlia, avessero ragione? Gli sembrava che Chiardi, suo malgrado, si fosse tradito. La contraddizione tra le parole del primo giorno e queste ultime era evidentissima. Come sempre, voleva fare il misterioso. Anche con lui? A che scopo? E il suo istinto poliziesco vedeva presentarsi, nell'ombra, una bella impresa da tentare: afferrare il filo che Chiardi gli aveva messo in mano con quell'involontaria contradizione, e penetrare, guidato da esso, nel labirinto dei fatti e nel cuore di lui e poi, all'ultimo, dirgli sorridendo:—Perchè non sei stato sincero? Non sei riuscito a sviarmi. So quanto te, e forse meglio di te stesso, come stanno le cose!—Sarebbe stata una gran soddisfazione, una bella rivincita!

* * *

Ma appunto in quei giorni Bedini aveva dovuto assentarsi da Roma, e la sua curiosità era stata acuita durante i tre mesi di lontananza, dalle lettere che Efisio Chiardi gli scriveva ogni settimana regolarmente; lettere di due pagine dapprima, poi di quattro, poi di otto, e che avrebbero raggiunto la grossezza di un volume, se la missione di Bedini presso la Biblioteca Nazionale di Firenze non fosse finalmente terminata.

Con la scusa di tenerlo informato dei pettegolezzi romani, del circolo dei loro amici specialmente, Efisio Chiardi gli parlava soltanto della signorina Nerucci che gli ispirava crescente e sempre più profonda pietà.

«Ma sai che è un bel caso questo! Non vorrei affatto occuparmi di lei e invece sono costretto a non occuparmi quasi di altro. Quella strega della sua mamma sembra vada attorno unicamente per far sapere a tutti la mia disgrazia; parla più di me che di sua figlia. Sono oggetto della sua commiserazione; mi copre di ridicolo. Ora non posso più stare un minuto senza che qualcuno non mi dica compassionevolmente:—Coraggio! Lascia andare. Non c'è lei sola al mondo!—Protesto, mi arrabbio, e faccio peggio. Nessuno vuole credermi; devo passare per forza da innamorato infelice!»

E alcuni giorni dopo:

«Sono furibondo. Ho incontrato Babolani, il gran chiacchierone; lo ricordi? Quel coso lungo, magro e col naso storto, che qualche tempo fa aveva tentato di fare il *reporter* di giornali, ed ora fa l'agente pubblicitario per non so quale ditta. Non lo vedevo da un secolo. Mi ha rotto le scatole due eterne ore! Capisci? Ora viene in scena anche il padre! Babolani dice che il signor Nerucci gli ha parlato di me. Elogi, al solito, della mia delicatezza di sentire. Le mie condizioni? Oh, io esagero! Dovrei avere maggior fiducia in me stesso. E poi la sua famiglia potrebbe facilmente aiutarmi a trovare un impiego, caso mai! Con tante conoscenze! Sarei adorato in quella casa. I genitori, pur di vedere felice la loro figliola, farebbero qualunque sacrificio.

But no sacrifice is necessary. Why am I so obstinate? Don't I see the miserable condition I am in? Not only am I wasting away, my obstinacy consigns that poor creature to do the same! This is what I have to hear! That I'm wasting away! And I've never been so healthy, so cheerful, so careless! They are all driving me crazy. . . I sent him to hell!"

And finally:

"We found ourselves face-to-face! It was impossible to avoid her. She was alone. . . As soon as she saw me. . . I swear, I was so terribly afraid! What if she had approached me? If she had asked me. . . ? I don't know what I feared she could ever ask, at that moment, suddenly. But I do know that I had no idea what I would have answered. . . She seemed to me another woman!. . . A better one. . . I must tell you that I only saw her eyes. . . Those eyes that were always beautiful, I mean, big, expressive. In the past, it seemed to me that she was slightly abusing their great expressiveness, as a sentimental pose. You used to agree; but maybe we were both wrong. Now, I confide to you in the most secret intimacy of a letter, they were just beautiful, so pious, so imploring!. . . And so resigned! She gave me just one glance and moved away, with a dignified countenance. I must have seemed a lunatic to her. Lucky that no one saw us! Otherwise, who knows how many additions people would make to the legend of our unfortunate love!

"I now understand that unrequited love can even effect a miraculous physical transformation of its victim. Can you imagine that I, I! am willing to judge Amelia favorably, I, who because of her have had so many sorrows, so many troubles, so many annoyances! When I think of all the bile that she and her silly mother have made me spill! If I, therefore, biased as I am against her, must acknowledge the extraordinary transformation that has taken place in her person, it means that this transformation must be both profound and evident. I am happy for Amelia: Not all troubles end in harm, then! And so, when this little comedy of ours will finally come to an end – soon, I hope, for every good game should last but a short time, and this one has gone on too long! – Amelia will have to be grateful to me for that benefit, even though I caused it involuntarily; a very rare thing, because ordinarily dead loves leave behind an inheritance of hatred and disdain. . ."

"Too much philosophizing, my friend!" Bedini exclaimed, folding the letter. And how is it that Miss Nerucci, the disgusting, the insufferable Miss Nerucci, has now become Amelia, and she is not only good, but almost beautiful to your eyes?"

***

And Bedini could not wait to go back to Rome to tell his friend Efisio, to his face: "Come on! Stop it! Marry her if you want; or at least court quietly, like everyone else. Spare us all the grimacing and the histrionics aimed at commiseration!"

He found Efisio Chiardi waiting for him at the train station. He looked like a man on tenterhooks. Impatient of every little delay, seeing that no porter was approaching, he had grasped one of Bedini's suitcases and had started toward the exit when his friend told him, "I don't know about you, but I'm stopping at the restaurant. I'm starving."

Chiardi could not help a gesture of annoyance.

"Do you mind stopping for a bite?" Bedini said. "Of course, if you are in a hurry. . ."

"Yes, I am in a hurry to talk to you, to consult you."

E non occorre. Perchè mi ostino? Non mi accorgo dunque come mi sono ridotto? Mi consumo e faccio consumare quella povera creatura! Anche questo! Mi consumo! E non sono stato mai così bene in salute, così allegro, così spensierato! C'è da ammattire... L'ho mandato al diavolo!»

E all'ultimo:

«Ci siamo trovati faccia a faccia! È stato impossibile evitarla.

«Era sola... Appena si accorse di me... Ho avuto, ti giuro, una di quelle paure!... Se si avvicinava? Se mi domandava...? Non so che cosa temessi che ella potesse mai domandarmi, a bruciapelo, in quel momento. So però che non sapevo che cosa avrei potuto risponderle... Mi è sembrata un'altra!... In meglio... Già dovrei dirti che di lei ho visto soltanto gli occhi... che sono stati sempre belli, cioè grandi, espressivi. Allora, mi sembrava che lei abusasse un po' di questa loro efficace espressività, per posa sentimentale; lo dicevi anche tu; ma forse ci siamo ingannati. Ora, te lo confido con la più segreta intimità epistolare, erano proprio bellissimi, così pietosi, così imploranti!... E così rassegnati! Mi ha dato un solo sguardo ed è passata oltre, dignitosamente. Devo esserle parso uno stralunato. Fortuna che nessuno ci ha visto! Altrimenti chi sa quanti e quali aggiunte alla leggenda del nostro sventuratissimo amore!

«Ho capito in questa occasione che l'amore può persino operare il miracolo della trasformazione fisica della persona che ama. Figurati se io posso essere disposto a giudicare benevolmente Amelia, io che ho avuto per colpa sua tanti dispiaceri, tante noie, tante seccature!... Credo di essere diventato un po' verde dalla grande bile che mi hanno fatto venire lei e la sua sciocchissima mamma. Se dunque io, così prevenuto contro di lei, ho dovuto riconoscere la straordinaria trasformazione avvenuta nella sua persona, vuol dire che questa è proprio grande, ed evidentissima. Me ne rallegro con Amelia; tanto è vero che tutti i guai non vengono per nuocere! E così quando la nostra commediola finirà—presto, spero; ogni bel gioco dovrebbe durare poco, e questo dura da troppo!—Amelia dovrà essermi grata di tal beneficio, quantunque le sia stato causato involontariamente; cosa assai rara, perchè ordinariamente gli amori morti lasciano dietro un'eredità di odi, di sdegni...»

—Filosofeggi troppo, caro mio! esclamò Bedini, ripiegando la lettera. E poi, come mai la signorina Nerucci, l'antipatica, l'insoffribile signorina Nerucci è diventata ora Amelia, e non soltanto buona ma quasi bella, per te?

* * *

E non vedeva l'ora di tornare a Roma per poter dire sul viso all'amico Efisio: Su! Finitela! Sposatevi, se ne avete voglia; o fate all'amore tranquillamente, come gli altri fedeli cristiani, senza smorfie, senza posa per farvi compassionare!

Trovò Efisio Chiardi alla stazione. Pareva un uomo sulle spine. Impaziente di ogni minimo indugio, vedendo che non si avvicinava nessun facchino, aveva preso lui una delle valigie del Bedini e si avviava verso l'uscita, quando questi gli disse:

—Ma io ho bisogno di fermarmi al ristorante; ho proprio fame.

Chiardi non potè frenare una mossa di disappunto.

—Ti dispiace? fece il Bedini. —Se hai fretta...

—Sì, ho fretta di parlarti, di consultarti...

"You will talk while I eat, if you don't want to eat something yourself."

"Thank you!"

"What's happened to you? There, let's sit at that corner table. . . So. . ." Bedini said, as soon as he had ordered.

"Do you believe in the power of suggestion?" Chiardi began. "You are looking at a victim of it! You stare? You laugh? There is nothing to laugh at. Hearing day after day from everyone that I am an unhappy lover, forced from morning to evening and from evening to morning to think incessantly about my fantastic misfortune. . ."

"Well, well! I get it!"

"I could beat my head against the wall! It means it was destined to be so."

"Save your head, please! There was no need for so many rhetorical obfuscations to let me know that finally. . ."

"Rhetorical obfuscations?"

"Well, what would you call them? You wanted to be your usual secretive self, but you didn't succeed. I confess, since we are at this point, that I never believed in your denials, and I see with pleasure that I have not deceived myself. You found a good excuse for doing what you have always intended: the power of suggestion! Tell it to someone else but with me, save your breath. Meanwhile I can ask you now: 'This wedding, when?' No, rolling your eyes and pretending to be angry is useless."

"But I am seriously angry! The power of suggestion, yes, dear Bedini. And if I wanted to make you believe that I'm sorry about it, I'd be lying. As I was saying, I could beat my head against the wall, thinking of how I will look in the eyes of so many people. . . But after all, why should I care? I'm going to make happy a creature that deserves to be such; and I'll make myself happy as well, because it doesn't happen every day to be loved as I am loved. How it happened, I couldn't explain to you. Try one day, try another. . . One morning I woke up, just like that, utterly in love, much to my surprise. . . It was fate! If it were otherwise, I wouldn't now need you, and your help as a friend. . . I was waiting for you with impatience; I want to get out of this embarrassing situation so I need someone to go and explain, to go and apologize for me. . . It's not easy. I am relying on your diplomatic skills. . . I've been improperly rude to everyone, with my denials. . . It was the truth. But not any more. . . If this isn't the power of suggestion. . .! Stop laughing, please."

"Better, better this way!" exclaimed Bedini at last getting control of himself. He did not believe his friend would make him look ridiculous, though this was, indeed, a comedy.

And the next day, at about five o'clock, he visited Lady Carlotta, happy and smiling, convinced he was bringing her beautiful and unexpected news. He had thought it desirable, for diplomatic delicacy, to approach the subject gradually, and he had been puzzled when she suddenly got very angry when he mentioned the name of Efisio Chiardi.

"What this man did is an unmentionable infamy!"

"Now, now, my dear lady!"

"Married, with children! What was he thinking?"

"My dear lady! Married? Who?"

"He! He!. . . We discovered it by accident."

—Parlerai mentre io mangerò, se non vuoi prendere qualche cosa anche tu.

—Grazie!

—Che ti accade?... Laggiù, a quel tavolino in disparte... Dunque...—soggiunse Bedini appena data l'ordinazione al cameriere.

—Credi tu alla suggestione? — cominciò Chiardi. —Eccone qui una vittima! Mi guardi negli occhi? Ridi? Non c'è niente da ridere. A furia di sentirmi ripetere da tutti che sono un innamorato infelice, a furia di esser costretto, dalla mattina alla sera e dalla sera alla mattina, a dover pensare incessantemente alla mia fantastica disgrazia...

—Bene, bene! Ho capito!

—Darei la testa contro il muro! Vuol dire che era destinato così.

—Rispàrmiati la testa! Non occorrevano tante precauzioni oratorie per farmi sapere che finalmente...

—Precauzioni oratorie?

—Come vorresti chiamarle? Hai voluto fare, al tuo solito, il misterioso, ma non ci sei riuscito. Ti confesso, giacchè siamo a questo, che non ho mai creduto alle tue negazioni, e veggo con piacere che non mi sono ingannato. L'hai trovata bene: Suggestione! Serbala per gli altri. Io intanto ora posso domandarti: — E questi confetti, quando? — È inutile stralunare gli occhi, fingere di arrabbiarti...

—Mi arrabbio seriamente! Suggestione, sì, caro Bedini. E se volessi darti a intendere che ne sia dispiacente, mentirei. Dicevo: darei la testa contro il muro, pensando alla figura che farò presso molte persone... Ma, infine, che dovrà importarmene, è vero? Rendo felice una creatura che merita di esser tale; e rendo felice anche me, perchè non capita tutti i giorni essere amato come sono amato io. Come sia accaduto, non saprei spiegartelo io stesso. Picchia oggi, picchia domani... E un bel mattino mi sono svegliato, proprio così, innamorato cotto, con mia grandissima maraviglia... Era destino! Se fosse diversamente, non avrei ora bisogno di te, della tua opera di amico... Ti attendevo con impazienza; voglio uscir subito da questa situazione imbarazzante. Bisogna che qualcuno vada a spiegare, vada a scusarmi... Non è facile. Conto sulla tua abilità diplomatica... Io sono stato d'una crudezza sconveniente nel negare a tutti... Era la verità. Oggi non più... Se non è suggestione questa...! Non ridere, te ne prego.

—Meglio, meglio così! — esclamò all'ultimo Bedini, convinto che il suo amico non gli avrebbe fatto fare una parte ridicola quantunque si trattasse di commedia.

E il giorno dopo, verso le cinque, si presentava alla signora Nerucci lieto e sorridente, sicuro di apportarle una bella e inattesa notizia. Aveva creduto opportuno, per finezza diplomatica, pigliarla molto larga, ed era rimasto interdetto vedendo scattar infuriata la signora Carlotta appena egli aveva pronunciato il nome di Efisio Chiardi.

—Quel che ha fatto costui è un'infamità senza nome!

—Rifletta, signora mia!

—Ammogliato, con figli! Che cosa si era immaginato dunque?...

—Signora! Ammogliato, chi?

—Lui! Lui!... L'abbiamo scoperto per caso.

"It can't be!"

"With a real witch, too, of whom he now is ashamed. . . In his village of Oneglia!"

Poor Bedini didn't know what to say. His awareness of Chiardi's secretive habits made him uncertain. It seemed to him impossible, however, that his friend could have been so brazen as to put him in the middle of such an indelicate matter. . . But Lady Carlotta wouldn't let him speak, repeating, "An unmentionable infamy! Fortunately, my daughter has already come back to her senses, and will marry a gentleman worthy of her next month!"

Bedini left the Nerucci home, relieved that his diplomatic nous had saved him from appearing to be an accomplice in such an awful deception and furious at Chiardi. Married to a witch he was ashamed of. Unbelievable!

Efisio Chiardi was waiting for him at the *Caffè del Parlamento*, with a cup of coffee that had cooled in front of him and an illustrated English newspaper in his hand that he browsed distractedly.

"That was fast!" he told him.

"Listen!. . . If it is true. . ." Bedini stammered.

"What?"

"If it is true that you have a wife and children. . ."

"I?"

"In your village."

"I. . .?"

"You should know, to start with, that the lady will be a bride next month!"

"Oh, Dear God!. . . But it's an infamy!"

"Lady Carlotta says so, too."

"Who could ever invent. . .?"

"Such things are not invented!"

"What wife? What children? I am a bachelor, a true bachelor!. . . I swear to you!"

"It's useless for you to protest. . . Perhaps it might be, what can I tell you, a sort of pretext to justify the change of heart in Lady Carlotta and her daughter. . . It wouldn't be a bad idea!. . . Oh, women!"

"But how? Must it end like this? Now that I. . ."

"You, too, will console yourself! In this world, you can console yourself for anything!"

"No, I have to prove my innocence. I don't want people believing me capable of such cowardly action! And I don't want to, no! No! Have my happiness stolen from me. . . I love her. . . you know. . . I love her, now!"

"As you'll love someone else. One love will cure you of another! As to finding out where this lie came from. . ."

"This slander!" Chiardi cried out, forgetting they were in a café.

"Calm down! You're making a scene. Let me take care of this."

"Who is this worm? Name him. I want his name! We'll settle the score between us!"

"I can't tell you. My astonishment was such that I forgot to ask Lady Carlotta who was going to marry her daughter."

"I'll find out; it won't be a mystery!"

—Non può essere!

—Con una bruttona, di cui ora si vergogna… Al suo paese, ad Oneglia!

Il povero Bedini non sapeva che cosa rispondere. Il contegno misterioso del Chiardi lo rendeva perplesso. Gli sembrava però impossibile che il suo amico avesse potuto spingere la sfacciataggine fino al punto di mettere in mezzo anche lui e in una faccenda così delicata… Ma la signora Carlotta gli chiudeva la bocca ripetendogli.

—Infamità senza nome! Per fortuna, mia figlia è già rinsavita, e sposerà, tra un mese, un gentiluomo degno di lei!

Bedini uscì di casa Nerucci rallegrandosi che la diplomazia lo avesse salvato dall'apparire complice di un brutto inganno, furioso contro Chiardi… ammogliato con una bruttona di cui si vergognava, come gli aveva affermato la signora Carlotta.

Efisio Chiardi lo attendeva al Caffè del Parlamento, con una tazza di caffè che gli si era freddato davanti e in mano un giornale inglese illustrato di cui sfogliava distrattamente le pagine, senza neppure guardarle.

—Hai fatto presto! — gli disse.

—Senti!… Se è vero…—balbettò Bedini.

—Che cosa?

—Se è vero che tu hai moglie e figli…

—Io?

—Al tuo paese.

—Io?…

—Intanto sappi che la signorina, tra un mese, sposa!…

—Oh, Dio!… Ma è un'infamità!

—Così dice pure la signora Carlotta!

—Chi ha potuto inventare?…

—Certe cose non s'inventano!

—Ma che moglie! Che figli! Sono scapolo, scapolissimo!… Te lo giuro!

—Tanto, è inutile che tu ti affanni a protestare… Sarà, che posso dirti, un pretesto per giustificare il voltafaccia suo e della sua figlia… Non è pensata male!…. Oh le donne!

—Ma come? Deve finire così? Ora che io…

—Ti consolerai, va' là, anche tu! Ci si consola di tutto a questo mondo!

—No, devo scolparmi; non voglio che mi si creda capace di così vigliacca azione! E non voglio, no! no! lasciarmi rubare la felicità… Io l'amo… capisci… io l'amo ora!

—Amerai un'altra. Chiodo scaccia chiodo! In quanto a scoprire da dove sia venuta fuori questa fandonia…

—Calunnia!—urlò il Chiardi, dimenticando di essere in un caffè.

—Zitto! Non far voltare la gente. Lascia fare a me.

—Chi è costui? Tu lo sai: voglio il nome! Ce la sbrigheremo tra noi due!

—Il mio stupore era tale in quel momento, che ho dimenticato di domandare alla signora Carlotta chi sposava sua figlia.

—Lo saprò; non sarà un mistero!

"Do you want to add ridicule on top of ridicule? Let me take care of this. And if I find something suspicious. . . But you have to admit that all this could have happened simply, naturally. . ."

"To saddle me with wife and children I don't have. . . Simply? Naturally. . . Bedini! Ah! You wanted to test me! Do I guess right? Tell me. Did you want to ascertain if I really love Amelia?"

"Don't go imagining things; not at all. You have a wife – and one so ugly you are ashamed of her – and children, plural. . . according to Lady Carlotta. And someone wants to prevent you from committing the crime of bigamy. . . according to Lady Carlotta. I have not invented anything; I wasn't testing you. . . And be a man! Who knows, perhaps one day you'll thank whoever this is for preventing you from committing a great foolishness. The power of suggestion, you said. Your will doesn't enter into it. Not even your heart. Your vanity, forgive me for saying it, probably does enter into it quite a lot. Perhaps even interest, unknowingly, a bit. . . And if the suggestion ends? And if you found yourself again as you were before?"

"I was an imbecile, then, I was blind. . . It can't end like this! It must not end like this! You'll see! You'll see!"

"Let me take care of this, I tell you again. Give me two or three days. You know what I'm like when I decide to find out something!"

Curious people are like great scientists or great inventors in that chance always helps them in a surprising way.

The culprit had been Babolani, the big gossip Babolani. Two days later, he bragged about it with Bedini, whom he had met by chance. "What can I tell you, my dear sir! I was feeling sorry for that girl. So I thought, *there is no other way to cure her.* And I told her father. . . I didn't tell a lie, you know. . . Efisio Chiardi has a wife and children. . . But he isn't *our* Efisio. From the village of Oneglia, though; I believe in that village everybody is called Efisio and everybody is called Chiardi. Isn't it true? And it worked perfectly, beautifully! No doubt my friend, Chiardi, will thank me profusely. It all turned out even better than I'd hoped. The young lady, you know? She is getting married. She consoled herself quite quickly, unless she is marrying him out of vengeance. Women are capable of anything! You know how these things go! All I had to do was "confide" to five or six people: 'They say Efisio Chiardi has a wife in his village, so ugly that he is ashamed of her, and he has children. . . Did you know?' And all six of them went to Nerucci to claim credit for such an important discovery. And that's the way it's done!. . . If I hadn't thought I was doing him a favor. . . Why are you laughing? What's so funny?"

"I laugh," Bedini answered, "because I realize that in this world far more comedies happen than are written."

"And funnier, too, you should add," said Babolani.

"It depends."

For Chiardi, this one in particular was not very funny. But he straightened himself out; and when he meets, arm in arm with her husband, she who had sworn to be his or no one else's, he cheers himself as one who has escaped a great danger, exclaiming: "Oh! She was too ugly! And she will get worse!. . . He can have her!"

THE END

—Vuoi aggiungere ridicolo a ridicolo? Lasciami fare. E se scopro qualcosa di losco, giacchè devi anche ammettere che tutto questo può essere avvenuto semplicemente, naturalmente....

—Appiopparmi moglie e figli che non ho?... Semplicemente? Naturalmente?... Bedini! Tu hai voluto mettermi alla prova! Indovino? Dimmi. Hai voluto convincerti se amo davvero Amelia?

—Non fantasticare; niente affatto. Hai moglie—e brutta da vergognartene—e figli... secondo la signora Carlotta... E c'è chi vuole impedirti di commettere un delitto di bigamia... secondo la signora Carlotta. Non ho inventato niente; non ho voluto metterti alla prova... E sii uomo! Chi sa se tu non debba un giorno ringraziare colui che forse ti impedisce di fare una grande sciocchezza. Suggestione, hai detto. Dunque la tua volontà non c'entra; il tuo cuore, nemmeno. La tua vanità, scusa, probabilmente c'entra molto; il calcolo, inconsapevolmente, un pochino... E se poi la suggestione finisse? E tu ti ritrovassi com'eri prima?

—Ero un imbecille allora, un cieco... Non può finire così! Non deve finire così! Vedrai! Vedrai!

—Lasciami fare, ti ripeto. Dammi due, tre giorni di tempo. Tu lo sai; quando mi metto in testa di scoprire una cosa!...

Ai curiosi succede come ai grandi scienziati o ai grandi inventori: il caso li aiuta in modo sorprendente.

Il colpevole era stato Babolani, il gran chiacchierone Babolani. Due giorni dopo se ne vantava con Bedini incontrato per caso.

—Che vuoi, caro mio! Quella ragazza mi faceva pena. Allora pensai: Non c'è altro modo di guarirla. E dissi al padre... Non ho detto una bugia sai?... Efisio Chiardi ha moglie e figli... ma non è lui, il nostro Efisio. Di Oneglia però; credo che in quel paese si chiamino tutti Efisio e tutti Chiardi. Non lo credi? Ed è andata bene, magnificamente! L'amico Chiardi dovrà accendermi un bel cero di ringraziamento. È andata anche, se vogliamo, troppo bene. La signorina, lo sai? prende marito. Si è consolata presto; se pure non lo prende per dispetto, per vendetta; le donne sono capaci di tutto! Guarda com'è il mondo! Ho confidato a cinque o sei persone: «Dicono che Efisio Chiardi ha moglie al suo paese; così brutta, ch'egli se ne vergogna, e figli... Che ne sapete?» E tutte e sei sono andate dai Nerucci a farsi un merito della scoperta. Guarda com'è il mondo!... Se non fosse stato a fin di bene... Perchè ridi?... Che pensi?

—Rido—rispose Bedini—perchè mi accorgo che in questo mondo si fanno più commedie che non se ne scrivano.

—E più divertenti dovresti aggiungere—disse Babolani.

—Secondo.

Per Chiardi non fu davvero molto divertente questa qui. Ma egli ora fa il bravo; e quando incontra a braccetto del marito colei che avea giurato di essere sua o di nessun'altro, si consola come da scampato pericolo, esclamando:

—Oh! Era troppo brutta! E diventerà peggio!... Se la goda!

FINE